BOOK IT

A LITERARY LOVER'S ANTHOLOGY

EDITED BY

CM PETERS

Print ISBN: 978-1-948780-14-8
Cover illustration: Lee Moyer

Contents

INTRODUCTION....7
BY THE BOOK....9
LOVE AT THE LIBRARY....17
A PAGE OUT OF HIS BOOK....39
STARTING A NEW CHAPTER....54
NO LOITERING....70
LAW OF LOVE....96
QUEEN OF THE LIBRARY....106
LATE FEES....133
A RARE TOME....146
THERE'S NO PLACE LIKE BROKEN REACH....159
LAST DAY AND FINAL PAGE....178
SEEING THE STORY....187
THE IN-BETWEEN YEARS....199
WRITING ONE'S OWN STORY....217
ABOUT SINCYR PUBLISHING....243

INTRODUCTION

CM Peters

I am a firm believer that romance and books go hand in hand. What is more special than to write about the one you love? I'm a sucker for a good romantic story, whether in a book or on the screen. And when the chance came to work with SinCyr Publishing on a romance anthology, I felt it was destiny.

The thirteen authors that surround me in this anthology know their romance well. From Katey Tattrie, who explores romance after a tremendous loss to K. Parr who delves into the new love of a librarian and his single dad customer, or to Aila Alvina Boyd's trans college professor discovering new love after a long, rough patch; all the authors have shown their true colors when it comes to love.

Some authors are budding, others well-established, but that is irrelevant when it comes to matters of the heart. In Book It, you will find these authors have woven amazing stories around books, librarians, bibliophiles, and romance readers.

Being a romantic to the core, I'm delighted to present Book It to you. May it bring a little more romance to your life.

BY THE BOOK

Marie Piper

Maddie Caldwell smelled like lemons and honey. It was everything Arlen could do not to drop the book of Stevenson poems he'd been deep into reading when her scent reached him just a few seconds before she did, darting in through the back door of his small bookstore.

"Did it come?" Maddie glanced around to make certain they were alone in the store. She rose on her tiptoes to look over the shelf that split the room into two parts. Satisfied in their privacy, and with her brown eyes shining, she leaned her elbows on the counter so she could talk to Arlen in a quieter voice. "You'll be my hero if it did."

Arlen nodded and slipped a small leather-bound volume from a drawer and into her hand. Maddie snatched the book and bent down to hide it in her crinoline.

Arlen tried hard not to think about her crinoline. Maddie was the prettiest woman he'd ever laid eyes on and he always tried ever so hard not to think about her in any way other than proper. He looked toward the front window of the store to distract himself. It had begun raining, and he watched people scurry down the main dirt street of town to escape the drips. "Yep. It just came in yesterday."

"Good timing," Maddie beamed as she stood up and smoothed her skirts. A few drops of water dotted the shoulders of her brown dress. She'd come the longer way around the building to use the back door rather than be seen coming in the front way. How he wished she could just use the front door like anyone else.

"You in town alone today?"

"Never. Clyde's with me today, though."

"Does he know you're here?"

"Shoot, Clyde's no doubt drunk at the saloon already. I'll fetch him at lunchtime and drag his sorry behind home. I actually prefer when he comes, 'cause he don't give a damn what I do with myself. Jonas watches me like a hawk. What are you reading?" She peered at the book on the counter beside Arlen.

"Robert Louis Stevenson. It's called Underwood, a collection of his poems."

"Could I read it?"

She didn't mean would he lend it to her. Arlen knew she still worried about her reading skills. "If you can manage that Shakespeare, you can manage this."

"I only struggled a little with The Tempest. Oh, how I loved it."

"I'm glad to hear it." In truth, he'd seen some of Miranda in her, alone and isolated from most of the world. He'd given her the play in the hopes it might bring her some sort of strange comfort.

"I can't wait to read Romeo and Juliet."

"Your Pa hasn't caught on, has he?"

Red curls danced on her shoulders as Maddie shook her head with glee. "None of them pay much attention to what I do so long as there's a hot supper on the table and the washing gets done. While they're out with the herd and after supper, I have lots of time to read."

Everything she ever said about her home life sounded like she was a hired girl and not the daughter of one of the richest families around. The Caldwell's could afford a girl, so keeping Maddie tied to the stove must have been Pa Caldwell's way of keeping her away from the eyes of the men in town who had noticed her beauty for a long time. "Must be lonely."

"Without the books, it would be. Arlen, I swear you're my white knight."

A hot flush came to Arlen's cheeks. "Anything for my favorite customer."

Maddie patted her hip. "Does this one have a happy ending?"

He winced. The ending of Romeo and Juliet was the exact opposite of happy, with the two lovers ending the play dead together and all their families devastated. "Do you really want to know?"

Maddie waved her hands and shook her head again. "No. Don't you tell me, in fact. I will find out for myself."

Footsteps on the walkway outside interrupted them. Arlen turned to the front door to see Mrs. Weatherspoon coming in, but when he looked back Maddie was gone out the back door, vanished like a ghost. The elderly widow sought a book by Nathaniel Hawthorne, but while Arlen assisted her, his mind was elsewhere.

The first time Maddie had walked into Quinn's Books, she'd looked as nervous as a spooked filly. The shock of seeing her in the store had frozen Arlen for a minute. Most of his customers were older women looking for novels, or men looking to buy a copy of the newspaper or the Almanac or maps.

Maddie had gone immediately to the farthest shelf from the door as if she could escape Arlen's eyes. He'd watched her browse the volumes, tracing her finger over a few of the gold-pressed titles or peeking inside another.

When he'd asked if he could be of any assistance, she'd jumped about a foot high.

It had only taken a moment to realize the young woman could hardly read, and that she was deeply ashamed of it. But she wanted to read. More than anything, Maddie wanted to read.

So Arlen gave her a primer, one of the schoolbooks he ordered for the children at the schoolhouse, and sent her on her way with a quick lesson in sounding out the letters. She had returned two weeks later having conquered the primer and determined to learn more. So he'd given her another book, and she'd returned again. She read everything he handed her, regardless of subject or story, Dickens and Poe and travelogues and a book about George Washington...

They went on and on that way for the better part of two years until the sneaking and the secret meetings were the most exciting part of Arlen's day, for in between all the pages and whispers, he had fallen madly in love with Maddie Caldwell and her impossible spirit and will of iron and her love for anything written in ink or put on pages. At the risk of her own safety, she persisted.

After the day of the Romeo and Juliet hand-off, ten days went by. Maddie did not come into the bookstore. It was a strangely long time between her visits. Arlen smoothed the cover of Shakespeare's A Midsummer Night's Dream that she'd also ordered with her meager allowance, and wondered what was keeping her. Something more than small had to have happened at the ranch, or she'd have sprinted in to collect it at least twice by now. He paced the store, looking out the window hundreds of times and thinking practically every woman was her.

He saw Pa Caldwell walk down the street one time, but not Maddie.

A few more days passed. He swept the floor probably fifteen times just for something to do. But Maddie didn't come. Something was definitely wrong.

Arlen made a decision. Probably a stupid one, but he made it nonetheless.

When two weeks passed with no sign of her and no word—he felt certain she'd have sent word if she could—he set out on foot as the sun went down and began walking in the direction of the Caldwell ranch.

He walked the three miles from town across the sloping plains, unnoticed and quiet. It was a pleasant walk—he liked long walks anyway—and the stars shone like candles flickering in the great big sky.

Had he taken leave of his senses? His mother would have told him he was crazy if he'd written to tell her what was happening in his life. For all he really knew, he was nothing to Maddie but the man who got her books. They'd never spoken too much about anything other than books and stories. No one would call him a handsome man, for starters. He was too skinny and wore spectacles and lacked any of the cockiness that he'd always thought women liked in a man. Arlen knew Maddie had grown up in town, and she knew he was from Minnesota, but what kind of anything was that? They were strangers.

But then again, Romeo and Juliet had been strangers too.

"And look what happened to them," he muttered to himself.

A crow cawed and Arlen sucked in a breath for he'd been sure he'd been spotted.

What was he planning to do anyway—whisk her away and run off? He barely even had a plan, and he knew it was a foolish one. Still, he kept on walking. His feet would not have let him turn back.

By the time he reached the fences of the ranch, it was dark. Covered by the night, no one looking out at the fields would have seen him. Everything was still. Everything was quiet.

He told himself he wasn't doing anything wrong. He was worried, was all.

The grass rustled. Arlen sucked in a breath and crouched down in the dark.

A big brown dog lumbered out of the night in his direction. It walked slow, huffed a few times, stopped a few yards away from Arlen, and barked just once.

"Hey now, Frank," Arlen said, reaching out a hand to give the beast some pets. Probably everyone around the territory knew Frank, and Frank knew everyone. Arlen had given him more than a few pieces of jerky over the years, and Frank remembered a friend. If the Caldwells had owned any other dog, Arlen wouldn't have made the trip. Big old Frank was more a lover than a fighter and took the ear scratches for a moment before wandering off somewhere else.

Arlen approached the sprawling yellow house. Ma Caldwell had passed some five years earlier, but she'd adored the pretty things in life, flowers and lace and colors that looked like sunrises. She had never walked down the street of town looking anything less than a queen. The house with the white shutters and the extensive garden stretched to the side of the house carried on her memory.

Arlen saw tiny pink roses and heliotrope among the neat-trimmed gardens. Maddie tended these plants as well as the vegetable garden, and it was the one part of her shut-in life she didn't complain about.

She was somewhere in that big house. How to get to her?

Lamplight shone bright from a few windows. Big trees surrounded the house, and Arlen circled slowly until he saw an open window up on the second story. He waited behind the tree for a moment and listened with his eyes closed until he heard a woman's voice.

Of course Maddie's room was on the second story.

Creeping around the Caldwell place in the dark was as stupid as an idea could be. In addition to Clyde Caldwell, eldest brother and notorious for getting into fights over next to nothing, Pa Caldwell was a sharpshooter and the twins, Eddie and Jonas, were rodeo roping champions. If it all went wrong, if he fell and broke his leg or was spotted and unable to get away, Arlen could be strung up in the middle of town and used as target practice before dawn.

He climbed the tree.

It wasn't easy. He wasn't eighteen anymore, and he'd never been a muscular man, and his shoes slipped a few times on the bark of the tree, but he managed to pull himself up the branches until he was even with what he hoped was Maddie's room. A deep sigh of relief came from him when he saw the lace curtains and other feminine decorations that told him he had guessed correctly.

The curtain blew aside in the breeze. He saw Maddie sitting at a small desk near the window, a book on her lap. The way her eyes never strayed from the pages made him stop breathing. Goodness, but she was astonishing. It wasn't just her beauty. Her very spirit seemed to sparkle and shine. With the book in her hands and a few moments of peace from her family, she was happy. He imagined the two of them sitting side by side in rocking chairs by a fire, reading peacefully as the years went by, and he'd never wanted anything more.

Like Romeo, he'd never seen true beauty before this night.

He panicked. He'd be interrupting her. Immediately, he wondered if he'd done the wrong thing. What if she screamed and alerted the world? What if she didn't want him to be there?

Love was worth the risk, he decided. Moved by something other than his sense, maybe the spirit of the poet, he spoke, "But soft, what light through yonder window breaks?"

The book flew into the air. Maddie started to scream, but when she realized who was sitting in the tree outside her window she clapped her hands over her mouth and stopped herself. The book fell to the ground and she shot a scared look at the door before turning back to the window. "Arlen!"

"Hello."

"You're plum crazy to come here like this. How'd you get up here?"

He stated the obvious. "I climbed the tree."

"Why?"

Arlen pulled A Midsummer Night's Dream out of his pocket and thrust it at her. "This came in and you didn't come to get it."

Maddie looked at him as if she'd never seen him before, then looked at the book in his hand and smiled. She leaned out the window to take it, and he held tight to a branch and leaned closer to her. From this position, they could just about whisper in each other's ears.

She sighed. "None of them have had any reason to go to town, so there's no way for me to go to town. Pa went once and I begged him to let me come along but he told me I needed to see to the carrots. The carrots! Carrots barely need any attention at all. My brothers haven't been around too much, working on new roping tricks. I'm bored out of my shoes, Arlen. I'm trapped up in this house like...Juliet."

Arlen grinned. "So you like it?"

She whispered. "It's a wonderful story."

It wouldn't end wonderfully, but he wouldn't tell her that just then. Not when he could see the strawberry color of her lips and the way pieces of her hair blew loose from her ponytail. "This one's wonderful, too. It's about faeries and magic."

"I could use some magic," she said. "Let me get my purse. I have to pay you."

"No you don't," he said, reaching out a hand to touch hers.

"But I do."

"I won't take your money, Maddie."

"Most men would bring flowers to a girl, you know," she said. But she was smiling.

"I came out here because I was worried something had happened to you."

"Nothing ever happens to me, Arlen. Or at least nothing ever did before tonight." Before he could think another thought, she leaned out the window as far as she could. Deliberately, swiftly, she put her soft strawberry lips on his.

Maddie Caldwell kissed him.

He nearly fell out of the tree, but she reached out and touched his face. Her thumb brushed against his cheek.

It felt like faeries and stars danced just for them. It felt like eternity was theirs for the taking.

The perfect moment didn't last. Men's voices carried up in the hallway, breaking into the magic as if shattering a mirror. With enormous eyes, Maddie pushed Arlen away from her and to his death. "Go quickly. They mustn't find you."

His hands scraped at the bark of the big tree branch that held most of his weight, but his heart was singing and exploding. Invincible, Arlen leaned in and kissed her, a bigger kiss, one that meant the whole world and promised a future brighter than she could imagine. For one moment, she didn't resist.

Slipping his lips to her ear, he whispered. "I love you, Maddie. I have for a long time."

She pressed a hand to his chest. "Pa won't care about your noble intentions if he finds you here. He'll only care about your hide."

Arlen grinned as he retreated into the tree, for he noticed she was blushing and grinning just the same as he was. "Do you love me back?"

"Go!"

"Not until I have an answer."

The voice in the hall was closer now. "Maddie!"

"Just a minute, Pa!" Desperately, she faced Arlen again. "Go. I won't be responsible for you when he shoots you." Arlen didn't move. Maddie glared at him. "You're damn lucky I love you, Arlen Quinn, or I'd shove you right out of that tree and not think twice about it."

No words had ever been prettier. "Come to me as soon as you can."

"I will. I promise." He slid down the tree, faster than he'd planned to.

"Arlen!"

"Yes?"

"Does Romeo and Juliet have a happy ending?" She asked it as if she needed to know.

He would not lie to her. "No." The sadness on her face inspired him. "But I swear on the stars, Arlen and Maddie will."

Her hand went to her mouth for a moment, and then she pulled her windows shut.

Arlen reached the ground and pressed his back against the far side of the tree. If anyone looked out her window, they wouldn't see him. He heard voices inside, hers and her family's. He waited a good long while, until the lights in the house were almost out, and then began the walk home.

Like Maddie had said, nothing had ever really happened to Arlen before either. He'd come west from Minnesota looking for something more than a life as a farmer and had opened a book shop purely so he could be around books all day long and have a good reason. And those books, his favorite thing in the entire world, had brought him Maddie. They had brought him love.

"I am in love with Maddie Caldwell!" He shouted to the sky, throwing his head back and laughing at the stars.

One particular star seemed to wink at him.

"I see you, sir." Arlen winked right back and laughed the rest of the way back to town.

LOVE AT THE LIBRARY

Kat Ryan

Elle pushed her laptop back and stretched her neck to the right, then left. The satisfying pop resounded in the quiet nook of the library. For a Saturday afternoon, there weren't many patrons milling around. Damp leaves spiraled down from the trees outside the window. Glancing at the riot of leaves, she smiled. She knew the crisp air outside heralded in the season of fall in the Midwest. After a longer than typical summer in Illinois, Elle was grateful for the return of sweater weather. The old home that was the library of this small town made her feel cozy, safe. Since coming to town last month, she had frequently sought solace in this building.

Glancing up, Elle caught a glimpse of the other reason she had become what was surely one of the library's most frequent visitors. Mmmm. Nate Roberts was what her untrained eye could only estimate as six foot five inches of a glorious distraction. Tugging her laptop back towards her, Elle attempted to look busy while watching Nate out of the corner of her eye. From her spot at the table in front of the windows, she could see the circulation desk where he was talking to a teen.

The young boy looked up at Nate, then back down at the stack of books in his hand, then nodded as he moved away from the desk and out the door, clutching his stack of books to his chest. Elle glimpsed the cover of the top book. Excellent choice. She'd read Aristotle and Dante Discover the Secrets of the Universe when it had come out because of her sister's recommendation. Ava was an English teacher at the local high school and had a never-ending list of books for Elle to read. The vibrations from her phone pulled her back to the present. Speak of the devil, she thought as her sister's name flashed up at her. Quickly, she tapped to open the text.

Ava: Hey stranger, you coming over tonight? Dinner?

Ava: I mean, you moved to town and I barely see you. I'm beginning to forget what you look like.

Elle: Overreact much? I saw you three days ago for coffee.

Ava: Three days, that's too long. I spend my days with seventeen-year-olds who believe they are the center of the universe. I need to see my little sis. That's why you moved here after all. Right? Come over.

Elle: Writing now. Maybe later?

Ava: Writing where…

Elle: …

Ava: You're at the library again.

Ava: For God's sake, Elle, ask the guy out.

Elle: If he wanted to ask me out, he would have. I don't need to embarrass myself.

Ava: Grow a pair, baby sis. You have talked about nothing but that glorious hunk of man since moving here a month ago. I asked around, he's unattached—

Elle: YOU ASKED AROUND?

Ava: Shh. You're in a library.

Ava: So, is he as beautiful as ever?

Elle glanced over at Nate to see that he was looking over a stack of books on the front desk, typing something into the computer. Her eyes tracked from his tousled brown hair, to the stubble on his jaw, to the henley that stretched across his lean chest, to his jeans that cupped what she knew from advanced study was a glorious ass. Yeah, you could say he wasn't a chore to observe. Her phone vibrated again.

Ava: Well…

Elle: Out of my league.

Ava: Shut up.

Ava: Clearly, I need to come down and kick your ass. You are gorgeous.

Elle grinned at her phone in reply. Ava was gorgeous. Elle knew she was pretty, but her sister with wavy brown hair, long lean legs, killer ass, and breasts to die for, was what society elevated. Ava took after their dad in height. Elle was a mirror image of their mom. Long thick brown hair, freckles dotting her nose and cheeks, and an hourglass figure that would have been gentle curves on someone taller than her five-foot-three stature. Elle heard a lot of 'Baby got back' in middle school. Thanks, Sir Mix-a-Lot. Grateful you liked those big butts.

She got ready to reply to her sister, only to jump in her seat as the sound of a throat being cleared came from above. Raising her gaze from her phone, she saw faded jeans, a forest green henley, and Nate's beautiful face smiling down at hers. Her heart threatened to vibrate right out of her chest.

"Sorry to startle you," he said, his eyes gleaming. "You look lost in thought over here, Ms. Jones. Anything you need?"

"Elle," she murmured.

Nate grinned, his eyes dancing with amusement. "I know, Elle. Just teasing you. Anything you need?"

She felt a thrill travel through her when he said her name. It was crazy, she knew. She'd been here enough that she knew all the staff and they were all beyond welcoming, but the way that Nate said it, mmmm. It warmed up her core.

"Elle?"

She shook her head, bringing her attention back to Nate. He was looking at her with a bit of concern. Good grief, she must have zoned out there for a minute.

"What?"

With a bit of smirk Nate said, "Just checking to see if you needed anything."

"No…" Elle wanted to groan out loud. She sounded breathless, like she'd just run a race. What on Earth was wrong with her? It's just a hot guy, she told herself, and he was only doing his job. But after observing him for the last two months, her body had decided to switch into overdrive at his proximity. The scent of him threatened to overwhelm her. He smelled like soap and the outdoors, somehow mixed together. She had a strong desire to bury her face into his chest.

Chill, Elle. Nate was kind; he had been all month. She'd spoken to him on and off, getting to know him better bit by bit, but nothing told her that he was interested in her in any way beyond some subtle flirting. Elle closed her eyes and sighed, wishing she had some of Ava's courage to call upon right now.

Her phone vibrated its siren call from the table, causing them both to look down. She saw a text from Ava come in.

Glancing back to Nate, she whispered, "Sorry, it's my sister."

Nate looked down as her phone lit up again with Ava's message, paused, then grinned. "I'll let you get to it. You know where I am if you need anything."

Mutely, Elle nodded and looked down at her phone, already feeling the loss of a guy that wasn't even hers. Those feelings vanished when she saw the text that was currently lighting up her screen from Ava.

Ava: Saddle up, Elle. I'm sure Mr. Nate Roberts would be perfectly fine with you jumping his bones. Get to it, girl. Come over when you're done. Love you!

Elle let out a small gasp. Holy. Shit. He hadn't seen that message, had he? Had all of it been visible on her phone? Feeling the heat in her cheeks, she allowed her gaze to travel back up from the table.

Yep, still standing there, book in hand, watching her. Terrific. As their gazes locked, Nate took a step, bringing him even closer to her spot at the table. Dropping his hands to rest on the table, he lay the book down. Even while swimming in mortification, Elle noted his muscular forearms. She devoured romance books on a regular basis and they often waxed poetically about forearms, which had always puzzled her. Looks like she just hadn't been around the right guys. Wow. Lesson learned.

Nate rocked her world as he leaned down across the table and whispered, "FYI, your sister's plan sounds good to me." Standing up, he shot her a wink and then headed across the room to meet Gabby, another librarian, coming down from the offices upstairs.

Elle worked to regain her regular breathing, controlling the urge to drop her head to the table and just give up the ghost. Seriously? Ava and her timing could not possibly be worse. Allowing herself one more quick glance in his direction, she looked up to find Nate watching her from where he now stood with Gabby as she sorted a cart of books into piles. If she wasn't mistaken, his gaze intensified as they continued to stare at each other.

Whoa. What the heck was going on?

Gabby was doing some type of dance around the circulation desk as she sorted books from the cart into two stacks—yes and no. The GSA club at the local high school was trying out a book club this month at their group meetings. One of the teachers reached out to his boss, Grace, and asked for recommendations of young adult books featuring LGBTQIA characters. The hope was that the books would either serve as windows into the lives of gay students for the straight allies or mirrors for the gay students to feel a little less alone. Nate watched Gabby tap her chin on the spine of a book as she looked back and forth between the two piles.

"What's up, Gabs?"

She paused, mid tap. "I'm debating the merits of Every Day by David Leviathan. I mean the main character, A, doesn't really have a gender. Instead, every day they wake up in a new body. I'm not sure it would fit in this list we're creating."

Nate considered the book for a moment. "Well, it likely depends on what they want this list to accomplish." Gesturing at the book in her hands, he continued, "That one would certainly be a good jumping off point for conversations on gender identity, being gender fluid, etc."

Gabby nodded. "You're absolutely right. Not sure why I didn't look at it that way." Dropping the book on her yes stack, she jerked her head towards Elle with a smirk. "She's back."

Nate glanced over at Elle, then back at Gabby. "Yep. Your point?"

Gabby wagged a finger at Nate. "Uh-uh, mister. Don't play innocent with me. If you think that Grace, Emma, Tim, and I haven't noticed the fact that you've been mooning over Elle each time she's come in for the last month, you're crazy."

"Mooning? Seriously? What are you, eighty?"

"Don't start, Nate. She's cute and super sweet. She sat and debated the merits of various Hallmark movies for a half an hour with Tim the other day, and you know he can go on and on for days. That alone speaks volumes of her character."

Nate glanced over at Elle. She couldn't overhear this, could she? He lowered his voice in case. "Not denying she's sweet, Gabby. Haven't met sweeter in some time." He cleared his throat. Was he really showing these cards? He'd never hear the end of it, and yet he couldn't help himself as he continued. "And hell, cute doesn't even begin to cut it. But she's new in town. I don't need to descend on her like a vulture. Give it time before you try marrying her off."

Gabby peered up at him. "You, sir, are one stubborn pain in the ass.

That girl looks at you like she wants to climb you like a tree. Get your ass in gear, my friend."

Nate laughed. That was Gabby, blunt as usual. He hesitated, wondering if he should share, then decided he had nothing to lose. Looking over at Elle, he jerked his head towards the back of the library where the house's original kitchen still stood. Figuring that would give them some privacy, he headed back to the kitchen and the coffee pot where someone typically had a fresh pot ready, even now as evening was descending. Gabby interrupted him before he could ask her if she wanted a cup.

"What's with the change in venue, Roberts?"

Looking back towards the main library and seeing that they were indeed alone, he went ahead and let Gabby have it all. "I saw a text on her phone."

Gabby's brows drew together, "Continue, Mr. Snoops-a-lot."

"Not snooping, saw it accidentally when I glanced down. Elle said she was texting with her sister. The text that I saw on her phone said something about how she should jump my bones." He couldn't help the grin that lit up his face as he thought back to seeing his name on Elle's phone, much less the content of the message. Elle jumping him? Where should he sign up?

"See," Gabby hissed. "This is not an unrequited attraction here, Nate. You need to ask her out."

Nate shook his head. "I gave her a bit of an opening and she didn't bite, Gabs. Not in the market to force myself on anyone."

Gabby looked skeptical. "Tell me more about this opening you supposedly gave her."

Nate's body hummed with energy as he recalled Elle's cheeks flushing at his words just a bit ago, highlighting her freckles. God, she was sexy.

Leaning out of the kitchen, he looked around the shelves of nonfiction books to see Elle's back as she typed away at the table in the front. She paused, leaning her head on her hand as she twirled some hair around a finger before resuming her typing. Watching her, he wondered what it was that she was working on today, not that he was complaining about her presence.

"Editing," Gabby whispered from the vicinity of his shoulder.

Looking down, he found Gabby standing right next to him, following his line of sight to a certain gorgeous woman typing away fifteen feet from them.

"Excuse me?"

"You asked what she was always working on. She's a freelance editor."

"I asked that out loud?"

Gabby grinned at him as she bumped his hip with hers, "Sure did, big guy. And what have you been doing for the last month that you didn't know that?"

Nate didn't answer her, not because he was ashamed of not knowing about Elle, but because he knew more than Gabby was aware. Nate knew that she was an editor, but Elle had also shared her dreams of writing a book. He wasn't sure if that was something she told everyone, though, so he bit back a retort to Gabby as he watched Elle write. He remembered the first day he came in and saw Elle typing in front of the window. It had been like a punch to the stomach, she simply took his breath away. He had gotten almost no work done as he found his eyes drawn to her repeatedly. He found himself in a trance-like state, watching as she twirled her hair while typing, occasionally wrinkling her freckle-scattered nose. Thinking back, he could picture her head nodding in time to whatever music was flowing through her earbuds. And then there was the first time she stood up and he saw those curves. Holy shit. He was grateful that he'd been sitting at the desk because his body reacted as if he was still a teen who couldn't control his reactions. Damn.

"Earth to Nate," Gabby called.

Not pulling his eyes off of Elle, Nate merely mumbled, "What?"

Gabby chuckled before tugging him back into the kitchen, "Let's make a plan, my friend. We need to get you this girl."

Elle sat staring at her computer, stewing. She should be finalizing the edits for the article she was working on, but all she could think about was Nate and Gabby. She'd seen them talking at the circulation desk before they headed to the kitchen in the back and her heart had sunk. Elle had gotten to know Gabby pretty well over the past month and loved the vivacious person she was, but now Elle was wondering if she'd missed something. She had thought that Gabby was single. Hell, she thought Nate was as well. Was there something between Gabby and Nate that she hadn't seen? Ugh, misery. Her stomach felt like it was tied up in knots, which was ridiculous. It wasn't like she had any claim on the man.

The bell over the front door pulled her out of her thoughts. Glancing to the front room, she felt tension flood through as her sister's mischievous grin met her gaze. What in the ever-loving hell?

"Ava," she hissed. "What are you doing here?"

Ava sauntered towards the table, glancing around as she got closer. "Well, where is he?"

Elle rolled her eyes, "Are you serious? There is zero reason for you to be here. You need a hobby."

Plopping in the chair across from Elle, Ava grinned. "Baby sister, you are my hobby. Besides, I have a reason to be here beyond getting you some action."

Elle didn't like the devilish glint she saw shining back at her. "What are you talking about?"

Gabby chose that moment to come out of the kitchen, coffee mug in hand. "Hey, sorry we weren't manning the store. Coffee waits for no one, you know?" She grinned at Elle, then looked at Ava. "Hey, Ava, are you here for the booklist? It's not quite finished, but I'd be glad to go over what we have so far."

Elle's eyebrows drew together as she gave Ava one of her patented stares, "What booklist?"

Gabby glanced at Elle, then Ava. "I didn't realize you knew each other. Ava is heading up the GSA at the high school. We've been pulling some books for their new book club and were going to go over the titles with her later today."

Elle's head spun to Ava and raised one brow. She wanted to call bullshit. Nope, she wanted to scream it. There was no way that Ava just randomly reached out to the library for help with a booklist. Beyond the fact that her school had a librarian, Ava devoured books. She could make a booklist on her own in minutes.

"Umm, Ava, can I talk to you for a minute?" she managed to ground out.

The wattage on Ava's grin increased exponentially. "Sorry, sis." Gabby's eyebrows shot up at that endearment. "I was swinging by to tell you that I had an appointment that I forgot about tonight and couldn't do dinner."

Ava looked over at Nate who was moving from the back of the library to join them, then glanced back at Elle. "Say, crazy idea here. Since I bailed our dinner plans, maybe you could meet up with Gabby and," gesturing at Nate, Ava continued, "Nate, is it? You all could have dinner instead. They can share the titles they were thinking of with you. We can talk about them later and I can get your input. Sound good?" Ava stood up, looking like she was going to make a fast exit.

Before Elle could say not so fast, Gabby began nodding as she tapped her chin absentmindedly. "Great idea, Ava." She looked over her shoulder at Nate. "Nate, I have that thing tonight. Do you mind getting Elle up to speed on the books we were thinking about? If we have a core group of titles that we want to go forward with, I can request as many copies as we need through the inner library loan website and have them for you by the end of this week or beginning of next."

Nate looked completely confused. Elle would feel bad for him if she wasn't so pissed at her meddling big sister right now. What the literal hell? Ava was clearly setting her up and somehow Gabby had decided to join forces with her? She interrupted Ava's reply to Gabby with a terse, "Ava, porch. Now." Without looking back, she stormed out.

The sound of the front door closing behind her made her whirl around to see Ava moving across the porch with a wide grin stretched across her face. She allowed herself a moment of insecurity at her gorgeous sister's appearance. Elle was typically pretty confident in herself, but today was not her day. She growled at herself in irritation, not the time for that. Refocusing on Ava, she snipped, "What the hell was that?"

"Tsk-tsk, Elle-belle. Where is the gratitude?"

"Gratitude? What do you think you're doing here?"

Ava looked to the heavens like she couldn't even remotely understand Elle, "Um, setting you up? Come on, that guy is dreamy. You can thank me later."

"Arrrggghhhh!" Elle threw her arms up in frustration and began to pace. "You always do this, Ava. Always! Why do you insist on meddling in my life?"

Leaning back against the porch railing, Ava watched her meltdown. "I wouldn't need to meddle if you'd get to work. You will be old and grey before you ever make a move on the hot librarian in there and you know it. I don't want you to end up with a house full of cats, Elle. You deserve that guy. You've talked about nothing else for the last month."

Elle ran her hands through her hair. "There is so much to work with here, I don't even know where to start. One, I would have made a move in time if I felt like it. Two, cats are cute, but I'm allergic, dipshit. And three, what's up with asking them for book lists? I know damn well you didn't need help with that—"

Ava raised her hand up, "Actually, I did. I mean, I wanted to bring the public library in as partners in these book groups because I want the kids to see that more people care about them in town than a few teachers at the high school."

Elle, paused, considering that, "Okay, that's not a terrible idea."

"I know. And also, might I add, you are full of shit. You wouldn't have made a move on that guy, you would have second guessed yourself ten ways to Sunday."

"It doesn't matter anyway," Elle started.

"Why? Because he couldn't possibly be attracted to you or some other bullshit nonsense you have in your head? Get over yourself, Elle. You're gorgeous, funny, loyal, and any guy would be lucky to get a chance at you." Elle couldn't help but note that her sister looked pissed.

"You're sweet, Av. Thanks for always backing me."

"Of course," Ava dismissed. "You do the same for me. But quit stalling. Why are you telling yourself that this guy you've been drooling over for the past month can't be yours?"

"Many reasons," she said as she threw her hands up in frustration. "Today's top one would be because I think there's something between Nate and Gabby," Elle's stomach dropped, even as she said the words. God, it wasn't like anything had happened between them over the last month, just sweet conversations. Why did she feel like she already lost something then?

"Um, excuse me. Not meaning to eavesdrop here, but I did anyway…" Gabby stuck her head out of the library and a wide grin stretched across her face. "Nate and I are just friends; he's like my big brother, so eww." Gabby scrunched her nose as she laughed, then wagged her eyebrows at them. "Just saying, if you're wanting to jump a certain 'hot librarian,' I am happy to cheer you on. Might I suggest tonight's dinner as an excellent starting point?"

Good lord, Elle dropped her head back to look at the ceiling as she let out a groan. Could this get any worse? Of course, the universe decided to answer her just then, and the answer would be yes, yes it could.

"Ahem, excuse me." Nate stepped around Gabby to join the group on the porch, otherwise known as Elle's current circle of hell. "One, just saying, if the 'hot librarian' is in reference to me, thanks. Two, Elle, how about that dinner?" Nate was looking at her with a look she couldn't read, but holy hell, it made her lady parts light up. Embarrassment and arousal were warring internally and she had no idea which side would win.

"Um," she squeaked out, "this is a bit mortifying."

Ava knocked her shoulder into Elle's, "What my sister means to say is yes, dinner sounds great." Ava squeezed Elle's arm as she moved from the porch railing to the door. "Gabby, do you still have those books on hold for me?"

Gabby slid inside after Ava, her voice floating back to the porch, "Yep, they're at the desk."

Elle locked eyes with Nate, feeling heat flood her cheeks. Where did they go from here?

Watching Elle's face flush was an ego boost, he couldn't deny. This girl had occupied any spare place in his mind for the past month. Her curves, freckles scattered like constellations, mesmerized him. However, the attraction was more than that. He noticed how she interacted with everyone in the library. Her smiles as she watched the kids that came in for story time. How she twirled her hair when lost in thought. Over the past month, he found himself drawn to her when she was at the library, asking questions and getting to know her a bit more each day. He knew her family included her parents, who were currently living abroad, and her sister, though he hadn't put it together that the sister was Ava. He knew she'd lived in Chicago after college and dreamed of being a writer, though she was currently earning a living as an editor. More than anything, he wanted her to agree to come out to dinner with him, but he worried that might be a hard sell.

"So, dinner?" Nate asked, crossing everything he could that Elle would say yes. He felt the air still in his lungs as he waited for what seemed like an eternity.

He watched her take a fortifying breath. "Yes," she closed her eyes as she nodded. "Yes, dinner sounds good." Long exhale. "God, I'm sorry. I'm sure I seem like an idiot." Her head slumped forward a bit. She looked so uncertain, he couldn't stand it.

Nate took a step forward. Then another. He reached the spot where she leaned against the railing on the porch and stood in front of her, not touching, but close enough that he could smell her perfume. It smelled like salt air combined with the woods and hit him in the gut as uniquely Elle. He wanted to lean forward, bury his nose in the nape of her neck. That would be a hell of a way to make her head for the hills. Controlling himself, he gently put his hand under her chin, tilting it up until her eyes met his.

"Elle?"

"Yeah?" she whispered.

He found himself studying her eyes. They were a caramel color with what appeared to be a freckle in one iris. God, they were beautiful. "Sweetheart, you are not an idiot."

Elle's eyes closed, then she looked back at him, not moving from their position. "Thanks for saying that, Nate. I certainly feel like one this afternoon." Her eyes fluttered shut as her tongue poked out and slid over her lips.

Damn. He knew she wasn't doing that to be provocative, but he certainly felt that as his jeans began to get a bit snug. "Babe, you're killing me."

Eyes snapping back to him, her brows drew together. "What?"

An internal debate waged on how forward he should be. And yet, he struggled holding back. Without meaning to, his thumb traced her lips. "This," he said with far more emotion in his throat than he meant to share. To hell with it.. "Sometimes when you're writing, you twirl your hair and bite your bottom lip. I've thought a lot about these lips over the past month..."

Elle let out a small gasp, "Seriously? You've thought about me?"

Nate let his hand drop from her face, but didn't move back from his spot in front of her. "Elle," he groaned. "Hell yes, I've thought about you."

She looked at him with her head tilted. He would kill to be able to read her mind right now. The right corner of her lip slid under her teeth and he prayed for willpower in his pants. Jesus, what this girl could do to him.

"So you really are good with going to dinner with me?" she whispered.

Laughter burst out, unbidden. "Did you not hear my comment earlier? I was down with the plan on that text message from Ava. And I am absolutely thrilled with the idea of dinner. But how about you? Those two seemed to have masterminded a date for us. Are you good with it?"

Elle grinned, seeming to stand up a little taller, though he still towered over her. "Yep, I'm good. Where do you want to eat?"

Grabbing her hand to tug her through the library so they could gather their stuff, he looked over his shoulder and said, "How about my place?"

Elle's eyes widened and he fought back a grin.

Moving quickly, they passed the circulation desk rounding the corner and heading to the table where Elle's laptop and bag still resided. Nate noted Gabby and Ava were perched on chairs there, watching their approach with some amusement. All they needed was some popcorn.

"Pretty proud of yourself?" he whispered to Gabby as Elle tossed the strap of her bag across her body, sliding the laptop inside.

Gabby watched Elle, then looked at Nate, "You guys getting dinner together?"

He nodded.

Gabby's grin was wide as she replied, "Then yes, I'm pretty proud of myself."

"Damn straight," Ava inserted herself into the conversation.

"Where are you two headed for dinner?" Ava asked.

"Ava," Elle sighed. Nate had a feeling that might be a common response. Ava seemed to be a force of nature.

"My place," Nate replied. Ava leaned to the side and high-fived Gabby. Nate forced back a laugh. Elle appeared to be mortified. "Do you actually want us to go over any booklist, or was that all a ruse?"

Gabby slid a document across the table. "That's a copy, so feel free to make notes on it and bring it to work tomorrow. We can finalize the list then."

"Yes, ma'am."

Gabby rolled her eyes, then looked over at Elle. "Elle, you're in luck. Nate here is an excellent cook, so don't let him go the lazy route and order pizza or anything."

Elle glanced at Nate, "You cook?"

"You bet I do." Nate slid a hand over his stomach as it let out a growl. Elle's eyes tracked his movements and her gaze heated up. That's it. He needed to get her out of here and away from prying eyes. "Let's go."

As Elle and Nate made their way up the walk to his house, she wondered if he was able to hear her heartbeat. It seemed to her that people in the next town over would surely be wondering where that loud thumping sound was coming from. Taking a deep cleansing breath, Elle took in Nate's place. He lived about three blocks from the library, away from downtown, in a small cottage. The brick walkway leading up to his house had a gentle curve. Leaves were scattered across his lawn, weighed down from the light rain showers early in the day. There were three windows facing the street and the lights that were already on in his front room that made the entire place glow with warmth and a feeling of welcoming. Nate pushed the door open and gestured for her to go ahead of him.

She stepped into a room that immediately felt like home. The space was wide open with white planks running horizontally throughout. There was a worn leather sofa by the front windows and an armchair perfect for curling up with a book. Bookshelves wrapped the lower half of the room. What appeared to be barn beams gave some separation between the living room and the kitchen area with a large island dividing the two. She could see a small but open cooking area. Books were strewn in several spots, urging her to sit down and grab whatever was nearest to read.

Nate smiled. "The lights are on timers." He placed his hand on her lower back, gently steering her into the room and closed the door behind himself. He dropped his bag on a bench and kicked off his shoes. "Beer?" he asked, moving towards the kitchen.

"Please." Elle mirrored his actions with her belongings before heading towards the island.

With his head inside of the fridge, Nate pulled two beers out. "IPA work for you?"

Elle nodded. Taking the beer from him, she took a small drink.

Nate looked up at her with a shy grin. Wowza. A strong desire to slide her arms around his waist and lean in overtook her. She held back, but barely.

"Nice place," she finally said, feeling awkward.

"It Was my grandparents' house. I inherited it when they passed." He glanced around in what looked like wonder.

"Happy memories here?" she asked.

Nate nodded slowly before catching her eyes, "Hell, yes. Lots of great memories. My grandparents were a trip. My grandma loved to tell dirty jokes. My grandpa was happy just watching her. They were pretty awesome."

"Sounds like it."

"Yeah," Nate cleared his throat. "Grandma passed a few years ago. Cancer. Grandpa died in his sleep just a few months later. My mom guessed he just didn't want to be in this world without her..." he trailed off, but then his voice returned. "But hell, they were in their eighties, had long, full lives. I try to remember that, when I wish like hell I could have one last dinner with them here."

Elle looked around his home. While certainly on the small side, the space was used exceptionally well. She could easily imagine a family growing up here. "These were your mom's parents?"

Nate stood from the counter, placing his beer on the island before turning to the cabinets and rummaging through them. "Yep.." He smoothed his hand over the worn butcher block counters. "I spent a lot of time here growing up. When my parents let me know that I could live here, well, I couldn't turn that down." His voice lowered, "It makes them feel closer in some way, you know?"

Elle nodded, then scanned the room thinking of something else to talk about that wouldn't bring up emotional memories. Glimpsing the stack of books next to the couch, she settled on a topic. "Clearly you like books," she said, jerking her head towards the living room.

Nate's laughter warmed her up. "I read Hatchet by Gary Paulsen in fourth grade and I was hooked. I'd convince my grandpa to take me camping and talk to him for hours about how I'd survive if I crash landed in the wilderness."

Elle watched as Nate's gaze landed on the trees just outside of the kitchen windows. Damn. She thought he was attractive when she watched him in the library. But this? Relaxed in his home, sharing memories that left him vulnerable? This was kryptonite to any remaining willpower she had. She just hoped he was being honest at the library earlier, that whatever was between them wasn't one-sided. She didn't know if she could handle otherwise.

Nate wasn't sure what it was about Elle that had him spilling all of his feelings within minutes of having her inside of his home. He'd much rather return to the conversation they were having on the porch of the library, if only to get that close to her again. Yet, he didn't want to rush her, or make her feel like the only reason he asked her back here was physical attraction. There was that, certainly, but this seemed like it was possibly so much more.

Elle had moved to the living room and was scanning the stacks of books he had on the floor and on the shelves. Turning, she asked, "So, do you have a favorite type of book?"

Nate organized the ingredients for dinner, pulling items from the fridge and cabinets so he'd be ready to go. "Not sure I have a favorite type, I'll read anything. If I'm just reading for me, I'd say I probably gravitate towards books that have a bit of suspense."

Elle returned her head to the side tilt she had going on while she scanned the spines of the books. Murmuring, she said, "Like Patterson."

Smiling at her typical assumption, he said, "Yeah, I think I have a few James Patterson's in there, but I also have authors like Mary Higgins Clark that I used to read with my grandma."

Elle's cheeks flushed. "I didn't mean to presume…" her voice trailed off.

Pulling out a skillet, Nate tried to think of a way to put Elle at ease. She seemed so tense, uncertain. "Elle, it's just books. I mean, we could pull up my list of books on my eReader and discuss my favorite romance authors. Books are books; you aren't going to offend me in this conversation. Promise. Now, how do you feel about chicken in a cream sauce?" Elle stood across the island from him and he couldn't help but note that her mouth was open, as if in surprise. It was freaking adorable. "Thoughts on chicken?" he prodded.

Elle's eyes refocused, then narrowed. "Umm, where do I start?"

"Chicken."

She smirked. "Chicken is good. Now, let's get back to this professed love of romance books."

Quirking an eyebrow at her, he turned to place the skillet on the stovetop. Dropping a bit of butter into it, he began to dredge the chicken in flour as the pan heated up. "Professed love? Nope, I said it outright. Romance books are some of my favorite things to read."

Nate moved to check on the skillet to see if it was warm enough then turned to see why Elle had gone radio silent. She stood there, brows drawn, watching him. Damn, she was gorgeous. What was even more attractive was that she seemed to have no idea how she affected him.

Looking at Elle, he was hit with the idea of what could be. For a month, they had danced around an attraction. He had wondered, at times, if it was one-sided. Lately, he had felt more certain that he wasn't alone in that. And yet, as he told Gabby, somehow, he knew this thing between them was not something to rush. Elle wasn't someone to rush. He wanted to savor this, every step of this beginning.

But man alive, it was hard.

"Elle, you look like you have something to say," he said. He grabbed some chicken and placed it in the skillet, hearing the sizzle that told him he had waited just long enough to get the perfect brown on each side. Looking over his shoulder, he prodded. "Come on, out with it."

Elle shook her head slowly, then paused before moving forward to claim a stool at the island. Sliding onto it, she said, "I just hadn't pegged you as a romance reader."

Nate assembled the white wine, cream, and cut lemon to the side of the stove. Grabbing some chives, he began to chop. "So, are you someone who looks down on romance books as smut?"

Elle began to stumble over her words, she was trying to reply so fast. "That's not, I mean, I wasn't trying to say that."

Taking a breath, he slid his hand across to capture Elle's in his. He almost forgot what he was going to say as he looked into her warm, brown eyes. "Let me try that again. "What I should have said was that I love romance books. How do you feel about them?" He traced his thumb back and forth across her hand.

Not moving her gaze from his, she bit her lower lip, then whispered, "I love them."

"What do you love about them?"

"The HEA, I mean, the happily ever afters."

"I work at a library, Elle. I know all about HEAs. Hell, Gabby and I run the romance book club filled with half of the retired ladies in town. Occasionally, a man will join us, but not often, unfortunately. So, I get that I'm not the typical market for a romance book. Doesn't mean I can't appreciate one."

Elle began to move her thumb over Nate's hand, grazing over his palm. Damn if that didn't make him want to vault the island to get to her. Just as he began to convince himself to round the island and kiss her senseless, he smelled the chicken.

"Crap," dropping her hand, he spun around and grabbed the spatula. He scooped up each piece and moved it to a plate he had to the side, checking the bottom to see if he had burned it. Hmm, a little browner that he would have liked, but not bad.

"So what do you like about romance books?" Elle asked as she watched from her perch.

Nate poured the wine in the skillet, allowing it to come to a boil before it reduced. "What's not to like? As you mentioned, I'm a sucker for a HEA. But also, I think some of the best books out there right now are romance books. I mean, you can read smart characters like anything from Penny Reid, crazy and hilarious stories from Kristen Ashley, gorgeous historical from Courtney Milan, and that's just a start."

"Damn," Elle let out in a breath.

"What?" Nate asked as he poured cream in with the wine and swirled it together before adding some lemon juice and chives. He heard Elle stand up and turned to watch her. He could sense the hesitancy in the way she leaned forward, then paused. As much as it killed him, he stood still. He felt like she had to be in charge here, she needed to decide to make a move.

Elle was trying to locate some confidence and move herself around the island. She took a step, then another, and before she knew it, she was toe to toe with Nate.

"Hey," she whispered, gathering all of her courage, and staring at his socks. She began to look away, then glanced back at the script on the socks. Carpe diem.

"Hey," he said, placing a finger under her chin and lifting it up so he could meet her gaze. "Glad you decided to move over here."

She slid her toes across his foot. "Apparently, I'm working on seizing the day."

Nate slid his hands to her hips, tugging her closer to him. "Are you now?"

Come on, Elle. You've got this. "Yes, I am." For the past month Elle had fantasized about a moment like this. Seeing Nate, at first, was an instant attraction. Hell, she could just call it a bit of lust and she wouldn't be lying. But then, as they talked, she began to dream. What would it be like to go on a date? What would it be like if there was something more? But that wasn't something that happened to her. Ava, yes. The irony of the world was that Ava was perfectly happy dating casually and had no desire to be in a long-term relationship whereas Elle was ready for commitment. Beyond ready.

"I was just thinking about something else I like about romance books," she said, gathering all of her courage and staring into his eyes. They looked like melted chocolate right now and were locked on her.

"What's that?" he asked as his hands caressed her sides.

Elle felt her face flush even as she knew she was going to say it. She knew that she'd regret only the chances she didn't take. "Sex scenes," she said, before biting the corner of her lip and watching for his reaction. She wasn't disappointed.

Nate groaned, "Shit, Elle, do you know what you do to me?"

"What?" she asked, fascinated.

He pulled her hips flush with his and she could feel him, rock hard, against her. Damn.

Nate let go of a hand to rake his fingers through her hair, stopping to play with the end. "Elle, would you be ok with me kissing you?" he asked as he twirled her hair.

Her heart beat louder than a bass drum as she got her answer out, "I'd be pissed if you didn't."

"I'm so glad to hear that," Nate whispered.

Elle held her breath for a moment, waiting to see what he would do. Nate smoothed a thumb over her eyebrow before letting his hand drop down to tilt her chin in his direction.

"Elle, breathe," he said with a grin.

As her breath whooshed out, he dipped down and his lips met hers. Holy hell. At first, they were soft, gentle. His teeth captured her bottom lip as they sucked it into his mouth, then let go. Then his tongue traced the seam of her lips before she parted them, letting him in. The kiss began to build as her hands roamed, from his back to his front. She tugged his shirt out so they could slide up his stomach and to his chest. She considered throwing her leg around his hip and pulling him closer, but thought that might be a bit much. Nate moved his lips down her neck, sucking in a spot gently right at the nape. Then, just as she began to pant, he pulled away.

"What?" her head was spinning. Every hot scene she had read from a Kate Canterbary novel flashed through her mind. She wanted to try them all. Right now.

Nate leaned down and kissed the tip of her nose. Keeping his hands on her hips, he nodded at the island behind her. "Want to sit here as I finish this up?"

"Um, sure?" Elle started to put her hands back to help herself up, but Nate put her up there before she could even get started. Well, that was kind-of hot, but what the hell? Had that been a test? Elle thought, to hell with this, and simply asked. "What was that?"

Nate was stirring the cream sauce on the stove, flipping the chicken over that was sitting in it. "That was amazing, that's what that was." He placed a lid on the skillet, then turned back to her.

Thank god, she thought, as her heart rate began to return to normal. "I agree. So why in the name of all that is holy are we stopping?"

Nate gave her a look that made her want to whip off her top, lay back on the island, and let him do anything his heart desired. Slow your roll, Elle. He stepped over to meet her legs, moved them apart so he could stand right between them, and lightly grazed her lips with his.

"Elle, I'm not in a hurry..." he started.

"What if I am?" she got out like the hussy she was beginning to wonder if she was.

He chuckled, but then put a finger on her lips. "I like you, Elle. A lot, a whole lot."

She pulled his finger off her lips so she could respond. "I like you, too." Then she placed his finger back.

Nate stood there for a moment, just staring at her. She could tell he was trying to figure out how to phrase something, so she waited.

Clearing his throat, he began. "Elle, I don't want a night. I don't want you just to jump me—" her face started to heat up, she could tell. Nate kissed her nose, then continued. "I mean, I'm all for that, but I want to start slow. I want to savor every experience with you. I want to make out on my couch to the point that I'm going crazy, but we still wait."

Good grief, so how long was he talking about waiting? It wasn't like she'd been with a lot of guys, but she certainly wanted to be with this guy, and the sooner the better. She didn't look up because she was pretty sure every thought was visible on her face right now.

"What I'm saying is, I don't want to rush. You're important to me. In one month, in quiet conversations at the library, I have gotten to know you. I know I would like to explore more with you." He gently helped her eyes meet his. "Do you understand?"

"Are you asking me to go steady?" her voice cracked as she immediately wanted to slap her forehead. Who the hell says go steady? She did apparently, that's who.

Nate's eyes sparkled. "If we were in middle school, I could pass you a note that asked you to check yes or no about going out with me." He kissed her brow, then leaned back to watch her. "What do you think?"

Elle felt some wetness in her eyes. This beautiful man wanted to be her boyfriend? He saw a possible future with her? Yes, she wanted all of what he was offering, and so much more. "I think I want whatever you're ready to give me."

Her phone took that opportunity to vibrate across the counter from them. She glanced back and Nate said, "Check it, I need to stir this sauce one last time."

Tugging her phone towards her, she saw Ava's name on the screen. Opening the text, she saw several messages she hadn't heard come in.

Ava: I'm feeling bad that I pushed you to leave with Nate. I mean, what if he's an axe murderer?

Ava: I mean, hottest axe murderer ever, but I'd still feel bad.

Ava: Elle, hello? I'm going to need a proof of life before I can go about my night.

Ava: You're just messing with me now, aren't you?

Ava: Seriously, do I need to get Gabby and storm the castle?

Elle started laughing as she read the texts. Nate grinned at her and cocked an eyebrow, so she handed her phone over to him. Scanning her texts, his smile grew before he handed it back to her.

"What are you going to say?" he asked, leaning back on the counter behind him and regarding her with a smile.

Elle paused, looking at her phone, and then at Nate. Smiling, she picked up her phone, fingers flying, and sent a text. She held her phone out to him once more. He moved back to his spot between her legs and looked at her phone.

Elle: No storming the castle. Following earlier directions and plan on jumping his bones. Turning my phone to "do not disturb" for the rest of the evening. Love you.

"I approve," Nate said, sliding her phone onto the island. Immediately it began to vibrate.

"I need to turn on do not disturb," Elle murmured.

"Let her message," he growled. "The dinner has about twenty more minutes and I have plans."

Elle marveled at the feelings of completeness that came over her. "I thought you wanted to wait. Care to share?"

"Waiting doesn't take everything off the table, my beautiful Elle," Nate murmured, his lips following her throat down and kissing the tops of her breasts where her shirt dipped down. "I plan on getting to know you a bit at a time."

Letting her head drop back, Elle felt arousal wash over her. "Sounds good."

"Elle," Nate's voice was deeper than usual. She pulled her head up to meet his eyes.

"Yes?" She bit her lower lip, waiting.

"This is just the beginning," he said, his eyes full of promise.

"I can't wait," she said as her phone vibrated again in the background. Thanks for the shove, sis. I've got this now, she thought. Looking at Nate, she knew that whatever lay ahead, she was ready to experience it with her hot librarian.

A PAGE OUT OF HIS BOOK

K. Parr

Hot Dad was back again.

With thick muscles, a neon blue Mohawk, abundant piercings, and colorful tattoos that crept down his neck and arms, he presented as exactly Max's type—tough-looking on the outside, gooey on the inside.

From behind the cart of graphic novels he was shelving, Max witnessed the gooeyness in action while Hot Dad, in ripped jeans and a flannel button-down, played house with his daughter in the children's area of the library. The girl couldn't be more than four and shrieked with joy whenever her dad sampled imaginary food or helped 'chop vegetables'. The sheer earnestness of Hot Dad's encouragement made Max's insides squirm like a colony of fuzzy ants.

Oh, to be treated so tenderly, to have such kindness and love directed toward him. Hot Dad was the rugged yet soft hero of Max's beloved romance novels, and Max was the heroine swooning onto a settee.

Except unlike book heroines, Max was doomed to remain invisible. Who would notice him—a scrawny library page with thick glasses that made his eyes bug, brown curls that were always too frizzy, and drab clothes that hung off his skinny frame?

With a sigh, Max pushed his glasses further up the bridge of his nose and returned to his cart. Luckily, shelving afforded him the opportunity to fantasize as his body moved on autopilot. He picked up where he left off, dreaming of carding his fingers through Hot Dad's Mohawk, of counting each piercing along his ears and lips, of tracing the tattoos and learning their meanings.

An ear-splitting squeal preceded a small projectile ramming into the back of Max's legs, and he let out an 'oof' as he blinked down at Hot Dad's daughter.

She put a finger over her mouth. "Shh! I'm hiding." She dropped down to crawl behind his cart.

"You know, the library isn't a playground," Max started—his usual spiel to kids who ran around uncontrolled.

And then Hot Dad rounded the corner.

Max's whole body flushed hot, then cold, then hot again.

"Boy, I sure wonder where Erika went." Hot Dad's gaze flicked down to his daughter's wriggly butt sticking out from behind the cart, then back up to Max. "I can't find her anywhere." He winked, and Max's soul transcended the earthly plane.

Erika giggled.

"Hey, Max, you didn't happen to see which way she went, did you?"

Those perfect pierced lips had spoken his name. For a split second, Max was too mesmerized to understand how Hot Dad could know who he was. Then he remembered he was wearing his library badge and lanyard. Duh. He shook out of his daze. Time to act like a normal human being. "Nope. Didn't see her. She definitely didn't come this way." His voice squeaked, and his cheeks twitched into what he hoped was a smile.

More giggles.

Hot Dad scratched his chin. "So strange." He marched to the cart and made a point of looking everywhere but where Erika was hidden. "She just disappeared."

"No, Daddy, here I am!" Erika launched herself at her father.

He caught her and spun her in the air. "Well, well, well, there she is." He set her down.

She pouted. This close, Max could see the resemblance. She had her father's round nose but a slightly darker skin tone and black hair. Her two pigtails swung as she shook her head, whining. "I wanna stay up."

"You're too heavy. You're gonna break my back."

Erika crossed her arms. "But, Daddy."

"Uh-uh, you get fresh with me and we're going home. Actually, it's close to lunchtime. Want to go eat?"

Erika collapsed onto the floor right where Max needed to shelve. She covered her ears.

Max made an aborted attempt to get back to his duties.

"Sweetie, you're in this nice man's way."

"Um. It's fine." Max's voice was strangled.

"No, it's not. Erika?" Hot Dad sighed and tapped his foot. "Come on. Get up. Now."

She refused to listen, and instead rolled onto her side.

"I'm going to count to three. One, two, three."

She didn't budge.

Hot Dad shot Max an apologetic wince. "Sorry. I think she's hungry."

"It's fine," Max said again. An idea occurred to him, and he knelt beside her. He lowered his voice to a conspiratorial whisper. "Hey, would you like to see one of my favorite books in the whole wide world?"

Erika slowly uncurled, her gaze intent on Max.

"It's a book I used to read when I was a kid. It's about dragons and princesses and unicorns. Do you like any of those things?"

She nodded and made a poor attempt to copy his whisper. "I like unicorns. And dragons and princesses."

Warmth bloomed in Max's chest, thrilled he'd distracted her from a tantrum—and successfully aided Hot Dad in the process. "Sounds like the perfect book for you then. Follow me if you want to see it." He led Erika and her father to the picture book section, where he removed a book from the shelf and held it out to her.

Erika snatched the title and sprawled on her stomach so she could flip through the pages. She mouthed words as the curly letters and sparkly images seemed to suck her in.

"My nieces demand I read that book to them every time I visit," Max added to Hot Dad, momentarily forgetting he was speaking to one of the most beautiful men he'd ever seen. "I know the whole thing by heart." He froze as the situation caught up to him. He was talking to Hot Dad. Like, actually speaking, with words coming from his mouth. Should he not be doing that?

"How old are they?" Hot Dad asked.

Max blinked at him. "Who?"

"Your nieces?" Hot Dad raised an eyebrow.

Max resisted the urge to slap himself. "Right. They're seven and five."

"Nice." Hot Dad's amused grin made the edges of his eyes crinkle. "Got any kids of your own?"

"Nope. It's just me." Max gestured to his body with a strange jerky motion that made him mentally cringe. Why did his limbs choose that moment to be awkward and gangly—and why would he draw so much attention to his less-than-ideal self?

Hot Dad didn't seem repulsed. In fact, he gave Max a quick once-over before scooting around Erika to stand closer to him. "I haven't seen you before. Of course, I'm new to the area. Just moved here a few weeks ago." He stuck out a hand. "I'm Presley."

His hand was calloused and warm in Max's grip. "I'm Max," he blurted, despite the fact that Presley already knew his name. They pumped once, twice, and when they pulled apart, Max's brain stalled. Presley. The rockstar name suited him. Max's mind spun with fresh fantasies of Presley on stage, sweating, his impressive biceps bulging as he commanded the audience with his body and music.

Presley said something Max didn't catch, and he jolted back to the present, his cheeks hot. "What?"

"I said I like your pins."

Max glanced down at his chest, where his nametag hung below a series of Pride pins, including his pronouns. "Oh. Thanks." He'd been terrified to wear them at first, but most patrons didn't even see him to begin with, so his fear turned out to be moot.

"I need to get me some of those," Presley added.

Max's mouth dried. Did Presley mean to say...did he...was he…?

A blaring guitar riff made Max jump.

"Shit." Presley dug a cell phone out of his jeans pocket. Then, seeming to realize his faux pas, he flinched. "Shit, sorry. Sh—sorry! It's her mom. I gotta take this. Can you watch her for two seconds?"

Max couldn't do more than nod before Presley darted into the hallway. Numb and still processing Presley's possible coming out, Max stooped to check on Erika's progress. He recognized the page—the dragon and princess had just realized the knight was a bully and they should work together to defeat him.

"I love that part," he said. "What do you think?"

Erika scrunched her face, thoughtful. "I like the princess's dress."

"Ah, yes. It's very sparkly, isn't it?"

"Purple's my favorite."

"Me, too."

Presley's return cut off the rest of their conversation. "All right, it's time to go, missy. Let's check out that book. Your mom just brought home lunch."

Erika perked up, and the promise of food seemed to energize her into standing without protest.

"Thanks," Presley said to Max. "We'll see you around." He gave a little wave before ushering Erika toward the circulation desk.

Max waved back until he realized they weren't watching him anymore. He lowered his hand, then hastened to the cart he still had to shelve in the graphic novel section. Once there, he took a moment to brace himself on the cart and breathe, his head hanging.

He'd had a conversation with Hot Dad. He'd learned Presley's name, and Presley had commented on Max's pins. It was the first time a patron had noticed them—had noticed him. But it had to be a fluke. A once-in-a-lifetime chance. Plus, Erika's mother remained in the picture. It wasn't like Presley could ever be with someone like Max, even if he wanted to be. Which he didn't. Even though he'd maybe kind of indicated he might not be 100% straight, and maybe kind of checked Max out?

Max's pathetic heart skipped a beat. What if?

For the rest of his shift, his mind swirled with new domestic fantasies centering on Max in Presley's hefty arms with Erika tucked in between them, reading a story together.

Before leaving, he made a mental note to stock up on romance novels featuring single dads.

It wasn't a fluke.

A week after their initial meeting, Max was shelving juvenile nonfiction in the stacks, far from the main area of the children's floor. In his darkened corner, he put away books about animals and wondered if Presley had pets. Was he a cat person or a dog person? Max was a plant person, although he'd always hoped to get a big enough place for a cat someday.

"Hi."

Max startled so badly he smacked into the shelf behind him. Thankfully, the massive stacks were bolted to the wall, so he merely hit the wooden shelves instead of knocking books over. He rubbed the sore line on his back and spun to face Presley and Erika.

"Erika, don't sneak up on people like that," Presley said. "Say you're sorry."

Erika scuffed her feet. Her hair was in a long braid that she toyed with as she apologized.

Presley reached out a hand to Max. "Really, are you okay?"

Max waved off his sympathy. "I'm fine. Just jumpy." He glanced past them. "Um. Is there no one at the desk to help you? I can call for—"

"No, we came to find you," Presley cut in.

Max felt like he'd actually fallen on the ground. Or perhaps the ground had surged up to swallow him. His body tingled, and giddiness coursed through his veins until he had to look away for a moment for fear of smiling too widely at the pair.

They'd purposely sought him out. They wished to speak to him.

"Erika and I wanted to thank you for suggesting what's become her new favorite book. Right?" Presley patted his daughter's head.

Erika wound around her dad's leg and raised her chin. "I've read it one million times."

Presley huffed a laugh. "Not quite, but sure feels like it." He glanced at Max. "You weren't kidding about memorizing it. We've read the book at least once every night before bed, and I've got the beginning down pat." Presley gave a mock shudder.

"Wait until the story finds its way into your dreams," Max blurted. He faced the cart and pretended to check that the books were in order, all the while berating himself for being so odd. He wasn't lying, though. After perhaps the fiftieth instance of reading the text to his nieces, he'd dreamed of dragons and sparkly princesses. Of course, that was probably more the influence of the cold medicine he'd been taking at the time.

Presley laughed. "God forbid." His eyes were slightly desperate as he asked, his voice pleading, "But do you know any other books we can try?"

Max did. He had a whole repertoire of picture books stored in his brain—ones that held both child and adult appeal. He'd read them all to his nieces. "Of course. This way. Hopefully the book I'm thinking of is on the shelf."

⁂

Like clockwork, Presley and Erika returned the following week and tapped Max on the shoulder while he was shelving early chapter books.

This time, he was ready for them. The duo appeared to prefer Tuesday mornings, so Max had made an effort to shower, comb his hair, shave, and wear clothes that fit him, including a maroon polo he received from his sister last Hanukkah; she said the color made his blue eyes pop. He'd already gotten several compliments from his co-workers and he didn't miss Presley's lingering gaze when he and Erika appeared.

Erika was chattier than their previous visit and wanted to describe to Max what they'd read recently, despite him being the one who gave the books to her. It turned out that, although Max knew each story well, he didn't realize the skateboarding cat had friends who lived in outer space because they were aliens.

"You have an excellent imagination," Max said once she'd concluded.

Erika beamed, showing off her two missing front teeth.

"I like to think she gets it from me," Presley said.

"Are you a writer?"

"Me? No. But I am an artist." Presley held out his arms to show off his tattoos. Max could finally make out the details of a beautifully inked green snake eating its tail on one arm—an infinity symbol—and intricate vines interspersed with white and pink flowers on the other arm. The vines extended to his neck, and other colors peeped from the collar of his t-shirt.

Max shivered and tore his gaze away from the enticing view. "These are your designs?" He yearned to touch but held himself in check.

"Yeah. Drew them myself, then had my co-worker do the rest for me."

"So, you're a tattoo artist?"

"Yeah. You ever think about getting any?"

"Tattoos?" Max let out a slightly hysterical sound. "No. I'm a wimp. I think I'd faint. That's why I don't have piercings either, though I really like them." He didn't add, especially on you.

Presley shrugged. "If you want it badly enough, you can make it happen. Believe me, I've given tattoos to very squeamish people, but they left happy they went through with it."

Max's cheeks burned. He couldn't tell if Presley was teasing or trying to inspire him. "Well, I should get back to shelving before my boss yells at me."

"Oh. Sorry. I guess we better head out anyways. Got any more book recommendations before we leave?"

"For you? Always." Max brought them to their favorite section and helped them pick out books.

As he and Erika turned to leave, Presley added, "I like that shirt by the way. It's a great color."

Max ducked his head. "Thanks." And for the rest of the day, he floated on air. He even smiled at himself in the bathroom mirror.

The third and fourth weeks taught Max new facts about his favorite patron duo.

For example, Presley also worked part-time as a hairstylist and did his Mohawk and the dye job himself. He preferred coffee to tea, had two cats, and liked to fix old cars. Erika, meanwhile, was exactly four years old on August 18th, loved macaroni and cheese, wanted to be a dragon when she grew up, and had lots of stuffed animals.

During their fourth visit, Max ran into Presley and Erika on his way to the staff room. He'd just removed his glasses and was on the hunt for a cleaning cloth to wipe off a smudge.

"Whoa, hey, I almost didn't recognize you without your cute glasses," Presley said.

Max made some sort of face at him—he had no idea what his expression could've been—and fled to the back. Once safe, he located his glasses kit and robotically cleaned his lenses while the word 'cute' reverberated through his mind. Presley thought his glasses were cute. Cute. Did that mean he thought Max was cute by extension? He'd liked Max's maroon shirt, right? And if he weren't interested, would he so openly state his opinion in a public library? Max's fantasies were starting to blend with reality, and he didn't know what to do about it.

Max only heard about Presley and Erika's fifth visit when he came back from vacation.

"Two of our patrons asked for you. They were bummed to not find you," were the first words out of his boss's mouth when he got to the children's floor.

The librarian smirked. They both knew exactly who she was talking about. "I told them you'd be back this week."

Max's face flamed. "Oh. Okay." He turned to his shelving cart.

"And Max?"

He paused, his hands on the bar. "Yeah?"

"When you get done with that, can you work on this month's book display? Those patron friends of yours couldn't stop talking about your excellent recommendations, and I think we should highlight some."

Max stared at her. "Am I allowed to?" He thought he'd only ever get to shelve books.

"Absolutely. Be creative. I'm sure your display will be great." She shuffled papers on her desk, then peered at him. "I'm excited to see what you create. We're always looking for new ideas."

"Thanks." Max gulped. A fizzy feeling burst in his stomach—excitement. He couldn't shelve fast enough.

After finishing his cart, Max spent the rest of the afternoon on the display case, which was the first thing patrons saw when they entered the children's floor. He chose older books that were excellent but forgotten in the face of shiny new covers and arranged them standing on the glass shelves, tilted toward the center. To accentuate his selections, he cut out shapes from neon construction paper and pasted them in a starburst pattern like fireworks behind each title.

He was no artist, but when he finished, he stood back to admire his work. Not half bad, if he did say so himself. A hot rush of pride shot through him. He hoped people would check out the books he'd chosen.

"Oh hey, you're back," came a familiar voice that had Max smiling before he even turned around.

Presley stood without Erika, juggling a large stack of books in his arms.

"Hey." Max didn't know what more to say. He busied himself scooping scraps of paper into neat piles.

"I was hoping to run into you. Erika was sad you weren't around last week, though your co-worker gave us some great books, too."

"I can see that." Max waited for Presley to bring his items to the return slot, but instead, he hesitated.

"Heard you were on vacation. Did you go somewhere nice?"

"Yeah. My whole family goes to this ocean cottage every summer. The kids have fun, and I love reading on the beach." And if he read novels where he pictured Presley as the hero and Max as the heroine, well… He'd yet to find a rockstar romance where one of the characters had a child, but the holiday cozy he'd brought included the main couple and their little girl making a mess while they laughed and baked cookies. Under the sweltering sun, Max had been warm on the inside and the outside imagining himself, Presley, and Erika in the characters' places.

"Sounds awesome," Presley said. "What kinds of things do you read? I'm looking to get back into it. Been a long time since I read a book."

Oh no. Max's throat locked. He couldn't tell Presley he mostly read romances. "Umm. I don't know if...if they're things you'd…"

"Try me." Presley's tone was soft, his expression kind.

Max swallowed. "I… I read. Romance novels." His voice came out tinny.

Presley cocked his head. "What'd you say?"

"Romance novels," Max choked before dashing off to grab a trash can and sweep the paper scraps inside. He couldn't look at Presley. His whole body was on the verge of combusting.

"Oh," Presley said. "Um. I read a few romance books, back in high school. I stole them from my cousin's house. It was nice reading happy endings for once, after all the shi—stuff I went through."

Max dared to peek at Presley's face. "Really? I like happy endings, too. Especially when characters who think they won't find anyone end up discovering the perfect person for them." He snapped his mouth shut, terrified he'd said too much.

Presley shuffled on his feet, redistributing the books in his arms. "Yeah, I like that, too. And I think I'd be interested more in..." He bit his lip and surveyed the surrounding area as if verifying they were alone, which they were. Then he whispered, "Gay or bi romances."

Max's mouth fell open. Was this confirmation of what he'd guessed? He stepped backward and stumbled over the trash can, spilling its contents everywhere. He bit back a curse as he knelt to clean up. "S-sorry. Oh gosh."

Presley bent to help but seemed to forget about the books he carried. They tumbled onto the floor in a cascade he failed to catch in time. Then they were two grown men kneeling in a giant mess on the children's floor of the library.

"Oh no!" said a child, and Max and Presley turned to a mother who'd just stepped off the elevator with a toddler in a stroller. Her eyes widened at the sight of them while the child clapped his hands. "Clean-up, clean-up!"

Max met Presley's gaze and they simultaneously burst into laughter.

Several minutes later, everything was back in its proper place. Max accompanied Presley to the circulation desk to return his books.

"Where's Erika?" he asked as they took turns dropping the books in the slot. His boss shot him a thumbs up when Presley wasn't looking, and Max made a face at her to stop. She pretended to busy herself with her computer, completely unrepentant.

"She's at her mom's this weekend. Why?"

"No reason. I was hoping to hear what she thought of her latest books."

In unspoken agreement, they headed toward the picture book section.

"We're not together," Presley said.

Max jerked to a halt. "Huh?"

"Her mom and I divorced a while back. Part of why I moved to this neighborhood was so I could see Erika more."

Max nodded. That made sense. And right, he should probably stop nodding, but he couldn't. A barrage of fantasies assaulted him, surging with the hope that built in his chest like an expanding balloon. Was Presley available? Did Max have a chance?

"Hey, what about that display you were making?" Presley paused beside Max, so close Max felt the warmth radiating from his bare arms. He was wearing a tank top today, and Max couldn't think as those chiseled muscles pressed close. The scent of Presley's spicy deodorant and a hint of sweat filled Max's nose. Oh, how he wanted to curl up in that delicious musk forever and let the strength and confidence of Presley's solid form keep him safe, protected. But did Presley feel the same way? Did he want Max?

"Uh," Max said, and with a jerk, remembered he was pulling books for Erika. "Yeah. Um. The display's over here." He pivoted on his heel to lead Presley in the opposite direction. Their ensuing conversation was only book-related, and later Max couldn't recall a single word. Presley did check out half the display, though, which meant Max had to search for more items to replace the empty spaces. The task barely staved off the klaxon blaring in his mind, an alarm repeating that day's revelations. Presley was maybe gay or bi. In either case, he seemed to indicate he was into men. And Max was a man, so Max could ask Presley out. Or could he?

Max begged off work early, claiming illness, and spent the rest of the day tossing and turning in his bed as he rehashed every exchange.

Was Presley interested, or was Max just desperate and projecting his loneliness? At the same time, he couldn't deny Presley's admiring glances at Max's body, the way his first stop in the library was wherever Max was, how his face lit up when he managed to find him.

Max fell asleep with his own words on the tip of his tongue.

I like happy endings, too. Especially when characters who think they won't find anyone end up discovering the perfect person for them.

Max glared at the clock in the sorting room. Was his shift over yet? Tuesdays used to pass quickly, but ever since Presley and Erika stopped visiting the library three weeks ago, the day had become long and dreary.

His eyes glazed over as he alphabetized the children's DVDs on the cart in front of him. DVDs were easy to sort. He didn't need his brain at all, which was good. He could let numbness claim him rather than replay his last conversation with Presley for the thousandth time.

Max wished he knew what he'd done wrong. He must've said something to scare Presley away, although he couldn't imagine what. He'd agonized and agonized over every word until he lost sleep and had to call in sick, but no answer materialized. Better to think of something else, yet even his favorite romance novels failed to distract him out of his funk. He couldn't stop picturing Presley as each story's hero, and reading about them made tears prickle behind his eyes.

But the worst part? Erika. Max could only hope Presley hadn't completely given up on libraries and would bring his daughter to ones in nearby towns. A voracious reader like her deserved to be supported, not stifled by adult miscommunication and mixed signals. Max sniffled then startled at the sound of the sorting room phone ringing. He glanced around, but no one else was there to answer it, so he pulled the receiver off the cradle.

"Hello?"

"I need you upstairs," said his boss. "Leave the cart. Just bring yourself."

A cold feeling wormed into Max's gut. He wasn't going to get fired, was he? Sure, he'd been slower than usual since his afternoon with Presley, but he'd gotten compliments on his book display, and his boss had started sending more patrons his way for children's book recommendations. Was she angry at him? Had he misjudged her pitying expressions?

"Okay. Be there in a second." He hung up.

As Max hastened up the stairs to the children's floor, he tugged on his new shirt's sleeves. His thoughts careened with worst-case scenarios, too many to pin down. He must've made a grievous error and was going to be reprimanded. His heart in his throat, he barreled out of the stairwell and straight into a patron.

"I'm so sorry!" Max gasped and reeled back from Presley.

"Hey." Presley sounded equally breathless. "Thanks for coming up."

At her desk across the floor, his boss grinned at Max. Oh. Was that why she'd called him?

"Hi." Max forgot every other word in the English language, too ensnared by Presley's fond gaze. He had such long eyelashes, and tiny freckles dotted his nose.

"I wanted to give you this. I meant to last time, but I..." Presley rubbed the back of his neck. "Sorry it's been so long. Erika was sick, and I got behind at work and then my co-workers called out... Anyways, here." With his other hand, he held out a library book with the due date receipt sticking out of the top.

Max blinked at it. "Are you returning it? The book slot's over there."

"I know. But I wanted to return it to you." Presley raised his eyebrows.

"Um. Okay? I'll go put it in the slot." He grabbed the book, but Presley held on.

"No! Just." Presley rolled his eyes. "Look at the receipt."

Max frowned. Normally he crinkled up the receipts and tossed them in the recycling bin—they were for patrons, not library staff. He slid the smooth slip of paper out of the book, then read it. Nothing unusual on the front, but when he flipped it over, someone had scrawled a bunch of letters and numbers in blue pen.

Coffee? Text me 555-890-6178 -Presley

Max couldn't breathe. He met Presley's gaze but didn't know how to form words.

"I didn't get your romance book recommendations last time, but if you're interested in meeting outside the library, I'd love to hear them." Presley's expression was tenuous, hopeful.

It hit Max all at once. Presley was asking him out. A jolt of joy tingled from his scalp to his toes. "Yes!" he said, far too loud. He lowered his voice. "I'd like that." He smiled and couldn't seem to stop.

His boss pumped her fist into the air.

Presley blew out a long breath, then grinned. "Awesome." He gave an awkward salute as he backed toward the exit. "Text me."

"I will." Max's cheeks hurt as his smile somehow widened.

"Cool." Presley bumped into the door frame on his way out, and Max's heart burst with a desire so fierce he barely kept himself from screaming. As soon as Presley was gone, Max raced to the staff bathroom and locked himself in a stall where he performed a silent dance of celebration—until he smacked his funny bone and reality returned. He hadn't screwed things up. Presley wanted him. They were going to get coffee. Max didn't even like coffee, but he did like Presley.

They would make this work.

SIX MONTHS LATER

Max finished his book display, and already parents buzzed around, ready to grab that month's themed items—books on or including forests, replete with paper trees and leaves he'd spent several hours cutting out. As soon as Max stepped back, the adults descended, and a mother called him over to provide recommendations for her first-grader, who didn't like to read. Then, after he'd showed her some suggestions, he brought her to the circulation desk to check them out.

As an official library assistant, he did far more than shelve books.

Behind the desk, Max chatted with other patrons coming and going, their little ones clinging to their legs or fast asleep in strollers. He also signed up a few adults for the romance book club he was starting the following month—yet another new responsibility he was more than happy to tackle. He was even thinking of applying to grad school for a Masters in Library Science. Hard to believe that only six months ago, Max was only an invisible shelver hiding behind his book carts, and now he basked in the spotlight.

Time flew, and when he next glanced at the clock, Max realized the late hour. He bustled together his things with only a minute to spare, and as expected, his ride announced itself with a loud presence.

"Max!" Erika hurtled toward the desk with Presley running to keep up.

"Erika, what did we say about using your indoor voice?" Presley asked.

Erika hooked her chin on the edge of the circulation desk and stared at Max. "I gotta be quiet in the library."

"Right." Max booped her on the nose with a chuckle before removing his employee badge and stowing it in a drawer. "But not too quiet." He straightened and caught Presley eyeing him appreciatively.

"You're wearing the sweater I bought for you," he said.

"It's called a cardigan, and it's perfect." Max spun around to show how well the garment suited his skinny frame. Paired with his glasses and nice khakis, he looked like a real librarian.

Presley whistled. "I'll say."

Max blushed, then faced Erika who was fiddling with a pencil on his desk. "How was preschool?"

As Erika babbled about her day, Max waved a hasty goodbye to his co-workers and emerged from behind the desk. He offered his hand to Erika. She squeezed tight, still chattering. Presley grabbed Erika's other hand, and with her swinging between them, they left the library in the perfect imitation of a scene right out of a romance novel.

STARTING A NEW CHAPTER

Katey Tattrie

Anna had been working on her computer, doing the inventory, when the sounds of frantic barking drew her attention outside the shop. She frowned; the little bookstore was on the town's main street, and rarely were there dogs sounding like that.

Wrapping herself in the shawl from the back of the chair, she went to investigate. Outside the clothing shop next door, backed up against a tree trunk, was a dog barking furiously at the people who had boxed him in.

"What's going on out here?"

"There's a stray wandering, and no one can get close enough to grab him," the owner of the sandwich shop down the block replied. "Managed to get him stopped here but can't get any closer."

Anna frowned at the group of adults, then looked at the dog. It was a Rottweiler; his head was bowed, and his tail tucked between his legs. He kept raising one of his back paws off the ground, alternating with the opposite front one, and Anna could see blood on the ground. With the freezing temperatures, she guessed his paws were likely near frozen. As the dog continued to bark, she spotted a glint at his neck and shook her head; a collar and tags. "He's not a stray, he's just scared," she corrected.

Reaching back, she acted on a hunch and opened her store's door wide.

"C'mere, boy," she called out softly. The dog stopped barking and studied her warily. "Everyone back up and give him some space," she advised, then called softly to the dog again.

"Anna, this isn't a good idea," the sandwich shop owner said as the group watched the dog bolt for the open door.

"He's wearing a collar, and is frozen," Anna replied. "He's just lost."

Once inside, she closed the door and flipped the sign to closed, before she turned to see the dog had gone straight to stand in front of the electric fireplace she had by the cash desk; his whole body shivered as he stood there, warming up slowly. "That's what I thought," she murmured. "You're just cold, aren't you, boy?"

Anna walked slowly to the back of the store and opened the storage closet. Grabbing several blankets and the first aid kit from inside, she returned to see the dog hadn't moved but continued to watch her. Smiling slightly, she spread out a plush blanket in front of the fireplace, then patted the ground. "Come on, let's get you warm," she said to him. The dog limped over slowly and flopped with a loud sigh. Anna chuckled and wrapped another blanket over him cautiously, letting the dog catch her scent before she reached over the top of him. But the big dog nuzzled her hand and whined.

"Okay, big guy, let's see what you've done to your feet, okay?" Anna said uncovering first his front, then back paws, to see the left front and right back one cracked and bleeding. He tried to lick them as soon as she touched them, but she shooed him away. "No, no, none of that. Let's clean them properly."

She filled a basin with water and antibacterial soap, and a second one with just warm water. Then she grabbed washcloths, and returned to clean him up. Though he groaned, the large animal never once growled at her, which impressed Anna; she knew he had to be uncomfortable. She gently rubbed in a salve, then covered the injured feet in socks and taped them around his legs so the dog could not pull them off. Finally, she grabbed a bowl of water and checked his tags. Up until now, she hadn't been worried about anything other than his health; now she realized he likely had an owner who was also concerned as he lapped up the water with vigor.

The ID tags themselves made her burst out laughing. On one side, it read 'Oh shit, I'm lost'; something Anna had heard of, but never seen before. The other listed his name was Bear, and his owner's name and number.

Pulling her cell from her pocket, she grinned as Bear laid his head on her lap while she dialed. When the other end picked up, the man sounded frantic. "Hello, is this James Hill?"

"You found Bear? Is he all right?"

"He is," Anna assured quickly, and heard his long sigh of relief. "I own The Attic Nook bookstore on Second Street, just around the corner from Julia Avenue."

"I should be able to find it easily enough," James replied. "I won't be too long."

"No rush,'" Anna replied easily, stroking Bear's massive head. "I think he's hungry though; I have a roast beef sandwich, is that something he's allowed to have?"

"He absolutely can, but don't feel you have to; I can feed him when I get him home. He eats like a monster!"

Anna laughed and nodded. "I imagine so, but I don't mind. I've turned the closed sign, but the door is unlocked when you get here; just come in."

She was glad they sat next to the mini-fridge since Bear seemed in no mood to move from her lap. Pulling out the sandwich, Anna grinned when the dog's head rose with interest from her lap. "Are you hungry? Did your afternoon adventures leave you a bit peckish?" she teased.

After he had scarfed down the food, Bear wiggled onto his side, head still on her lap, and Anna reached into the cash desk to grab one of her personal books. She opened it and started to read aloud to the dog, waiting patiently for his owner to arrive.

James opened the door to the shop, and said, "Hello?" even as the bells overhead announced his arrival.

"Over here," the woman's voice called.

Walking over, James found his dog wrapped in blankets, his head lying in a woman's lap, though it raised, and his tail began thumping on the floor at the sight of his owner. "Bear! You scared the hell outta me, boy!" He knelt and rubbed the dog's ears gently. "I can't thank you enough for finding him. I'm James."

"Anna," she introduced with a smile.

James moved to pull the blankets off Bear, noticed the socks on his two legs and frowned. "What happened?" The dog, unhappy at being uncovered, snorted and pulled the covers back over himself with his mouth.

Anna laughed at his antics and started to stand. James held out a hand and she took it, letting him help her to his feet. Her eyes widened when she realized just how tall the man was once she was standing next to him. "How about I make us a coffee and tell you how I found Bear? I promise, it's nothing serious, and he'll be fine. But his feet are gonna be sore for a few days."

James frowned slightly but nodded. "He doesn't seem interested in moving anytime soon, so that sounds good."

Since the coffee machine made single cups, it took little time, and Anna motioned them to comfortable armchairs nearby. She explained how she had heard the commotion outside and coaxed the dog inside. "Two of his paws were bleeding slightly; probably a combination of the cold, and the salt down on the sidewalks. I…used to have a dog, and it was always rough on their feet. I cleaned him up and rubbed in a salve, but they're horrible for licking it off."

"Hence the socks," James said with a chuckle.

"It looks ridiculous, but it saves their stomach," Anna agreed. She studied the man across from her while she took a mouthful of her coffee, smiling while she watched the expressions flit across his face. He studied the books from where he sat, his hazel eyes fixating on certain titles and his lips twitching when he noticed certain ones. "How did Bear get out?"

James grimaced at her and shook his head. "It was such a stupid mistake," he admitted. "I'm moving into my house today, and I had Bear closed into a room, so we could leave the front door open. The movers opened the wrong door, and he slipped out."

"Am I keeping you?"

"No, my brother took over the move when Bear got out," James assured. "And when you called, I checked in; things were nearly done. Alex told me it was fine, just to look after Bear."

"He's a beautiful dog," Anna commented, grinning to see the animal sprawled in front of the heat and snoring softly.

James seemed to notice the same and chuckled. "I'm thankful he let you look after him; he's a rescue and can be nervous around people."

"I actually wondered when I saw him outside." Anna stared at the dog and smiled fondly. "He wasn't happy with everyone around him. It's why I just opened my door to give him an escape; I thought one-on-one he might be a little better."

"You've definitely been around dogs," James agreed.

Anna laughed and nodded, offering to refill his cup. While she made them each a fresh coffee, she asked, "So, you're just moving into town?"

"Back into town," he corrected. "Lived here all my life; moved away for school and stayed gone for a job. Came back to work with my brother in construction; it's the family business. I'm just not sure what I'm going to do with Bear."

"What do you mean?"

"He's not used to being left alone all the time," James explained. "During the week, I'll be at work with Alex, and his wife works as well, so there's no one to check in on him. I'm worried about separation anxiety."

Anna chewed her lip for a second then let out a sigh. "I know I'm a stranger but, what if you brought him here?"

James turned to look at her. "What do you mean?"

She shrugged and looked down at the dog. "Well, we already know he likes me. I can walk him on my lunch, and he could hang out here during the day. The area behind the cash desk is more than big enough, and we've established he likes the fireplace."

James chuckled and stared at the dog for a minute, who was stretching and turned over before he turned back to her. "What will your customers think?"

"My customers won't care if there's a dog here again," she replied, then quickly averted her gaze.

James stared at her, then nodded slowly. Her face blushed deep enough to match her flaming red hair, and Bear whined at whatever emotion the dog could feel radiating from her. "Okay then," James agreed. "That would actually help me out a lot, Anna, I appreciate it."

She swallowed and nodded, looking up with a smile on her face. "When did you want to start?"

"I start work on Monday. What time do you open the shop?"

Anna grinned. "Shop opens at 9 am, but I'm here at 8 if you want to drop him off earlier."

James laughed and nodded. "That actually works out better, thank you. I'll give you my cell number, message me if anything changes or there are any problems?" He waited for Anna to pull out her phone and recited his number, then smiled and took her hand. "I really appreciate this." He studied her for a minute, then knelt and scooped Bear up in his arms. "Let's not get those socks wet, right, buddy?"

Grabbing the door for them, Anna gave him a smile. "I'll see you Monday morning."

Anna was cleaning up the blankets from the floor when the store's phone rang. "The Attic Nook, how can I help you?"

"Anna, is everything okay?"

She frowned at the concern in her best friend's voice, Anna paused what she was doing. "I'm fine, Beth. Why? What's wrong?"

"Joseph, from the sandwich shop, called me to say you'd taken in some stray dog, and that a stranger went into your store with the closed sign flipped," Beth said.

Even over the line, Anna could hear the frown in her voice. She sighed in return, rolling her eyes, and shook her head. "He wasn't a stray, he was lost," she explained patiently. Anna explained everything that had happened with Bear, and what she had arranged with James, to be looking after him during the week.

"That's Alex's brother!"

Anna shook her head. "Is there anyone in this town you don't know?"

"Not really," the other woman replied with a giggle. "Besides, we went to school with them; Joe still works with them, I think," Beth explained, referencing her brother. "Michael played football with them."

Anna paused then nodded slightly. "That makes sense," she said softly. The mention of her late husband always made her take a deep breath, even if the pain was slowly lessened over the years.

"I miss him too, Anna," Beth said softly.

"I know you do. We still on for dinner tomorrow?" she asked, changing the subject to a lighter one.

"You know it. Text me if you need anything. Love you."

Anna smiled. "Love you too."

Monday morning, Anna unlocked the store and went about hanging up her coat, turned on the lights, and grabbed a blanket to lay out for when Bear arrived. She was booting up the computer when a knock sounded at the door; she looked up to see James peering in the window.

James led the dog inside on a leash once the door was open and smiled down at her, a bag in the other hand. "Good morning, Anna," he greeted. "I can't tell you again how much I appreciate this."

"Please, I'm happy for the company," she insisted. She reached for the leash and unhooked it, laughed as Bear headed straight for the blanket and flopped down. Anna turned with a wide smile and shook her head. "It looks like he remembers this place."

"I'd say so," James agreed. "I brought a few of his toys, food, dishes, treats if you want to give them… But I realized we never discussed payment?"

Shaking her head at him, Anna's smile faded. "I don't want any money."

"Anna, you're taking time out of your day to look after Bear," James insisted with a laugh. "I have to do something to repay you!"

"I really don't need anything," she maintained. "You've brought the food over, so I don't need that, and treats. I'm not out any money, so I honestly don't need anything."

He frowned playfully at her, narrowing his eyes, and let out a soft sigh. "Well, let me make you dinner, then?"

"James…"

"It's the least I can do," James said with a smile. "I'll grill some steaks, something easy, Friday night. I need to be able to thank you for making my life easier, Anna, please?"

"All right, dinner on Friday," she finally agreed with a nod.

"Perfect. I need to go, but I'll see you tonight to pick Bear up. Have a good day, buddy!" James called, but the dog had rolled over onto his back in front of the fireplace and was sound asleep.

⁂

On Friday, Anna finished up a sale and answered her phone just before it went to voicemail. "The Attic Nook, how can I help you?"

"Anna, hi, it's James."

"Hey, how's work going?" she asked with a smile, glancing at the dog who was fighting with a rope toy on the blanket. The week had flown by, and the Rottweiler was extremely well-behaved. Her lunches were spent walking him or taking him across the street to the park to play and burn off energy before they settled back in at the store for the afternoon.

"Good, just...really dirty, actually," James replied. "I don't mean to be a pain, but would it be a problem if you brought Bear to my place tonight?"

Anna shook her head, realized he couldn't see it, and rolled her eyes at herself. "No, of course not. I'm coming for dinner, anyway. Five-thirty, right?"

"Perfect, it'll give me a chance to clean up. Thank you, Anna. 48 Cherry Hill Lane. I'll see you soon."

She checked the clock and knew it was only a few hours, and she had to finish the order for next week and finish checking the sales inventory. Anna nodded to herself; should be just the right amount of time.

Anna arrived at the house and parked behind the pickup truck. She opened the back door of her sedan and grinned as Bear bounded up to the front door excitedly, scratching at the kickplate. She followed the dog up and was about to knock when the door opened.

James' hair was still wet, and he seemed out of breath as he said, "Anna, hey! Thank you so much for bringing Bear. Come on in."

"It's not a problem," she said with a smile. "Turns out, it's literally on my way home."

He took her coat and hung it while Anna took off her boots. "Well, I appreciate it. I ended up so covered in drywall dust today, I didn't want to show up at the bookstore like that. I looked like I'd been coated in powdered sugar!"

Anna burst out laughing. "And I appreciate you not tracking that into the store; I wouldn't want to have to clean that up."

"The steaks have been marinating all day, but it's a little early to start the veggies; unless you're hungry now?" James asked.

"No, it's early still," Anna confirmed. "But really, you didn't have to make dinner. I'm happy to look after Bear."

James frowned at her and motioned her to follow him into the kitchen to get drinks. "You won't take money as payment; you at least have to let me make you dinner!" he insisted. He opened the fridge and motioned, grinned as she said water was fine and poured them each a large glass before they moved to the living room.

"So, you said Bear wasn't used to being alone before you moved?" Anna asked.

James nodded and settled onto the couch, smiling as Bear settled across Anna's feet. "My ex and I broke up, but we had been living together," he explained. "She wasn't working, so she was always home. They didn't get along all that well, mind you, but…"

"But at least someone was there," she finished. "I didn't mean to pry."

"No, not at all," he said with a dismissive wave. "I would have been back here sooner, this house was bought, and Alex was looking after it, but… She kept making it difficult to sell the one we were living in so I couldn't leave."

Anna grimaced. "I'm sorry. That must have been challenging." She studied the boxes still scattered around the living room and grinned. "You seem to still be unpacking?"

He chuckled and shook his head. "I can't seem to get into the mood after a long day at work, and don't quite know where I want everything," James replied, running a hand through his hair. "I'm…particular about how I want to organize things. This weekend will likely be trying to get everything put in order."

"Well, a lot of them seem to be labeled books; I could always help you arrange those?" she offered. "I do have a bit of a knack for that."

James studied her, the playful light in her blue eyes, and nodded. "You do, don't you?" he countered. "It would be a bit of an all-day job, though; I have quite a few."

Anna nodded and stood, laughing when Bear moaned and shifted to let her move. She paced around the living room to study at least half a dozen boxes all labeled 'books', as well as movies and music. "Well, it is the weekend, if you want a hand; I have staff to work Saturdays for me; the store is closed on Sundays. But I don't want you to think you have to invite me."

"Honestly, having seen the bookstore, I'd love to have your help," James said with a nod. "How does ten tomorrow morning sound to you?"

"Perfect. Now, did you want some help getting the veggies chopped?" Anna asked.

⁂

Anna arrived the next morning with pastries, bundled in her long winter coat; the winds outside howling. James ushered her inside, took the box from her hands and her coat, then urged her to go stand in front of the fireplace. "Warm up! I'll go pour us some coffee."

"And get some napkins; the Danishes are fresh and super sticky!" Anna advised.

James brought everything back out and they settled to eat. He pointed out that he had opened and separated the boxes into books, movies, and music, insisting that she didn't have to help with it all.

"Please; we'll just work and see how far we get, how's that?" Anna countered.

He chuckled and nodded. "You're very persistent, you know that?"

"Have you dealt with many redheads before?"

Throwing his head back to laugh, he said, "I'm afraid if I respond and make a fiery redhead comment, it might get me in trouble here!"

Anna wiggled her eyebrows at him. "Mmm, careful there, stilts."

Grinning at her quick comeback, James shook his head at her, though couldn't argue; he was nearly a foot taller than she was.

They washed up and started working. James spoke of his family; Alex and his wife, expecting their first child in the next few months, and how they had just discovered they were having a girl. The brothers had grown up across town, and their parents had moved to Texas once their father retired, to get away from the cold, but still came back every few months to visit. "I swear, Dad just likes to check-in on the business," James finished with a grin.

"If he started it from the ground-up, I can't say I blame him," Anna said with a shrug. "It's just as much his baby as you and Alex are."

"Yeah, true enough," he agreed. "Dad grumbles but admits things are going well. And you? How did you and Michael meet?"

Her head bowed to study the book in her hands, and she drew in a deep breath to steady herself.

"I'm sorry, Anna. You don't have to tell me," he said quietly.

Anna smiled and shook her head. "No, it's all right. I don't mind, honestly, it's just… It takes me a bit because I don't talk about it a lot," she admitted. "Michael and I met in college. I think you knew my husband?"

"I remember the whole family, yeah," James admitted. "Joe and I are the same age; Beth and my brother were in the same grade in high school."

Anna grinned; it was a small town, so she wasn't surprised. Michael was the youngest sibling, only a year younger than Joe. "They have a close family, which I love. I didn't really; my mom left when I was young, and I never knew her. Dad tried, but he had health issues and passed when I was in high school and applying for universities. Luckily, I got in on scholarships." She continued to work as she spoke. "Anyway, Michael and I were in several classes together for business and English; I was taking a general Bachelor of Arts degree but wasn't one hundred percent certain what I was going to do after. So, I took a wide range of classes; business, English, history, all so that I could try and decide what to do after. Michael was taking English and business so he could run the bookstore after he came home."

His tone implied he was impressed. "How many classes did you end up having together?"

"Most of them, actually, in our first semester," Anna admitted with a smile. "We spent a lot of time together and it wasn't long before we were dating. By the time university was over, I moved back here with him, and the family… Everyone is amazing. Dad… Don accepted me readily, Beth and I became, and still are best friends." Her face darkened slightly. "We'd been together for three and a half years by the end of school. We came back here, bought a house together, and got married. Daisy was our wedding gift to each other, a lazy yellow lab who loved Michael as much as I did; she followed him everywhere."

"Which is how you know so much about dogs," James said softly.

"She was a brat, but I loved her," Anna agreed. "She was so pale she was almost white. Anyway, when Dad wanted to retire, we bought the store from him, and Daisy used to go in with us. Michael loved fishing, and he and his brother Joe had been planning a trip up to the family cottage," Anna explained, frowning as she rearranged books on a shelf. "Michael was able to leave a day earlier and take Daisy with him; he wanted the extra day of fishing before Joe joined him. On Sunday, they were on their way home. Joe was following behind… The driver of the transport had a heart attack, and died instantly," she said softly, pausing in her unpacking. "He crossed the center line and ran into the side of Michael's truck. Joe said he never had the chance to react; Michael and Daisy were gone in a second."

When her voice died off, James walked over and placed his hands gently on her shoulders. "I'm so sorry, Anna," he murmured.

She smiled at the warmth in his tone and leaned slightly back into him for a moment. "Thank you," she said softly. "It was about five years ago now. Not long after it happened, I offered to sell the shop back to Don; I thought it belonged in the family." Anna stepped away and turned to face James and shrugged. "He insisted that it was still in the family. I'm still involved with family dinners once a month; Beth is my best friend. I lost Michael, but I didn't lose my family, and I love them for that."

James smiled and nodded. "I'm glad. They were a lot of fun in school and good people, and I'm glad to see they haven't changed."

Three weeks into watching Bear, James began to stay after work to have a coffee with Anna at least three of the nights if he wasn't too encrusted with dust from his job. She found herself looking forward to the end of each day to spend time with him, and Friday night dinners were becoming late nights of talking about books, movies, and anything else that held their interest.

James admitted he was looking forward to warmer weather to be able to take Bear for long walks, something Anna agreed she missed doing as well. Neither were a fan of the cold winter winds. Each loved mystery, spy, and science-fiction novels, but James had a penchant for thrillers, something Anna had never ventured into much.

Five weeks after they had first met, James walked into the shop at four-thirty. Anna glanced up at the clock and frowned slightly as she turned back to him. James chuckled and said, "We got off work early today," he answered her unspoken question.

"I was wondering! You're about an hour earlier than I expected," she said with a grin.

"I thought I'd come to spend the extra time with you."

Anna flushed at the deep timbre to his voice and leaned back against the counter as he came to stand in front of her. They had slowly been getting closer when they sat next to each other in the last few weeks, so she waited to see what he would do. Anna watched as James reached out to cup her face, his rough hands gentle on her skin. Her heart was hammering in her chest, even as she tilted her head up to meet his lips. The kiss was soft, and she had just reached up to grip his shirt when the bells of the front door sounded, announcing a customer.

She pulled away, her face flushed, and Anna looked over to see one of her regular customers. "Mrs. Anderson," she greeted. "Here to pick up that order, I'm assuming?"

The older woman's eyes sparkled, and she wore a knowing grin as she approached the counter. "Yes, my dear. Thought I would come and pick it up before you closed for the night. I won't keep you long," she assured with a wink.

Anna felt her face burning and cleared her throat as she rang out the sale and bid the woman a safe drive. She locked the front door and turned to James, who had moved to the back of the store to give her privacy while she worked, but the dark look in his eyes spoke volumes.

"I don't want to rush you," James assured. "I've talked to Alex, and I know you haven't dated since you lost your husband. We can move at your pace, Anna. I can wait."

She licked her lips and nodded. "I love the time we're spending together," Anna replied. "I don't want to lose that."

"You won't. I'm not going anywhere." James walked over and wrapped one arm around her waist, the other ran through her curls while he smiled down at her. "We're still on for dinner tonight?"

She started to nod, then groaned, rested her hands on his hips. "I can't tonight," she replied with a sigh. "It's the family dinner tonight at Dad's."

"Then how about brunch tomorrow? I'll make a frittata, potatoes, pancakes?" His fingers stroked her lower back and he watched her eyelids lower. "Any requests?"

"No, that all sounds good. How about I bring a fruit salad too?" she offered.

"I keep telling you, when I offer to cook, you don't have to bring anything," he said with a chuckle. "I enjoy it."

Anna smiled and nodded. "I know, but I like to."

The hand in her hair came down to stroke her neck and James nodded in return. "Fair enough. So, ten-thirty tomorrow?" When Anna nodded, James leaned down and pressed a soft kiss against her lips. "I'll see you in the morning, Anna. C'mon, Bear," he called, watching as the dog groaned and got up from in front of the heater.

She watched him leave and turned to check the last few boxes of the delivery that had arrived earlier in the afternoon. It was still an hour before she needed to be at the house for dinner and wanted to finish checking off the receiving form. A smile crept across her face when she saw one author's name on the list: James Patterson. Knowing James had been looking forward to the new release of the author's latest thriller, Anna set one aside and left a note for the staff in the morning, she finished checking things off and got ready to go home.

Anna always enjoyed dinner with her extended family. Though Michael had passed on, they treated her as if she were one of them, and there was never any awkwardness. Until her best friend brought up recent events.

"So, Mrs. Anderson says you and James looked rather cozy this afternoon," the blonde said with a knowing grin.

The wine glass paused on the way to her lips, and Anna felt the blush wash up her face. Taking a sip, she nodded. "I forgot you two were neighbors," she muttered.

"And Mrs. Anderson is a bit of a gossip," Beth confirmed with a giggle.

"Just Mrs. Anderson?" Joe teased his sister with a frown. He turned to the redhead and smiled. "Anna, the brothers are both amazing men. And you look happier tonight than I remember seeing you in a long time."

She chewed her lower lip and nodded. "I've been dog-sitting for him during the week since he moved back; his Rottie is a rescue who isn't used to being alone," Anna explained. "In return, because I refuse to let him pay me for it, he's been cooking dinner for me. We both love to read…" Her voice died off and she shrugged, staring down at her wine. "It's been nice to spend time with him, I just…"

Don reached out, his hand up, and waited for her to take it. When she looked to meet his eyes, the older man smiled at her and squeezed her fingers. "Anna, Michael would want you to be happy," he assured. "We want you to be happy. I know that boy, and Joey's right, he's a good one. I don't want you feeling guilty over this, you hear me?"

Anna smiled and nodded. "I hear you, Dad," she agreed. A small tightness in her chest eased; though the family had been gently pushing her to move forward, they were understanding in her reluctance. Now that she had met someone, Anna had been nervous about how they would respond; their blessing meant the world to her.

Anna arrived the next morning at James' house, her scarf wrapped up around her head as James let her in. He laughed and frowned at how she looked until she unwrapped herself, revealing her damp hair.

"You must be frozen!"

"I slept a little late, and with these curls, I can't exactly use a hairdryer!" she replied with a laugh. "That's why the scarf is so thick."

"Well, the coffee is just finishing, so let's get you warmed up."

She followed him through to the kitchen, the smell of hazelnut coffee filling the room. She opened the bag she had brought, handing over a fruit salad and watched as James rolled his eyes, then looked down at Bear. "I didn't forget you, don't worry," Anna assured, and handed over a large bone, laughing as he bounded to his dog bed excitedly.

"You spoil him," James scolded jokingly.

"Just like you do," she argued with a grin. "And, I have a surprise for you." Anna pulled out the book she had brought and watched his face light up. "It came in yesterday's shipment, and I knew you were looking forward to it."

James came around to hug her while he took it. "Thank you! I can't wait to start it."

"So, how about we make this a reading date?" she proposed softly. "I saw a few books in your library I wouldn't mind looking at. We can curl up on the couch and read after brunch?"

He smiled down at her. "Is that what this is? A date?"

She smiled slightly at him and put a hand on his chest. "It's been a long time since I've dated, and I've never exactly been a wild one. We already know one another from coffee at the store and dinners, and we both love to read. So, are quiet dates okay with you for now?"

He set the book down on the counter and pressed his lips against her forehead. "Any time I get to spend with you is more than okay with me," James assured. "I told you, Anna; your pace. I meant it."

The oven buzzed, forcing James to draw away to pull out the frittata. The pair sat at the breakfast bar and shared about their work weeks, before cleaning the dishes and pouring fresh coffee, then moved to the living room. While he added wood to the fire, Anna browsed his shelves and chose a book for herself.

Once James was settled in the corner of the couch, he reached to pull Anna down to lean against his side. She laughed and glanced back up at him, shaking her head. "What?" he asked with a grin, keeping one arm wrapped around her waist.

"I just wasn't expecting to read like this," she replied with a grin.

James smiled as she placed one of her hands over the one resting on her stomach. They stayed like that for hours, before Anna set her book down in her lap. Her mind couldn't help but drift back to days she and Michael would read; they were nothing like this. Her husband became engrossed in books, not aware of anything else around him; she was close to the same. They often sat in separate chairs, or at the very least, opposite ends of the couch. But James, every now and then, would nuzzle her hair and place a kiss on the top of her head, making her smile. As soon as she realized she was making comparisons between the men, Anna felt awful and let out a long sigh.

James closed his book and looked down at her. "What's wrong?" When she shook her head, he hugged her slightly and urged, "Come on, Anna. Talk to me."

"I was just sitting here, thinking back to when Michael and I used to read, and realizing it was so different from this," she admitted. "And I don't want to compare the pair of you, I really don't…"

"But you can't help it," he finished, smiling softly. "I can understand that, Anna; it's all right. I just want you to remember that we are different people."

Anna nodded and smiled slightly, looking up at him. "And that's fair, totally fair," she agreed.

Bear chose that moment to come bounding into the living room, a stuffed animal in his mouth. James laughed and shook his head as the dog jumped up to lay across Anna's legs. He felt her stiffen against him and frowned, staring down to see her eyes fixated on the Rottie. "Anna, what is it?"

"I've never seen him with that stuffed animal before," she whispered.

James craned his head and noticed Bear had brought his Paddington Bear stuffie with him. "It's his favorite. He usually leaves it in my room, on his bed," James explained. "I'm not sure why he brought it out."

Anna swallowed and reached out to pet the dog's head and let out a shaky sigh. She knew it was a common enough toy, but it had been one of her own dog's favorites; Daisy took it with her everywhere. Anna hadn't seen one in the years since.

He seemed hesitant, but guessed, "Daisy had one too, didn't she?"

"It was her favorite," Anna confirmed. Of all the times for the toy to appear, it was when she was feeling guilty about being in another man's arms. She leaned back until she was across James' chest and looked up at him with a small smile, reaching up to stroke his cheek and the stubble on his face. "Is it stupid to think that Bear brought it out as a sign?"

James smiled at her gently and shook his head. "Not at all."

She chewed her lower lip and studied his face closely. "I think I'm starting to fall for you," she admitted in a quiet voice.

"Good," he replied with a laugh.

"Good?" she asked in surprise.

"Well, I'd hate to think I'm the only one," he teased, leaning down to kiss the tip of her nose.

NO LOITERING

Sonni de Soto

Lena Moreno pursed her lips at the "No Loitering" sign that now hung, laminated, and boldly printed, on the wall. A companion to the new café policy that had been waiting for her and the rest of the staff from the Deadwood Books manager, William Litton, before he left for the day.

Well, that felt passive-aggressive.

"Any person or being in the bookstore, or adjoining café, for over two hours who has not made a purchase, will be asked to either make a purchase or to leave."

Running her hands frustratedly through her short, curly hair, Lena shut her eyes and sighed before reaching for a rag to wipe down the café counter. She'd been trying to ignore it since the moment she'd seen it. Determined to distract herself, she'd buried herself in the day-to-day tasks of her job. But, as she restocked pastries and disposable coffee cups, those words kept echoing in her head.

"Any person or being."

That felt targeted.

Lena watched her girlfriend, Callie, wander through the shelves. Like she'd been doing since Lena's shift started, an hour and fifty-eight minutes ago. Like she always did while Lena was at work. As a muse, Callie loved the bookstore, as well as the coffee shop. No matter the time of day, there seemed to always be someone inside waiting, wishing, for a little inspiration. And Callie was always only too happy to oblige.

Lena could see her coworkers' gazes flick from Callie to Lena nervously. Lena knew that, according to policy, someone would have to do something. And it should be her. She was the café manager and Callie was her girlfriend.

Lena hated being in this position. It reminded her too much of all the times she, as a Latinx woman, had ever been scrutinized or profiled in stores or by security. Growing up being treated as if she didn't belong, as if her very presence was suspect, simply for being brown, made her never want anyone to feel like that. Especially not her own girlfriend.

But policy was policy. Either she enforced it or someone else would. And, while she didn't think any of her coworkers—not even William—would be cruel about it, being asked to leave, being told that your existence in a space you thought you had every right to be in—should have had every right to be in—was incriminating, was humiliating. Better it come from Lena than some other, random employee. Right?

So she braced herself, forcing her body to stand a little taller, before heading over to Callie.

Her knees felt weak as she stepped out from behind the counter. Her stomach churning, she made her way through the café tables. She wiped her clammy hands on her Deadwood Books apron as she approached Callie, who was peeking over the shoulder of some person looking at the array of notebooks by the checkout counters.

Lena took a steadying breath. "Callie?"

It shouldn't be, not after years of being together, but it was still a little striking whenever Callie looked at her. Lena lost her voice for a moment, only able to stare. Callie's maple-shaded hair somehow shone under the fluorescent lights as if sunshine followed her everywhere. When her deep, teakwood eyes blinked at Lena, a bashful flutter replaced the heavy unease in Lena's gut. And, when her full, pink lips smiled, Lena wanted nothing more than to lean down for a kiss, workplace decorum be damned.

It should have made things easier.

But it didn't.

"Did you need something?" Callie's voice was melodic.

Lena swallowed, trying to find her own voice. She could feel everyone's gaze on her. All her coworkers. Even the person browsing the notebooks paused to listen in.

Lena glanced at the clock. Two hours and three minutes had passed. She had to say something. If she didn't, she'd be in violation of store policy. She could be written up or even fired for this. And she needed this job. They both did.

Callie, while beautiful and smart and charismatic in that way only a demi-goddess could be, wasn't exactly a good fit for the modern workspace. She was an effervescent embodiment of inspiration, overflowing with this necessary and wonderful but essentially chaotic force. As her one foray into the corporate landscape taught her when someone needed inspiration, it almost always felt great to finally find it, boosting productivity and exceeding project expectations. But, too much quickly got distracting, if not overwhelming, and could, within days, upend an entire office, making interns start revolts over mail delivery duties and CFOs leave partnership positions to start their own fashion lines.

It was actually one of the reasons why she and Lena worked so well together. Lena wasn't a creator. She wasn't particularly ambitious. She didn't paint or sculpt. She wasn't a student or a philosopher or in search of life's great answers. She was the type who would much rather enjoy a good book than write one. Lena had always thought of herself as remarkably unremarkable. And, while pretty much every other person she'd ever dated found that boring, it let Callie feel...well, normal.

It wasn't that Callie didn't love being a muse. Of course, she did. Inspiring people wasn't just something she did but was who she was. She was proud to be part of a timeless tradition of moving humanity forward, of shaping unspoken dreams into something people could share.

But so often it felt like her magic was the first, and often only, thing people—both magical and not—saw, for better or worse. There were always too many people expecting her to be and act a certain way. It was a juggling act, trying to navigate it. And, with the weight of all that, especially in a world that was more comfortable relegating Callie's existence to ancient mythology than modern reality, it was nice to come home and feel no more and no less herself.

Callie had once told her that, even after having read and inspired countless romance stories filled with enormous and dramatic grand gestures of love, the most romantic thing she could think of was a partner who made the hard stuff easier. Who made her feel safe in a world that, for a multitude of reasons, didn't always.

If she was honest, it often made Lena feel guilty, to be heroized for doing what felt like so little. Show up. Be a supportive partner. It never felt like enough. Callie deserved to be showered with gifts and effusive expressions of affection. But Lena wasn't a grand gesture kind of girl. She never knew what to do and felt silly trying to be something she wasn't. And, as guilty as she sometimes felt, she was grateful that Callie never expected her to be more or less than she was.

However, if ever a grand gesture was needed, it was now. Right? Here was this rigorous policy and it was her job, as Callie's girlfriend in shining armor, to slay the danger ahead. To fix the things and make the hard stuff easier.

So Lena licked her lips. "I, uh..."

If only she knew what to do or how to do it.

Feeling like she'd stepped into knight-sized shoes that just didn't fit, Lena stuck her hands into her apron pockets, the odds and ends she kept in there brushing her fingers. Her hands clutched her pen and pad that she kept for inventory notes and, in a flash of inspiration, she bolted up straight. "I was going to bring you something. Did you want a drink or a snack?"

Callie smiled. "That's so sweet! Thanks." She thought a bit before giving Lena her order.

Feeling as if she'd both cleverly cheated the system yet also foolishly lost to it, Lena took down the order on her pad, even though it wasn't as if she'd forget it during the fifteen-feet walk from the shelves back to the café. It didn't change the fact that the policy still felt unfair and wrong, but buying Callie something from the café herself was technically a legitimate loophole in the new policy.

It still didn't feel like a victory. Hell, Lena didn't even want to tell Callie about it; why, when it would only remind them both that their life—their love and happiness together—often came at a cost. "Great!" Lena plastered a smile on her face. Maybe Lena couldn't fix that, but she would do what she could to shield Callie from it. And, really, it seemed a small price to pay, especially when she factored in her employee discount if it meant not having to be the person who made Callie feel unwelcome or unwanted.

"I'll be right back with this."

It was a solution, sure.

Then why, as Lena headed back behind the counter, didn't anything feel fixed?

⁂

It'd been a slow day.

Callie hadn't exactly been keeping count, but it felt as if there had been fewer people in the café today and the few who'd been there hadn't stayed long.

Callie blamed the "No Loitering" signs hanging up all over the store. She'd noticed the one in the café first. Then more had cropped up by the bathrooms. Then by the entrance. Over the course of a couple of days, suddenly the signs seemed to be in every nook and cozy corner of the store, silently shaming people for overstaying their welcome.

How was a muse supposed to work, if there weren't people present to inspire? She sighed and sat down at one of the tables.

"Can I get you a drink?"

Callie winced at the sound of William's voice.

The man stared down at her, disapproval clear in his eyes. "Or a pastry. We have some seasonal soups and sandwiches right now as well."

Callie forced a smile. "May I have a glass for water please?" She watched the manager's face tense.

William crossed his arms over his chest. "We have flavored water. May I recommend the lavender-and-blueberry-infused energy spritzer?"

Callie's spine stiffened. William was well aware of who she was. What she was. He knew that muses didn't carry money. Why would they? Aside from the rare exception, muses didn't make much money. This wasn't a calling that one did for personal gain. Being a muse was a labor of love. It was the love of story and art personified. But, even though it might sustain and satisfy her on a psychic well-being level, it didn't exactly pay enough for luxuries. Callie's smile felt both sweet and sharp. "No, thank you."

William frowned and walked away.

Callie shook her head and turned her attention to the other people in the space. Callie dismissed the group of sleepy, stressed-out, summer-semester college students. While they were often good for a term paper or end-of-course presentation, pre-test cram sessions rarely required Callie's brand of inspiration. Same with the mall-workers on break. Even the photographer sorting through her latest shoot didn't feel quite right. Callie worked better with words than images, better with stories than academics. It was why she liked to linger in bookstores.

Except Deadwood Books seemed...well, pretty dead today and she supposed beggars couldn't be choosers. About to settle on the photographer, she suddenly felt something.

Ah, there it was.

She turned to one of the students who was staring off into space, a sweet-faced boy with too-long hair. A classic daydreamer. Callie leaned in and closed her eyes, opening herself to that liminal space where her powers met his ideas. She smiled at his thoughts. A girl. Of course. Callie's eyes dreamily blinked open, only half-seeing the blond girl reciting from her notes across the table from the boy. Callie could still see her as she was—pretty and outgoing—but, more than that, she saw how he saw her. The way her fingers twirled in her hair seemed to invite thoughts of how soft the twining lengths must be. Her voice was confident, ringing with the sound of truth regardless of what she said.

From his head to Callie's, she saw him imagine what it would be like to approach the blond girl at the end of the study session. The rest of the group would disperse, leaving only them at the table. He'd ask if he could buy the girl a coffee. He didn't even know how he would, what exact words he'd use, but he imagined himself being clever and undeniable. Her blushing acceptance was something he couldn't quite picture in his head but was something he'd clearly thought about a lot.

Callie could feel his hope and fear and desire all wrapped up in that one thought. It was almost overwhelming. She took a breath and pushed, making his visions clearer, adding details to the dream. The possibility of the girl's acceptance felt more thrilling, shaping her lips into a knowing, excited smile. And the possibility of her rejection sharpened, a cutting laugh slicing through him. Callie could feel his mind reel, filling and swirling with both—all—prospects.

"Here you are." William placed the tiniest plastic cup only half-full of water on the table in front of Callie, tearing her from the boy's mind.

Callie had to fight not to scowl. She looked up at the man, the new "No Loitering" sign framed by his stiff shoulders. Even Callie could recognize the unspoken, yet crystal-clear message. He crossed his arms over his chest. "Is there something else I can help you with? Help you find a book?"

Callie simply smiled, her face feeling as if it were about to break. "No. Thank you." Her words sounded clipped and insincere even to her own ears.

William shook his head. "If you're not going to buy a book or something at the café, I'll have to ask you to please leave."

Callie balked. "You're kicking me out?" Why? She wasn't hurting anyone. On the contrary. She was inspiring people.

And, okay, it wasn't like the boy ignoring his textbook was going to pen the next great American novel or anything. But, who knew, maybe their relationship would inspire the blond to.

"This is a business." William's tone felt patronizing as if he were speaking down to her. "If you're not going to buy something, you have no business being here."

As a muse, Callie rolled her eyes at that. She could imagine him coming up with that phrase and feeling so clever. He seemed the type to ponder putting that kind of thing on a bumper sticker or break room poster.

Callie huffed. Being a muse would be so much easier if she could be ethereal, could be invisible.

But ever since the magical community decided to step out of the shadows and try to coexist with the humans, things had gotten complicated. Things that had been taken for granted since the dawn of time were now being called into question. It didn't matter that beings like muses and fairies and nymphs had all worked in the world beyond the vision of man, doing necessary things like maintaining the cycles of seasons and society. No, now, while still shouldering the grand burden of balancing the cosmos, they were now expected to be bound by such mundanities as privacy laws, personal boundaries, and, apparently, loitering rules.

Medusa's head, Callie was a creative spirit! She should be free to go wherever she liked and touch the minds and hearts of whoever called her. She and her kind had shaped the course of human history; how had they been caught in fate's puppet strings? "But I haven't done anything wrong," she finally said.

"That's for me to decide." William turned to tap the digital tablet in his hand. "As it is, you've wasted enough of my time today. As manager of Deadwood Books, I have the right to refuse service to anyone, for any reason. I've asked you to please make a purchase or leave. Please do so."

"Or what?" Callie wondered, her brow furrowing.

He bristled and raised his voice, making her flinch. "Please don't cause a scene."

Callie looked around and, even though she didn't think she had been causing a scene, she noticed the table of students had stopped studying. The photographer was no longer looking at her pictures. Even some of the bookstore shoppers had stopped to watch. She could feel them all stare as a heavy hush swept over the store.

Feeling vulnerable and exposed, Callie couldn't block out their thoughts. In a jumble of suspicion and gossipy curiosity, she could hear people wonder if she was a criminal, if she'd shoplifted or vandalized something. Some even scrutinized her face, wondering if she was one of the many wanted criminals they'd seen splashed across the news. After all, no one was asked to leave by management unless they'd done, or were, something wrong, right?

A few of the store employees had been expecting this kind of confrontation for hours, some for days. Their thoughts were a dizzying mix of guilt, pity, and voyeuristic glee.

Callie could feel tears well up inside her. It was all just too much. She couldn't stand to see herself through all their eyes, to have their speculations and distortions erase who she was and mold her into only what they wanted to see her as. She tried to shut it all out, but she couldn't.

"Either make a purchase or please leave the store," William continued, "or I can call the police."

The police? Was he kidding? Except she knew he wasn't. "For what?" Except she knew that too. Even though she knew she wasn't breaking any laws, William didn't see it that way. He saw her and her kind as an invasion. He saw all supernatural beings as inherently unnatural. He didn't trust her or anyone like her and certainly didn't want them anywhere near him.

"For causing a disturbance."

Since when was sitting in a coffee shop a disturbance? If anything, he was the one causing a raucous. Not that the cops were likely to see it that way. After the reveal of supernatural beings, often with supernatural powers, the public, and especially the police, had begun to view all magical beings with suspicion. Even beings like her, with passive powers that couldn't possibly hurt anyone, made people nervous. No one liked the idea of creatures who could creep into a person's mind, learning all their thoughts and secrets, and use that to influence them.

It didn't matter that she could only stoke the flames of inspiration for ideas that were already inside a person. It didn't matter that muses had been a subtle, shifting presence in society since the beginning of time, far before humans ever became aware of it. It didn't matter that, in all that time, muses had never caused anyone harm. Humans were all so scared of what she might find in their heads. Or what suggestions she might leave behind.

And, with cops, it wasn't so much that she had the right to remain silent as they would do what they must to keep her quiet, afraid that anything she said or did could be used against them. Callie had heard stories from other beings like her—of species profiling or even human rights violations, not that they were human—and, as she imagined those kinds of things happening to her, an instinctive fear shivered through her even as embarrassed anger seethed.

Okay, this had all obviously gotten out of hand. Callie needed to calm down. Needed to calm William down. She looked around. "Where's Lena?" She could help. Lena, even as a human, had her own kind of magic that seemed to soothe and calm people. She was good at that. Surely, she could explain things to him.

"She's working." William frowned. "And, unless you're going to purchase something from her, it's inappropriate to be bothering her while she's on the clock."

Inappropriate? To talk to her own girlfriend?

Callie opened her mouth to challenge him, but he cut her off. "Lena has a job to do and she can't do it, if she's constantly being distracted by you. And, if she can't do her job, I'll need to find someone else who can."

Callie stiffened again, her eyes narrowing. Was he threatening Lena? Callie hated the idea of being a burden to Lena, but she couldn't deny that dating her often made things difficult for Lena. There were a lot of people in the world who were still adjusting to discovering magic existed in the world and not all of them welcomed the knowledge. And you could never be sure who those people were—your boss or your mother or your neighbor or your waiter—until they said or did something that made it painfully clear.

Callie had lived with it her whole life, but Lena hadn't. Sure, as a woman of color, Lena had dealt with discrimination too. But at least when people told her she wasn't human, wasn't deserving of basic human rights, she didn't have to deal with the sting of truth that, strictly speaking, they were right.

Callie wasn't human. And, throughout the course of magical history, her people had been treated inhumanely. Sometimes for the better, being worshipped as gods. Other times for worse, being hunted as monsters or burned as heretics. It had been why, for a long time, they'd hidden away, relegated themselves to myths and legends.

But, for better or worse, they were out now, unable to hide in this digital, hyper-aware world, filled with cellphone cameras, high-speed internet, and twenty-four-hour news channels. And they all, human and magical alike, would have to deal with it.

But Callie would not make Lena pay the price for William's feelings toward Callie's kind. He could hate her all he liked, Callie did not care. But he would not threaten Lena over it. That was it! She stood up, her fists balling tightly. "I want to speak to your manager."

William shook his head. "I am the manager."

She knew that. Hades knew he loved to throw his weight around enough to never let anyone forget. "But I want to speak to whoever is above you." Like the district or regional manager. Or even Deadwood Books corporate. "This is harassment." He couldn't kick her out of the store for no reason and he certainly couldn't threaten his employee.

"Well, you can't." William puffed his chest out. "What you can do is leave. Immediately."

Make me.

The words, childish and clichéd as they were, burned on her tongue. But, just as she was about to hurl them at William, she saw Lena rush toward them. She placed a cup of coffee in front of Callie so fast the dark brew sloshed over the rim of the cup and onto the table. "Sorry, it took me a bit longer than I thought to get you your drink. But here you go."

Callie's shoulders relaxed, Lena's mere presence seeming to ease the tension inside her. She didn't care what anyone said; sometimes, some mortals were positively magic. She wanted to reach out, to touch Lena. To even just hold her hand. But she had a feeling that displays of affection in front of this man would be taken as a sign of weakness rather than strength and, in the end, would end up hurting Lena the most.

So instead, she took comfort from the stalwart stiffness of Lena's spine, and the steady weight of her hand on the back of Callie's chair as her caffeinated savior turned to glare at William. "Is there a problem here?"

William's gaze zeroed in on the coffee cup on the table and sneered.

"No problem."

Yet.

Callie didn't need special powers to hear the thought in the man's head. She could read it all over his face and, she knew, this wasn't over. Not by a long shot.

⁂

Lena stared at the latest new policy pinned to the employee news board.

"Employees may only use their company discount on two café items per shift."

Crap.

Lena had never been the best with math, but even she could add up those numbers. She'd already been stressing over the past few days' tallied-up totals. Even if she bought the cheapest, most basic item on the menu—just a small, black coffee—with her discount, every two hours, for forty hours a week, it all added up quickly. As it was, she and Callie were barely making ends meet. The added expense was barely doable.

Subtract her discount and she didn't know what she was going to do.

Maybe it was time to revisit the idea of Callie working again. But then they'd have to talk about it and Lena had been avoiding that from the start.

Sure, they'd talked a bit about the sudden appearance of the signs and, after the incident, they'd discussed William, but it made Lena really uncomfortable. She hated that there were people in the world who hated Callie, not for who she was but what they thought she was. Nothing made her feel more helpless than the fact that the world didn't accept Callie or their relationship and there was precious little Lena could do about it.

While buying Callie a coffee or scone every two hours was her way of trying to fix the problem, it made Lena feel awful that she had to do it in the first place and that her so-called solution felt like trying to strap a Band-Aid on a broken world.

Some grand hero she was. Lena sighed.

She'd left Callie in the sci-fi section, who'd been drawn by some summer-break teenager researching cryptids for a comic he was thinking about starting. Knowing her, she could keep him bouncing from book to book, ravenous for information, for inspiration, all day.

If she could. If she was allowed.

Except, when Lena walked out onto the sales floor, there was William, with his ever-present tablet clutched in his hands. He caught her eye over the top of his frameless glasses. He held up his tablet so she could see it. She watched as the timer on his tablet counted down the hours, minutes, and seconds Callie had been in the store.

Lena's hands fisted at her side.

Jerk.

He put a timer on Callie! Was he timing anyone else in the store? What about the college students who wasted away hours between classes studying? Or the afterschool or summer-break teens who scoured the shelves for anything even remotely resembling porn?

Lena rolled her eyes. To be honest, William probably wouldn't set a timer specifically for them—that he reserved just for Callie, apparently—but he was probably thrilled with the prospect of having the authority to shoo them out of his store as well. He was probably wondering why he hadn't thought of that before. It was a handy way for him to rid himself of all the people—and beings—he deemed undesirable.

Lena was well aware of what William thought about Callie. Lena's coworker, Hannah, was sure that William was prejudiced against non-humans, considering some of his past policies and behavior toward non-human customers and the fact that none of the non-humans who'd applied to the store ever seemed to meet his standards. But he seemed to have a particular problem with Callie.

Lord knew he'd brought it up to Lena enough times over the two and a half years she'd been working at the café.

Not that he didn't have a point sometimes—the bookstore and café weren't a public space for gathering; they were a business after all—but Callie wasn't hurting anyone. She was helping people. Kinda. Maybe.

Lena assumed that Callie did. It was all a little fuzzy to her. Lena had never actually needed Callie to do her muse-thing on her. She'd seen Callie do it to countless people, but it was always a little different with each person. Different with each work.

Sometimes, it was like flipping a switch. She'd seen people go from wanting to smash their laptops or burn their notebooks rather than stare at the blank nothingness for one more second to, with just a look or a touch from Callie, burning a hole in the pages with a firestorm of words.

Other times, she'd see it sneak up on a person.

Lena watched as Callie's head turned toward a little girl, maybe five or six years old, who was fussing in line, while her mother tried to order an out-of-print book. Lena knew that red-faced look puffing the child's cheeks. She was five seconds from throwing an absolutely spectacular tantrum, her tiny sneakers kicking at the carpet as she wriggled impatiently by her stressed-out mother. Lena smiled as Callie breezed past, causing a rhyming dictionary on the impulse buy table to fall on the floor at the girl's feet.

The little girl paused and picked up the book. Confusion turned to wonder on the girl's face as she paged through it, softly speaking each word and marveling at the sounds. It was such a small thing, an inconsequential moment, yet it felt miraculous. Like Lena was watching the origin story of a great poet or songwriting sensation. She had a strange feeling that one day she'd hear that girl tell that story in a televised interview or in front of a sold-out stadium.

Lena was a mortal; she didn't think she was supposed to understand magic—the how's or why's of it all—but she recognized a miracle when she saw one. One worth protecting, whatever the cost.

Lena turned at a sharp tap behind her. William held up his tablet.

Two hours had passed.

And, so it seemed, had the time for magic.

Lena hated that William could so easily steal that feeling from her. That he seemed to be stealing her whole life from her. Lena was exhausted. She felt like all she did these days was work and sleep and worry. She tried to put on a good face for Callie, to act like nothing was wrong, but it was all starting to take a toll—taking on the extra expenses, handling William alone, making sure Callie never found out. It was all too much. Callie deserved a world that didn't hate her and this was the only way Lena knew how to give it to her, but the stress was wearing on her and she knew she wouldn't be able to keep going like this.

Callie and everything she brought to Lena's life was worth any cost, but neither of them deserved this. There had to be a better way. Lena just wished she knew what the hell it was.

⁂

Callie rode mutely in the car next to her silent girlfriend on the way home. Once back in their apartment, Callie cooked quietly in the kitchen all by herself, after Lena wordlessly walked away to lock herself in the bedroom. During dinner, Callie sat next to Lena and ate her food as soundlessly as possible, each chew and swallow seeming so loud in the taciturn tension.

Because they were two women in an interspecies relationship, it didn't always feel safe or welcome to show affection in public. Even when they first started dating, Callie's family worried Lena might turn on Callie, if the relationship went badly, using the public's distrust of magical beings against her, and Lena's friends worried over how she could know—for sure—that Callie wasn't using magic to snare her. Even among strangers, they just never knew whether some passerby might make something so beautiful as a kiss or an embrace into something dirty with a word or a stare. Or, Hestia forbids, something worse.

But, at home, they could be themselves. They could be and do and say whatever they wanted. So, in an apartment that was more often than not filled with laughter, chatter, and affection, the distant silence felt almost violent as it stormed through the space, stealing the couple's usually happy, homey sounds.

Was she still mad about the incident with William? Callie knew she shouldn't have lost her temper, but she couldn't help it. Lena had said she was fine with it, that she understood how Callie felt, but maybe things had gotten worse at work since then. What if William had taken his frustration out on Lena?

Callie should say something. As a muse, even from the kitchen as she finished washing the dishes, she could feel Lena's mind search for words as she paced the bedroom floor. Lena had something she needed to say and, well, helping people express themselves was what Callie did best. So she wiped her hands on the dishtowel and made her way to the bedroom.

She knocked on the door. "Is everything okay?" She heard Lena shuffle in the other room. "Do you want to talk about it?"

A sigh came from the other side of the door before it opened. Lena stood grim-faced against the jamb. "We need to talk."

Callie knew they did but, after so much silence, the words sounded so ominous. She wanted to close her eyes, to slip into Lena's mind, and take a peek at the words and thoughts forming there. To use her powers and the knowledge she'd find there as a shield against whatever words were coming her way.

But she wouldn't. Eyes defiantly wide, she walked into the room when Lena opened the door. She wouldn't use her powers against Lena. She shouldn't need a shield against her girlfriend. Lena would never hurt her. She loved Lena and Lena loved her. So Callie entered the room, trying to feel open to that love rather than left vulnerable in the silence.

Her eyes caught on a piece of paper, a small square ripped from the notepad Lena always carried around with her at work, with numbers scribbled all over it. Callie frowned. She was really more of a word muse than a numbers one. She knew that science and math took inspiration too, but it'd never been her strong suit.

Lena shook her head wearily, her short, thick hair falling over her face as it veiled her downcast eyes. "You can't come to the café anymore."

Callie frowned. "Why not?"

Callie listened while Lena explained the new policies that William had implemented along with his signs. Hateful man. She'd noticed him glaring at her whenever he was on-shift. She knew he didn't like her, didn't want her in his store. But to create new rules to keep her out seemed excessive.

She crossed her arms over her chest. If she couldn't go to work with Lena, where else was she going to find such a high concentration of writers and artists than a bookstore coffee shop? "How can he do this?"

Lena shrugged. "As long as we can't prove the new rules are discriminatory—and since they apply to any person or being, we can't—he can pretty much do whatever he likes, so long as it doesn't affect the store's sales performance."

Callie began to pace. "But, without beings like me, there wouldn't even be any books for him to sell in the first place." He needed her. Or at least muses like her.

Lena nodded. "I know, but I don't think that argument will convince him. Even if you could get him to agree that muses actually inspire authors like that, he'd argue that you don't have to do it in his store."

Callie threw up her arms. "But why can't I do it in his precious store? I'm not hurting anyone by being there."

Lena winced.

Callie stopped and stared at her. "What?" She could feel a flood of unsaid words churn in Lena's mind. "What?"

Lena hunched her shoulders, bowing her head low. "Look, you know I love having you around, but it's not like he doesn't kind of have a point."

Callie arched an eyebrow at that. "A point?"

Lena cringed. "Well, you spend all day taking up table-space in the café or wandering around the shelves, never buying anything and encouraging—compelling—other people to do the same. I mean, Deadwood Books is a business, not a public park."

It shouldn't hurt. They were just talking. But Callie ached, hearing Lena side with that spiteful man. Hearing his words cut from her mouth.

Lena plopped down on the bed frustratedly. "More nights than not, we've had to stay open long after closing time because you and your muser-of-the-day weren't ready to leave yet." She sat up straighter. "Oh, remember, that one guy who, I swear, wrote from open to close, went home, fell asleep, then came back to do it all over again for a straight week. He didn't look like he'd eaten, much less bathed, that entire time." She gave a disgusted sniff at the memory. "He chased away customers just by being in the store."

Callie cringed. Oh yeah. That guy. He, like well-aged cheese or fish cooked in an office microwave, had been an acquired taste that could probably only really be appreciated by the one enjoying the meal. But, by Zeus, it'd been so good. His imagination had been so vivid and bold. Admittedly, she may have indulged a bit too much with him. She looked at Lena sheepishly. "What if I promise to be better about that kind of thing? Do you think William could be convinced to let me stay?"

Lena shook her head. "You know how William is. Once his mind is made up, you won't change it unless it starts costing him money." Lena sighed sadly, reaching out a hand to her. Callie took it and sat down on the bed, gripping Lena's hand as she rubbed her thumb across the back of Callie's knuckles. Lena brought Callie's hand to her lips with a sorrowful resignation. "And, since he won't change, we have to. I'm sorry, but we just can't afford to have you be at the café all day. I've done the math. Even if it was just a small cup of black coffee every two hours, with two of those cups using my employee discount a day, we'd need to change our monthly budget too much to make it work. We can't reduce our rent or utilities, so we'd have to cut down on our food bill as well as on most luxuries."

Callie's grip on Lena's hand tightened, needing the connection. "But, if I don't go to the café, how will I inspire people?" She needed to do that. Not only because it was part of who she was, her reason for being, but it brought in money as well. Sure, it wasn't much but, every time someone she inspired sold a piece of their work, a portion of all those little hidden taxes and fees—that no one except the cosmic accountants of fate could really explain too closely or very well—went to her. It wasn't exactly steady or reliable income, but it certainly wasn't nothing. Sure, some months it'd be a few hundred dollars here and there, but at least a few times a year there'd be a sudden and inexplicable surge. And it all added up. If she stopped doing that, not only did she wonder if she could psychically survive the loss—she was a muse, after all—she didn't think they would financially make it either. "Can we really afford for me not to go?"

Lena groaned and shut her eyes. "I hadn't thought about that." She huffed. "Well, you could always go to another café."

"Until I get kicked out of that one." If William could do that to her, the girlfriend of one of his employees, why would a random stranger treat her any better?

Lena winced and wrapped her arms around Callie's slumped shoulders. "I don't know if we have any other choice." She rested her chin on the crown of Callie's head. "Unless I quit my job."

Callie sat back and looked at her quizzically. "That solves our money troubles how?" She may not be good with numbers, but even she knew an unsatisfying job made more money than no job at all.

Lena shrugged. "I mean, I'd find another one, of course." She winced again. "Eventually."

Callie couldn't ask Lena to do that. It was sweet of her to offer and she loved Lena for it, but it wasn't worth it. She leaned against Lena and laid her head against the other woman's shoulder. "No, you're right. Tomorrow, I'll find somewhere else to go." Maybe the library or the community college, even though those tended to be frequented more by readers than writers, consumers rather than creators.

But, looking at Lena, Callie knew it was worth figuring out another way. She loved Lena, loved the life that they had together. But life often changed and, if she didn't change with it, she risked losing everything. And she didn't want to lose Lena. Lena was worth any effort.

With that decided, Callie was in the mood to leave this world behind for a nicer, less complicated one for a bit. So she leaned closer to Lena, kissing her cheek, then the corners of her lips, before finally sealing Lena's mouth with her own. She took a deep breath, the steady strength of Lena's body as comforting as the sweet, floral scent of her shampoo and as exciting as the heat of their kiss. She closed her eyes, wrapped her arms around Lena's waist, and smiled. "Read to me?"

Lena smiled and kissed Callie's lips again, before reaching for the book on her bedside table and settling against the pillows. Callie curled up next to her, making space for herself in the crook of Lena's elbow. The feel of their bodies pressed close soothed her in a way nothing else could. The sound of Lena's voice, a little monotone but so sure, washed over her. Callie probably shouldn't like it, was sure most people wouldn't. Lena wasn't a performer. But that was kind of the point. This wasn't for some audience, it wasn't something practiced or meant to be shared. It was a moment just for the two of them. It was something that Lena only did—would only do—for Callie and that made it special, almost sacred. On that bed, with their bodies entwined and her eyes shut, Callie let Lena's imagination fill and soothe her while the world slipped away until there was nothing else.

Hannah leaned over the café counter and frowned at Lena. "I haven't seen your girl around here lately. Where's she been?"

Lena shrugged and kept restocking the pastry case. "She's been trying out some other bookstores and cafés." Last week, Callie had been rotating between the library, a mall bookstore, and a college coffee shop, hoping that avoiding being a familiar face in any given place would help her fly under the radar.

At first, she'd seemed really excited about it. Had seen it as a kind of adventure or exploration. But Lena knew Callie was a being of habit. She liked having a space that felt like her own. A sacred space of sorts. And, with every passing day, Lena could see the lack of that start to take a toll on Callie.

Lena hated it too. Sure, William and his "no loitering" policy were awful, but at least they were the awful she knew. Lena could be there to help mitigate some of the horribleness. She could play interference with William. Could take advantage of loopholes in the rules.

But, with Callie out of the shop, there was nothing Lena could do. What if Callie wasn't as under the radar as she'd hoped. What if some other pompous manager rudely asked her to leave, or even forcefully kicked her out? What if they called the cops? Lena couldn't be there to watch over her anymore. Stuck here, all Lena could do all day was worry about Callie and hope she was all right.

Hannah looked at Lena sympathetically. "William's a jerk." She sighed. "Callie knows none of us would narc on her, right?"

Lena smiled. "Thanks." She knew they wouldn't if they didn't have to. But none of them could protect Callie forever. If William found out that people weren't following his new rules, they'd all get in trouble. And she couldn't ask anyone to risk losing their jobs for them.

"God, that really sucks!" Hannah huffed and crossed her arms over her chest. "I mean, of course, it's unfair and William's a bigot." Hannah's nose crinkled as she slanted Lena a slightly guilty look. "Is it awful that I was really hoping Callie would help me out with the story I'm working on? I've been stuck on the ending for days now and she, you know, just by being there, does that thing she does."

"Inspires people." Lena smiled. "Yeah, she was good at that."

Hannah shrugged. "A couple other people have been asking too. Dave and Freddie were looking for her help the other day. A couple of customers have been asking around too. Even more, have been just making vague comments about something being off about the place lately."

Lena nodded. The teen from the other day had come back to buy the books he'd been looking at about cryptids but had thrown an unholy fit because none of the books on the shelves seemed the same now. He'd been so sure that they were different books, complaining that the pictures didn't seem as vibrant or the text as dynamic. He'd yelled at Freddie about how he'd sold a bunch of his stuff so he could raise the money to buy all the books he'd need only to find the books had changed. Poor Freddie had tried to explain that they hadn't changed that section's stock, but how could Freddie hope to explain the inexplicable.

The books hadn't changed. The bookstore had. There was something—someone—missing.

Hannah leaned over the counter again, before whispering, "Callie's been trying out new locations, huh?" Hannah shrugged casually, but Lena could see the strain of desperation in her shoulders. "So, where's she at today?"

Lena laughed at Hannah's lack of subtlety and told her, while the beginnings of an intriguing thought brewed in her head.

Callie jumped as the front door slammed open. "Callie!"

Oh no. Callie sucked in a breath and wondered what had happened now.

"Callie!"

She stood up slowly, but couldn't seem to make her feet move. She knew that she should go see what Lena wanted, but she just didn't know how much more she could take.

It hadn't been a good day. She'd been at the local college's library today but had to leave early when her inspiration had started a... small struggle over research papers. Who knew that sleep deprivation and deadlines made it so hard for college students to share? She'd snuck out as soon as the campus police showed up to stop the fight and check everyone in the library for a school ID.

She hated feeling so out of control. How had inspiring people, this wonderful gift she was born to do, become so complicated? When exactly had it begun to feel like a crime?

"Callie?"

She turned to see Lena peeking her head into the kitchen.

At the sight of her, Lena frowned and walked into the room, coming up to touch Callie's face gently, her thumb brushing against the corners of her frowning mouth. "Are you okay?"

Callie shook her head and forced herself to smile. "I'm fine." She had to be. For Lena, she would be, whatever the cost. She turned back to the pot of spaghetti sauce that sat simmering and forgotten on the stove. "What's up?"

Lena gave her one last unconvinced look before stepping away to pace the room a bit. "Okay, so I had a thought at work today." She took a deep breath. "What if you could come back to the café?"

Callie furrowed her brow and began to stir the pot. "What are you talking about?"

Lena's pacing increased, her form moving restlessly in Callie's periphery. "What if there was a way for you to stay at the café that played by William's every rule?"

Callie said nothing, she just stared as the sauce bubbled. She recognized this state well enough. The frantic movements. The jumbled thoughts. Lena was on the verge of a eureka moment. It was on the edges of her mind, just out of grasp but felt more real than anything in this world.

All she needed was a push.

Callie sighed. Okay. She turned down the stove and faced Lena. "And what way would that be?"

Lena smiled. "What if you worked at the café?"

Callie scoffed, leaning her back against the countertop and crossing her arms over her chest. "Work for William?" Never. Not only would he never hire her, she'd never apply.

"No." Lena stepped closer, her speech slowing as if she were imparting some great wisdom. "What if you inspired people at the café as your job?"

Callie shook her head. "What are you talking about?"

Lena's face scrunched up a bit. "I'm not altogether certain yet. But I know that Hannah was willing to scour the college campus in search of you today. Dave and Freddie too. And all three of them know at least another person who'd pay for your brand of inspiration." She smiled. "So why not let them?"

Charge for inspiration? Callie shook her head vigorously. No. She turned back to the stove, the mix of garlic, tomatoes, and basil filling her senses. No, that wasn't how being a muse worked. Being paid to do what she did would cheapen it.

Wouldn't it?

Callie bit her lip. "How would that even work?"

Lena waved her hand dismissively. "I don't have all the answers, but what if people seeking inspiration bought you something from the café?"

Callie went back to stirring the pot if just to give her hands something to do. "I don't know." It just didn't feel right. "I've never taken money from the people I inspire." She frowned into the now cooling sauce, so still without its simmering bubbles. "I mean royalties are one thing." That was getting her share of the cut. Upfront payment was another. She sighed and shut the stove off completely. "I mean, what if their poem never gets published or no one buys their book." She'll have taken their money and given back nothing of any real consequence. It didn't feel right.

Callie leaned back when she felt Lena's arms wrap around her, the warmth of the other woman's body comforting down to her soul. "I know it's not a perfect fix." Callie could feel the slight rumble of Lena's voice, feel the heat of her breath, against her neck. "I wish I had one for you." She sighed and gave Callie a squeeze. "But what if you thought of it like tithing."

Callie turned her head at that. "Tithing?"

"Yeah," Lena said as she rocked on her feet, making them both sway a bit as she thought, "you know, like how, in ancient times, people would leave offerings at temples and altars."

"Yes." Callie, as a goddess, was well aware of what tithing was.

"Well, think of this as a modern-day version of that. Two hours of inspiration for the price of a café item? That sounds like a deal to me, right?"

She supposed, but there was something else to consider. "What about William?" She shook her head and leaned forward, away from Lena's touch. "Even if this follows the rules, he'll never allow it." All he had to do was create new rules, new policies, and they both knew it.

"Then we'll figure it out." Lena touched Callie's elbow and gently turned her around. "Together."

Together. Callie shut her eyes and let herself get lost in that one word, the strength, and power of it. They could do it together, could be together. Wasn't anything worth that?

Callie took a deep breath. "Okay, where do we start?"

Despite the fact that Callie still wasn't sure about Lena's grand scheme, the smile that spread across Lena's face gave her hope.

So, when Lena asked Callie to inspire her, to use her powers on her, so they could turn Lena's vague ideas into actual plans, she did. Even though she worked better plotting stories than she did plotting schemes, she sat down next to her at the kitchen table, while Lena laid out an old notepad. Callie didn't understand why she felt so nervous. She'd done this countless times before.

But never with Lena.

It somehow felt more personal, more intimate with her. As she closed her eyes and opened herself to Lena, it was almost shocking to feel Lena's thoughts flow into her mind. She could see the beginnings of a website, where people could schedule appointments with Callie. The images felt electric, laced with Lena's excitement. Callie watched as Lena filled out page after page of the notebook, working out widgets and ad campaigns.

Callie had always thought that she knew everything there was to know about Lena. How she thought. How she felt. Why she did the things she did. But being in her thoughts gave Callie a whole new perspective. She never realized how often Lena second-guessed herself, too often shutting herself down out of self-doubt. It was such a gift to be the one who literally knocked down the walls that blocked Lena from her full potential. To be the one who let Lena dream.

They worked through dinner and well into the night. They argued the merits of one website builder versus another. They eagerly poured over site design customization. They gave up on trying to figure out a company name. For days, it went on like that. Getting up early to tweak the site before heading off to work. Lena put out quiet feelers at work, asking coworkers if they'd be interested in Callie's services, while Callie put up flyers around the college campus and public library. Then they'd come home and brainstorm over dinner before turning on the laptop to turn their ideas into something more tangible.

But, even after all their hard work, when the day finally came to open shop, Callie was not sure about this.

It felt weird being back in the Deadwood Books coffee shop again. Which, in and of itself, felt weird, considering how much time she'd spent in the place over the years. But, after two weeks of not being here—of not being welcome here—it felt wrong being back.

Her eyes scanned the store.

Lena placed a hand on Callie's shoulder and squeezed, making her body relax at the familiar, comforting touch. "It's another couple of hours until William's shift starts. He's not here." She shrugged. "And, even if he was…" She placed a small cup of coffee on the table next to Callie. "You have every right to be here."

Callie smiled gratefully at Lena but kept her hands clutched in her lap, afraid to even touch the coffee.

"Hi." A woman clutching a laptop came up to the table. "Callie, right? From Altared State?"

Lena nodded. "Yep, this is her." She pulled out the chair across from Callie. "Why don't you have a seat? And please remember, your session is for two hours, if you want additional time, you'll need to log back onto the Altared State website and schedule another session, which may or may not be the next two hours, depending on availability."

Altared State. An inspiration-on-demand site where, for the price of a café item, a person could sit down in this humble altar to the written word with an honest-to-minor-goddess muse.

Callie adjusted a bit in her seat before taking the woman's outstretched hand. "You must be Liza, you've got a magazine article that you need to finish by tomorrow, right?"

The woman nodded, shaking her hand. "That's me. So how does this work? I've never used a muse service before. I'd never even heard about it before Hannah mentioned it to me the other day. She swears by you and I'm running up against my deadline, so I figured, what could it hurt?" She nodded toward the coffee. "I see you have your drink already. So, what happens now?"

Callie smiled and closed her eyes, feeling her anxiety begin to ease as she slipped into Liza's mind in a ritual that was as familiar and necessary to her as breathing. "Now, you open up your laptop and just work."

Lena watched Callie shake hands with Dave before he closed his notebook and got ready for his shift. Lena was probably prouder of Altared State than she should have been, seeing as it wasn't really her business, just her idea. Callie was the one doing all the heavy lifting, but Lena liked the idea of being a helping hand. A digital tithing site. She should have thought of it sooner.

Already she was toying with the idea of adding an after-session option, where a person could go back to the site and tip Callie if they'd felt extra-inspired. As she turned to make a new drink, she took advantage of all the inspiration in the air and toyed with the idea of adding a rate and review option to get a few testimonials on the site to entice new customers.

William walked up to Lena, looking down at her from the other side of the café counter. "You know this isn't exactly following the rules."

Lena shook her head as she worked. "You can time it yourself. Someone has bought Callie a drink every two hours." Often, they brought her pastries or sandwiches too. "It follows your rules to the letter."

William's jaw tensed. "This isn't a personal office. She can't run a business out of our business."

Lena turned her head and nodded to a woman in the corner on her phone. "That woman is a wedding planner who comes in at least twice a week to set up interviews with potential clients." She turned again and nodded at a group of students at a table in the back. "Those kids come here to study every week, even during the summer." She looked at William. "We also have a slew of writers and graphic designers and artists and business people who all use this space to work. How is this any different?"

"For a few hours at a time." William tapped his tablet impatiently. "She's here all day. Every day! Sure, you're both technically following the rules now, but we both know, one way or another, it can't keep going on like this."

Lena felt her own body tense. All it would take is another new policy from him to ruin all their plans. Sure, with a little bit of ingenuity and inspiration, they could probably loophole their way out of trouble again.

But they shouldn't have to.

Lena nodded. "Do you know how much business the café has done today?" They both knew he had the store's sales totals on his tablet. He knew. "Sales are up almost ten percent." Not only did Altared State mean at least one drink every two hours was bought, Callie's clients often bought their own drink or snack. And, the more people saw other customers with café items, the more likely they were to want their own. The café was, after all, the ultimate impulse buy display. "She's also walked people around the store, helping them find research materials. Without being on your payroll, she's sold six books, a paint set, and three CDs."

Lena smiled when she saw William shift his weight uncomfortably. She looked back at Callie. "You could ask her to leave." Both Lena and William watched as Callie's next appointment, a frazzled-looking college student with too many papers and textbooks, sat down at the table. "But they come to see her. If she goes off to some other café, some other store, so do all their sales."

Lena wanted to whoop. This was what knights who slew dragons and superheroes who swooped in to save the day must feel like. William, for all his authority, had tried to take this space from Callie. To make the world just a little smaller for her. But, together, Lena and Callie had taken it back, because they belonged anywhere they wanted to be. And Lena was so glad to be back together.

With a smug sniff, she turned and grabbed the café au lait she'd made. "Now, if you'll excuse me, I have an order to deliver."

For the rest of her shift, William stayed on the other side of the store, fuming as he punched at his tablet, presumably crunching the numbers in hopes that Lena was wrong.

But she wasn't. She knew it. She might love reading more than doing math, but she understood the basics of business.

She watched while Callie said goodbye to her last client of the day before she grabbed her bag from behind the counter and headed to the table. "How was your first day working as an official Altared State muse?"

Callie smiled, settling something inside Lena that she hadn't even known was off. "It was amazing. I had a lot of people sign up for more sessions in the future."

Lena grinned proudly. "I knew you'd be a hit."

Callie stood up to wrap her arms around Lena's shoulders in a quick hug. "Thank you. None of this would have happened without you." Callie gave Lena a wry grin. "I hope it's all worth it."

Lena saw doubt and worry crease Callie's beautiful face as Callie stepped away from her. Lena wouldn't allow it. Reaching out to cup Callie's cheek, she pressed her forehead against Callie's and looked deep into her eyes. "I believe in you."

Tears welled up in Callie's eyes as she laid her hand over Lena's, holding her close to her cheek. "Thank you." She shook her head and shrugged as if, for once, Lena's eloquent muse was at a loss for the right words. "Thank you."

They seemed pretty right to Lena. "You know me," Lena said with a casual shrug, "just doing what I can to make the hard stuff easier."

Callie let out a small laugh before pulling her close to give her a kiss, lingering over the sweet press of lips. "My hero."

Lena kissed her back, reveling in the feel of it before deepening the kiss, workplace decorum be damned. Callie was her girlfriend and she wouldn't be made to feel like she had to hide. Not by anyone. Not for any reason. Not anymore. "I'm glad it went well." Lena gave Callie one more smacking kiss. "Ready to head home?"

Callie nodded and took Lena's hand as they walked out of the café. Holding Callie's hand as they passed the café's "No Loitering" sign, Lena felt, for the first time in weeks, the weight of that laminated slip of paper lift.

LAW OF LOVE

Felicia Nicole Hall

I run my hands through her hair. Taylor is fast asleep and my arm is tucked under the curve of her neck, too tight to pull away without disturbing her. I stay cuddled up close and stare out the window at the rising sun. I wonder how I ended up in my bed with this beautiful girl who came into my life only a few hours ago. I notice that the usual urge to check my phone the moment my eyes open is nonexistent. I realize that at this moment, I don't have a desire to focus my attention anywhere else. I close my eyes and let myself relive the night before.

I sit staring at the computer screen in front of me. My eyes burning from the light; it's been hours since I moved from this spot. I consider it my own little corner of the world. Since I started college two years ago, that small space in the library is where I spend most of my time. Wordy questions with vernacular I only know from hours of memorization stare back at me from the screen. I glance at the book next to me and resist the urge to pick it up.

Instead, running my hand through my messy, dirty blonde hair, I refocus my attention on studying the judicial processes and analytical reasoning that I doubt I'll ever be able to drill into my brain. With a dog-eared copy of Hemingway next to me, it takes a lot of discipline to stay focused. I flick the edges of the pages, longing to pick it up. Knowing I need to finish this practice test, I snap back out of it and eye the little bubbles in front of me, considering which one to click. I settle on one, hoping for the best. I scroll down and see the little arrow leading to the next page, 17 more questions to go. It's already taken hours to answer the first 13. I have a long night ahead of me.

I know I should get to it, but I decide to finally get up and walk around. I need to stretch and get away from this screen. I glance at the clock and see it's already after ten. Looking around for the first time in a while, I realize that, other than the librarian sitting at the front desk, I'm basically alone… not that I should expect a crowd. After all, it's a Saturday night on a college campus. What normal person would be spending it in the library?

I notice one girl sitting in a hidden corner nook. She's curled up in the big armchair with a book in her hands, wrapped in a blanket looking as comfortable as could be. I smile at the thought of that nook being her small corner of the world. Her dark hair is pulled back loosely, with pieces falling in front of her eyes, she mindlessly pushes them behind her ears every few seconds. She looks so engrossed in her book that she wouldn't even notice a stampede running through the room, but I'm thankful for this because she doesn't notice me staring and I can't seem to look away. For a minute, looking at her, all of my stress seems to disappear.

The ding of my phone snaps me back to attention and I look down at the dim screen, wondering who could be texting me this late.

Dad: Did you get your test results back yet?

I sigh, staring at the screen for a few seconds before slipping the phone back in my pocket without bothering to offer an answer. I've been waiting a week already for my pre-LSAT test scores, it feels like an eternity with my dad checking in every few hours. My college campus offers the test every few months to undergrad pre-law students. The test doesn't actually determine anything, it's just an idea of how I would do on the real LSAT if I were to take it right now. But to my parents, this score determines the rest of my life.

Nonetheless, the test was hard and I'm not expecting a passing score. My mind fills with anxiety all over again, I try my hardest to push it away as I make my way downstairs to the vending machine.

When I sit back down in my little corner, my first instinct is to look over at the beautiful girl in the opposite corner. I realize I've been here for over five hours and wonder if she's been there the whole time. I eye the books on shelves surrounding me, considering all of the possible stories and discoveries that lie within them. I sigh again as I try to force myself to refocus my attention to the questions in front of me, pushing everything else—my test results, the novels waiting to be read, and the girl in the corner—out of my mind.

"So, are you like a loner or something?" The voice next to me startles me. I had taken a break after question 25 and finally allowed myself to pick up Hemingway; I needed to lose myself in the stories of World War I before continuing to decipher the process of a criminal trial. I'm so lost in the book and the joy of allowing my brain to relax for just a little while that I jump when the beautiful girl from the corner appears next to me.

"Well..." I consider her question for a moment. Was she being serious, sarcastic? "Not really, but I guess I could ask you the same question." I give her a small smirk, letting her know that I'm teasing.

"Yeah, I kinda am now that I think about it," she plops up on the rectangular table that I've been working on. She pulls her legs onto the table in a swift motion, settling them in a criss-cross style. I'm surprised by her casualness; I even pause for a moment to make sure I don't know her from one of my classes; she's acting as if we're old friends rather than two strangers sitting in opposite corners of the campus library at midnight. I study her face in silence for a few seconds, confirming I've never met her before. I would have remembered her, the way her jawline meets her ear and small freckles fall across her olive-toned nose, assures me that she is too remarkable to have forgotten.

The girl finally breaks the silence lingering between us. "I noticed you over here and figured I'd come say hello. I couldn't resist the only other human spending their Saturday night in the library," she smiles.

"I've been here for hours, studying is pretty time consuming apparently." I smile back.

She looks at the book I had just placed down on the table near her leg. "Farewell to Arms?" she picks the book up and glances at my scribbled handwriting in the margins. "Are you studying for an English class?"

"Actually, that's my distraction. I'm taking a practice test online for the LSAT."

"Wow, isn't that a test you take after law school? Why are you practicing so early?"

"How do you know I'm not in law school already?" I ask with a grin.

"Good point. So are you in law school?"

"Nope." We both laugh. "My parents are just very strict about me being a successful lawyer, they're requiring that I take the practice test every few months until it's time for the real test, just to stay up to date and keep my mind sharp." I use my fingers to put air quotes around that last part.

"Wow, they sound…" she paused for a moment, searching for the right word, "…intense."

"Yeah, tell me about it." I looked back towards the computer, dreading my return to the last five questions.

"So, what's your name?" She bounces off the table and into the chair next to me, staring at me intently.

"I'm Dylan. And you?"

"Taylor," she says, extending her hand out, waiting for mine to meet hers.

"Nice to meet you, Taylor," I say, shaking her hand and looking back into her eyes. The sea of green sparkles with flecks of gold send an electric shock through my body. We break eye contact at that moment and I wonder if she felt it too. Her quirky and bubbly personality seems to dissipate and she looks down shyly at her fingers, picking at the skin around her nails.

I don't remember the last time I paid enough attention to a girl to notice the color of her eyes and the freckles across her skin. I haven't felt those tingly fireworks under my skin since I was in high school, falling in love for the first time. The feeling caught me off guard; I wasn't one for falling in love. Since I began college, I had a few casual dates and even one unexpected hook up at a party, but I believe I have only fallen in love once. My first girlfriend and I dated for the last three years of high school and only decided to go our separate ways because our colleges were many miles and a long plane ride away from each other. I hadn't thought much about the possibility of falling in love again. I was always too preoccupied with keeping my grades up, my parents satisfied, and my thirst for literature quenched. On top of that, I worked a part-time job filing papers in a law firm (insisted on by my parents, of course) and kept a simple social life afloat; I really didn't have the time to worry about a relationship.

"Hello?"

I snap out of my thoughts and realize Taylor has been trying to get my attention. I push the alarming idea that I've only known this girl for approximately five minutes and I'm thinking about the possibility of being in love with her, out of my head. What is the matter with me?

"I'm sorry, what did you say? I zoned out for a second there."

"I noticed." She let out an airy laugh. "I was just asking what your major is? I mean, I know you're preparing for the LSAT but I guess, technically your major could be a lot of different things."

"I'm pre-law with a focus in political science."

"Ahh." She looks as if she's studying me, almost like she doesn't believe me. She reaches for the book again, 'So, this is just like a hobby?"

"Yeah," I pause, "I've loved reading and writing for as long as I could remember. It might be the only thing that keeps me sane in this world." I shrug and wonder if that was too deep. I glance at Taylor, gauging her reaction.

"Writing allows me to let out my insane side, so I understand what you're saying." She picks at a peeling cuticle on her thumb. I'm surprised that delving into a deeper conversation didn't scare her away; she actually doesn't seem phased at all.

I look at Taylor and I feel those sparks traveling down my spine again. I'm thankful to realize that she doesn't sense my nervousness as she continues. "If writing is your passion, what are you doing with this?" She gestures toward the idle computer screen. I glance at it and remember the questions I still had to get through.

"You know how parents are," I scoff and let out a small laugh. I thought this would be enough of an answer but Taylor just stares at me quizzically waiting for more.

"Both of my parents are lawyers and both of their fathers were lawyers. If I wanted them to help me pay for college, I didn't have much of a choice but to carry on the family legacy." As soon as the words are out, I realize that it is the first time I ever admitted how I felt about my major to anyone other than myself.

"I never understood that," Taylor says as she continues picking at her cuticle. "Why do parents force their children to go to school, thinking it will give them better lives, but not allowing them to choose their own path?" It sounded like a rhetorical question, but she looks at me expectantly.

"I wish I knew." I sigh.

"I'm an English major. Neither of my parents care what my major is. They don't even know what school I'm attending, actually. Most of the time I consider it a loss on my part," she looks at me, "but now I'm not so sure." Taylor smirks, allowing me to catch the hint of sarcasm in her voice.

"I guess the grass really is always greener." I give a small smile as Taylor looks away from her thumb and straight into my eyes. She smiles at my comment, her teeth showing slightly. When our eyes meet, they lock for a second longer than they should and with that, I know that Taylor feels the sparks too.

I look at the clock and can't believe that over an hour of talking to Taylor has already passed. Somewhere in those minutes ticking by, our chairs ended up close together, our knees touching and our hands occasionally brushing against one another. I feel as if I had known her for my entire life. I suddenly can't imagine never knowing such a lovely smile.

"How many questions do you have left?" Taylor nods toward the computer screen glowing next to my face. I forgot that it was even there.

"Only five. The library closes soon. I should try to power through them," I say as I brace myself to say goodbye to Taylor.

"Let's go, I'll help you," she says, bringing her chair even closer so that we can both read the questions on the screen.

I'm surprised by her willingness to stay in the library into the middle of the night to help me study.

"Are you sure? I don't want to keep you awake," I say, desperately hoping that she knows I'm just being polite and secretly really want her to stay.

"I think my helping you is the only way you'll finish and not get distracted by Hemingway." She laughs a little. "Plus," she pauses, "I really want to stay," she catches my eye as the words fall out.

"Okay, if you insist, let's do this!" I smile back and know now that she is definitely feeling what I'm feeling too. We read the questions aloud and work through each one, taking our time. Taylor seems to take each question with such ease, and I wonder if she's taken law classes in the past. I choose not to interrupt our flow by asking right now.

"Are you ready to submit?" Taylor looks at me as soon as I press the little bubble for the last question.

"I guess I have to be," I say with a shrug, "at least it's only a practice test."

"I'm sure you did great," she reassures me. "You at least did great on those last five since I was here to help you." She winks and we both laugh.

"I'm ready," I say, and we both reach for the mouse to click the submit button. We pull away and Taylor lets out a nervous giggle.

"You do it. I wouldn't have gotten it done without you," I say, and Taylor reaches her hand out towards the mouse again.

As soon as she clicks it, a new page appears.

THANK YOU FOR SUBMITTING YOUR LSAT PRACTICE TEST. YOUR RESULTS ARE BEING CALCULATED. PLEASE DO NOT REFRESH OR EXIT THIS PAGE.

As soon as the screen pops up, Taylor and I both let out a little cheer and laugh.

"Shhhh," the librarian shushes us from her spot at the front desk. We immediately quiet down but look at each other and laugh, wondering why our volume matters when we've been the only people in here for hours.

"The campus library will be closing in fifteen minutes," the overhead speaker announces. I always spent late nights in the library but I never stayed long enough to hear the closing warning. It startles me, but Taylor looks unphased.

The little loading circle continued spinning on the computer screen. Taylor looks focused on the screen, waiting for the results.

"I guess after the results load, we should get going," I say, regretfully. Taylor was about to answer when she was distracted by the movement of the screen.

"Look! It's ready," she says, and I look at her, more intrigued by the glimmer in her eyes than the test score in front of me.

I finally look over to the screen and see the bold red number in the middle of the page.

65%

"That's not bad," Taylor says, keeping her positive attitude. I'm grateful for her encouragement but a passing score would be a 75% and even that isn't ideal.

I smile slightly at Taylor, who is still staring at me, waiting for my reaction. "You're right. Hopefully, I did better on the standardized one so that I could at least satisfy my parents with that."

Taylor looks as if she wants to say something but is holding back, I don't press her.

"Let's get going before they lock us in here," I continue. Taylor begins to fold the blanket that was once wrapped around her and puts her book into the small bag slung across her body.

"You should draw the line," she says. "Stop letting your parents decide your life."

Her bluntness stuns me for a second. I expect her to say more but she doesn't.

I push in my chair and swivel to walk towards the exit. "I wish it were that easy." Pushing through the wooden double doors, I change the subject. "Which way is your apartment? I'll walk you."

"Up the hill." Taylor points in the direction of the infamous huge hill right off of our campus. "I'll be just in time to find everyone passed out on the floor from my roommate's party." I notice the dread in her voice.

"Do you want to come to my apartment?" I ask her, hoping that she doesn't think it's creepy. "I mean, I'm not trying to be weird, you totally don't have to… I just thought since you didn't want to go home and we're both still awake, that maybe we could just keep talking… I could make coffee," I ramble on awkwardly, knowing I'm making the situation worse. I expect Taylor to tell me she'll walk alone back to her apartment now, but instead, she starts giggling and puts her hand over my mouth, playfully telling me to stop rambling.

"I would love to go to your apartment." She smiles, releasing her hand from over my mouth.

The walk back to my apartment with Taylor is easy. We laugh and joke, letting our arms brush against each other until our fingers finally intertwine. I have never felt a connection come so quickly and so easily with a girl before. Taylor is different, and the same goes for the way my heart catches fire each time she squeezes my hand a little tighter.

We walk slowly, turning a 15-minute walk into a 30-minute one, prolonging every moment we have together, neither of us wanting our time together to come to an end. When we finally reach my apartment, I dig in my pocket for the key, push the door open and flick the light on in a swift motion.

"Wow, I'm sorry. If I would have known I'd be having company, I would have cleaned up a little." I grab at the sweaters thrown over various chairs and couch armrests. All the while making a quick scan as I pray that I don't see any dirty underwear or socks on the floor.

I hear the door click shut as Taylor closes it gently behind her and makes her way into the room. I'm still frantically picking up various items that I left lying around. I see Taylor glance around the room as well, her eyes lingering on my bookshelves, clearly not worried about the mess. She runs her fingers over the books, thoughtfully reading each title.

"This is an awesome collection," she says.

"Thanks, I've been adding to it my entire life basically," I say as I make my way next to her. Her eyes remain on the books, slowly picking up one after the other, but my eyes linger on her. I watch as her mouth moves slightly, reading the summaries to herself. I watch her mouth and can't help but let my mind wander and imagine how her lips would feel against my own. I bite my lip and push a piece of her hair behind an ear. If my touch startles her, she doesn't let it show. Instead, she looks calm, turning her gaze away from the book in her hand and into my eyes with a gentle smile.

Our eyes lock and I feel the butterflies in my stomach. I feel the redness rush to my cheeks as I grow shy, wanting to break contact, but before I can think any further, Taylor's lips are pressed against mine and everything else melts away. I hear the book that was in Taylor's hand fall against the shelf as she lets it go and wraps her arms around my neck. Our kiss, that started slow and gentle, turns feverish and greedy as we want more and more of each other. I allow my hands to move over her body and hers follow suit. I didn't expect my night of studying and stressing over my future to end up here, but now it's happening and I'm so grateful our paths crossed. Taylor jumps up into my arms, locking her legs around me and I carry her to my bedroom, never breaking away from our kiss.

My eyes open for the second time this morning, realizing I fell asleep again. This time, I look out the window and the sun is high in the sky, a few hours have definitely passed. Taylor is still lying next to me but this time she's awake, reading a book.

"Morning, sleepyhead," her voice is airy and cheerful. I never saw someone so beautiful, even more beautiful in the late morning sunlight than she was the night before.

"Good morning." I smile sheepishly at her, my voice still groggy. I expect to feel the awkwardness of waking up next to a girl I just met, but it doesn't come. It just feels natural to be around Taylor, like it's meant to be.

I feel my phone vibrate under my pillow, I want to stay in this moment with Taylor and not let the real world back in yet, but knowing it could be my test result, I reach for it anyway. I see the email notification and sit straight up, nervous to respond to it.

"Is it the test results?" Taylor says excitedly and closes her book.

"Yes, I'm scared to open it. After last night, I definitely don't think I passed." I slide my phone open and prepare to see the answer, I don't want to push this off any longer.

Good morning, Mr. Bucknell,

Congratulations! We are writing to inform you that you have PASSED the Pre-LSAT exam.

I am shocked at the result, relief flooding my body. Taylor waits patiently for me to tell her the result.

"I passed!" I exclaim, and she kisses my lips with force and excitement. We break apart, looking shyly at each other.

"Congratulations, that's amazing! I knew you could do it," she says.

"Thank you. I can't believe it," I say, still staring at the email. I feel the relief wash over me again as I realize what I need to do now. The answer was always there, it had just taken me some time to figure it out. After all of my persistence and one night with an amazing girl that I'm pretty sure I'm falling in love with, everything makes sense. I finally proved that I could do it. I could pass the exams and I could live up to my family's legacy. But just because I could, didn't mean I had to.

I take a screenshot of the email and send it to my parents.

Look I passed! I'm so proud. But…I need to talk to you both later, I'm changing my major.

Taylor stands next to the bed, pulling on her clothes. I smile again at just the thought of her angelic smile and fiery eyes. I walk up behind her and hug her. "I know this cute little coffee shop in town, they also have shelves and shelves of books to read. Let's go get breakfast and explore. I'm not ready for this date to be over yet."

QUEEN OF THE LIBRARY

J. Leigh Bailey

Halfway through my raunchy performance of Katy Perry's Bon Appetit, I almost toppled from my six-inch platform boots. I didn't blame the boots. In fact, the red, glitter-covered, faux-leather boots absolutely made my slutty Strawberry Shortcake-inspired ensemble. My graceless stumble—followed immediately by the graceful recovery, obviously—was a hundred percent the fault of the man sitting at table number six. My boss. Adrian Markes.

He was a librarian, for Christ's sake. And while he had starred in every one of my X-rated fantasies the last few years, he was the epitome of the buttoned-down librarian. What the hell was he doing at a dive bar called The Hot Box on Drag night? Of course, as a librarian myself, I didn't have any room to judge. But I'd bet money the man in his boring pastel polo shirts and khaki pants sat at home watching the news or PBS at nine p.m. on a Saturday night. If I hadn't known better, I'd have figured he ate, drank, and slept at the library. Of course, I did my best not to picture him out in the real world. The dude was gorgeous. If he gave me half a sign, I'd have made a play for him years ago, but he didn't, and I loved my job too much to chance it.

Luckily, I knew my routine inside and out; my body moved from one step and dip to the next without conscious thought. A shimmy here, a shoulder shake there, followed by the seductive glide of satin gloves down my hips and over the mounds of tulle exploding just south of my crotch.

A flash of cash to my left pulled me to a nearby table. I winked at the grinning bride-to-be and snatched the five-dollar bill from her, tucking it into the shaft of my boot. Normally I'd flirt and play the part the audience expected from a drag queen called Allison Wonderland. Normally I wouldn't be caught dead within two feet of my boss—my freaking boss!—while wearing an orange wig and extravagant fake eyelashes. His presence threw me off my game, big time.

I had thirty seconds left in my song before I could flee to get ready for the next act. I could totally avoid table six. In fact, I could pretend that whole side of the room didn't exist.

Adrian's hand flicked up, a bill tucked between two fingers.

Damn it. If there's one thing a queen learns fast, it's how to differentiate currency values at a glance in bad lighting. And a ten-dollar bill… Well, one did not simply pass that up. The man next to Adrian—his date?—also held out some money. Not a ten, but a least a few singles. If I didn't sashay my way over there, people would notice. Especially the regulars. The last thing I needed was extra speculation. Not with him there.

So, I added an extra roll to my hips, widened my vibrantly red lips, and ducked my head just enough that the floppy pink hat with the fake strawberries perched jauntily on top partially shadowed my face.

His eyes lingered on my legs as I lip synced my way over. On the one hand, my legs were amazing (thus my preference for short, flirty skirts). On the other hand, boss. The appreciation edged with heat in his gaze stirred something hot and dark in my stomach. Something I quashed right away. If he knew boring Jack Brisbane hid under the paint and sparkle, he wouldn't be so appreciative. After all, I'd been working with the man for over three years, and not once had he given me a second glance. No matter how often I wished he would.

Unable to help myself, I added an extra dip and rotation of my hips when I reached for the cash, letting the edges of my pink skirt dance across his knees. And if one of my knees grazed his, oh well. I was only human, and I'd never have the chance to actually get all up in his personal space like this again. I may have also let my glove-covered fingers trail along the back of his hand as I plucked the ten-dollar bill out of his grasp.

His slashing dark brows twitched, and the edge of his mouth kicked up. Not a full smile, or a leer, or anything like it, but I'd cataloged enough of his expressions to recognize the knowing humor. Something low in my abdomen tightened and I had to move along before things got painful below my skirt. Believe me, taped and tucked was uncomfortable enough without adding the threat of arousal to the mix.

I relieved his friend of his money with less fanfare and managed to saunter back to the stage in time to fake-belt out Katy's last note. I flung my arms up, angled my legs sharply to draw attention to their length, and blew a smacking kiss to the audience. To one audience member in particular.

Adrian cocked his head, eyes narrowed in concentration. Shit. That couldn't be good. Had he recognized me? But then he turned and said something to his date/buddy/friend, and I ducked out of the way for Kiki La Coeur to make her grand entrance.

Half an hour later, I ignored the disappointment that Adrian wasn't sitting at his table as I completed my second tour around the room to a campy version of True Colors while wearing my trashy Rainbow Brite ensemble. I'd barely made it past the back curtain heading to the cramped room where the queens got ready when Maxine H2-Ho—the hostess of drag night at The Hot Box—grabbed my arm.

"Hey," she said, not bothering to modulate her naturally baritone voice. "Ricky's looking for you. He's got a line on a side gig."

"What kind of gig?" I asked Maxine.

She shrugged, sequins flashing in the muted backstage lights. "No idea."

"A brunch?" I suggested, then shook my head. "The brunch shows usually have their own list of queens. Why would they go through Ricky? It's not like he's our agent."

"Only one way to find out."

I tugged at the top of one of the thigh-high rainbow stockings that started creeping down a bit. The elastic was nearly shot, and I made a mental note to order a new pair as I made my way across the club. I wove through the crowd, keeping my smile bright, winking at any of the patrons who made a point of meeting my eyes. I also ended up stopping to pose for half a dozen pictures, so several minutes had passed by the time I slid behind the bar to a short hallway that led to Ricky's office.

Even before I pushed open the door, I heard it. The familiar quiet tone of my boss. I tried to ignore the inappropriate tic in my chest. I'd managed to push back the tiny crush I'd once had on him. I'd spent the last three years working with the man, and eventually, I'd stopped fantasizing about him taking me back into the stacks and… Nope, nope, nope. So, yeah, the fantasies didn't really stop. But I'd gotten damned good at ignoring them. So why did seeing him here bring all those feelings to the surface?

No, it was better to focus on more important things. Like what the hell was he doing here, talking to Ricky? And asking for me? Shit…does he know it's me? Is he going to fire me? I racked my brain to remember if there were any clauses in my contact with the library that prohibited a second job. Or some kind of morality clause that doing drag would violate.

I hesitated at the door, which pissed me off. Allison Wonderland was a brash, confident queen, who didn't hesitate in doorways. And even Jack, while not as fearless and assertive as Allison, wasn't some wilting flower who kowtowed around others. I straightened, edging my way forward.

Ricky waved to me. "Allison, come on in."

I snuck a glance at Adrian as I crossed the threshold. His date/buddy/friend wasn't there, which shouldn't have relieved me as much as it did. I relaxed a bit when Adrian showed no signs of recognition as I walked in. He wore his best impressing-a-future-donor face, the one that was 30 percent enthusiasm, 30 percent earnestness, 30 percent charm, and ten percent earthy appreciation. Okay, maybe I'd never seen that heat in his eyes when courting a donation, but it was definitely there now.

Whew! Where was the fan from my Mulan costume when I needed it?

"Gentlemen," I purred, modulating my voice carefully so as not to tip off Adrian. I also dipped my chin enough he wouldn't get a good look at my face, and he'd have trouble seeing past the heavy blonde bangs. Between the wig, the obvious contouring, and the voice, I hoped to maintain the right illusion. Only a few feet separated us—a lot of pressure for a face-full of cosmetics and a headful of synthetic fibers. "You wanted to see me?"

"Allison," Ricky said, "this is Adrian Markes. He runs the Evans Library in town. He's got an idea, and I think you're just the gal to make it work."

I loved that Ricky was as careful as anyone I've ever met about keeping the pronouns and names straight when working with queens. In drag, I was Allison Wonderland, and should be referred to in female terms. Not everyone remembered the distinction, but Ricky had worked with us too long to make that mistake. It had the added benefit of him not calling me by my given name.

I reached out and shook Adrian's hand. He held on a little longer than politeness required, and certainly longer than he'd ever done before when shaking my hand. "You have an idea, you say? Lovely. 'There is one thing stronger than all the armies in the world, and that is an idea whose time has come,'" I quoted.

Adrian's smile widened. "Victor Hugo."

I nodded. Trust a librarian to recognize the quote. "Very good. And what idea's time has come?"

"I'm interested in setting up a Drag Queen Story Hour program at my library."

I almost fell out of the glittery gold platform Mary Janes I'd put on to go with my rainbow thigh-highs. Twice in one night. A new record. To my credit, though, Adrian had never, ever, said anything about doing a Drag Queen Story Hour. Not once. I'd have remembered, obviously. "You are?" I asked, the words more a croak than a question. "I mean…that's cool. So cool."

Ricky gestured to my outfit. "When Adrian here mentioned what he was looking for, I knew you were the queen to make it happen. In fact, I can't think of anyone more suited."

"Is that so?"

Ricky wasn't wrong. Any other day, any other library, any other director, I'd have been all in. In fact, if I'd thought there was an iota of a chance of getting the library's board of directors' buy-in, I'd have suggested it a couple of years ago when Drag Queen Story Hours started popping up around the country.

"All your looks are centered on kids' books and cartoons. I mean, your Cruella De Vil is a thing of beauty, and your Alice in Wonderland is always a crowd favorite."

"Yes!" Adrian jabbed a finger in my direction. "That's exactly what I'm looking for. I believe strongly in the messages that Drag Queen Story Hour convey, and being able to tie the experience back into books would make it even better." He gestured at my costume. "Like this. It's perfect." His eyes caught on my legs again. "Perfect." He blinked. "I mean, in context and environment it can be highly sexual, but out of context, it's not at all inappropriate."

It took everything in me to not tug at the molded plastic of my very short skirt. Probably the skirt should have been at least a few inches longer to be appropriate for a library, but I understood what he meant. "You're sweet," I said, "but—"

"You'd be perfect." He fished something out of his pocket. "Take my card, please."

I couldn't not take it. "I appreciate you thinking of me, but I'm not sure I'm the right fit."

Ricky snorted. "Seriously? Didn't you approach some of the other girls about doing something exactly like this?"

I glared at him. This was not the time for him to be logical. Because, yes, I would love to participate. It would be the best possible combination of my two passions—libraries and drag. And bringing the message of diversity, acceptance, while at the same time providing unabashedly queer role models to children? Count me in. Except. Except.

"Well, of course, you're right," I said through gritted teeth. "But there are processes necessary to set up an official, affiliated Drag Queen Story Hour. I just don't know that I have the time to figure out the details."

"You won't have to worry about that." Adrian smiled with a shark-like intensity. "My assistant will take care of the details."

What now?

Last I knew, I was his assistant, and such a project had not crossed my desk.

"I'll have Jack reach out to you. Does that work? What's the best way to contact you?"

I blinked at him, wondering at what point I lost control of the conversation. Had I ever had control of the conversation?

Ricky, the bastard, chimed in. "Probably her website." He shot a glance at me. "Unless you have one of your cards with your stuff in the changing room?"

"No," I said weakly. "I mean, yes. I mean, no, I don't have any cards with me."

"Great. Website it is, then." Ricky clapped his hands, obviously proud of a job well done. "I'll just write that info down for you."

"I can't wait." Adrian reached out and I shook his hand out of habit.

"Expect to hear from Jack next week."

Right. I'll hear from Jack. Should I call myself on the phone? Or perhaps an email would suffice? I closed my eyes. How is this my life?

"Mornin', Jack," Adrian called out from his office on Monday morning as I strode resolutely into the library. I could do this. I could absolutely face my boss as Jack after Friday night's impromptu meeting. I'd had all day Sunday to come to terms with the fact that my boss wanted me—wanted Allison—to host a Drag Queen Story Hour at the library. "Can you come here for a minute? I have something I want to run by you before we open up."

A quick glance at the clock showed me we had more than a half-hour before we unlocked the doors, so I'd lost any shot at avoiding the conversation by claiming I needed to make sure we were set up for the rampaging hordes—or handful—of morning patrons.

"Sure thing," I said, tucking my shoulder bag under the front desk on my way to his office. I sucked in a breath to make sure my expression didn't give away anything.

Every surface in Adrian's closet-sized office was covered in books and files. When I reached the doorway, he was in the process of shifting a stack of catalogs off the single guest chair jammed in the corner. "Have a seat."

I tugged at my tie, tucking it tightly into the gray vest I wore. I settled onto the edge of the chair. "What's up?"

Instead of settling in his own chair, he perched on the edge of the desk. Which meant, much to my fascinated and somewhat distracted horror, that my direct line of sight was the khaki fabric pulled tight across his lap. I jerked my eyes up to safer territory. I needed to rebuild the shields that had allowed me to work with him without inappropriate fantasies, STAT. Saturday night had decimated those shields, hardcore. My face heated at the reminder of the fantasies I'd had last night. There was this one thing fantasy-Adrian had done with his thumbs that—

Adrian's voice jerked my brain back to the real world. "I've been toying with some programming ideas for next year," he said. "I didn't want to say anything until I'd gotten approval from the Board of Directors. There was some push back. Expected, of course, but part of me wished the board would be more progressive."

"Progressive?" I knew what he meant, of course, but as far as he knew, he'd talked with Allison, not Jack.

"Oh, right." Adrian smiled wryly. "I'm getting ahead of myself. I want the library to host a Drag Queen Story Hour. In fact, I want to make it a regular part of our monthly programming."

I choked. I'd nearly convinced myself that I could somehow manage to organize such a one-time event while at the same time keeping my alter ego under wraps. Maybe I'd call in sick, or schedule a family emergency. But such plots would definitely not work over the course of months.

Adrian misread my reaction. "You disapprove?" The coldness in his voice rivaled the November temperatures outside.

Yes, but not for the reasons you imagine. "Not at all," I said. "It's just… you got the BOD to agree?"

"On a trial basis." He pulled a folder out from a stack on his desk. "The good news is that after the upheaval last spring, the current Board is more open to the idea than in previous years. The bad news is they're still finding their feet."

The previous board chairperson caused a bit of a scandal by sleeping with not one, but two of the trustees. Then, to make things worse, he managed to embezzle several thousand dollars from the library. Fortunately, he was bad at both things and his indiscretions were discovered almost immediately. Unfortunately, he'd run the board like his own personal fiefdom, and now there was a bit of a power vacuum as the updated membership figured out how to function in the new environment.

"And by finding their feet…"

He rolled his eyes. "They're afraid to make any 'major' changes," he said, flicking fingers into quotation marks when he reached the word major. "They're afraid of community backlash."

I nodded. "I can see that. Naperville's not very progressive, and there are some big voices backed by big dollars who might throw a fit."

"Exactly. So that's why they've agreed to do it as a test. But they want to get one organized before the holidays, so they can see how it goes before making their final decision."

"But it's already November! That's not enough time to organize a whole new event. And what does by the holidays mean? Are we talking Christmas or Thanksgiving?"

"Thanksgiving," he admitted.

"Thanksgiving?" I slumped in my seat.

My mind cycled through dozens of arguments. I didn't even know where to start. "That's less than three weeks."

He cringed. "Actually, we've got a week and a half. The professional storyteller we had scheduled canceled, so we've got an open spot next Friday. This way we can get the initial feedback in time for the Board to discuss, and hopefully approve, the program at their December meeting."

"Impossible." Relief coursed through me. This gave me a solid, logical reason to say no. "No one could pull together something like that within a week and a half. I mean, we need a willing drag queen at least. And how would we get the word out? I just don't see how we can pull all this together in a week and a half."

"That's the good news." Adrian reached behind himself and grabbed a sticky note. I recognized my website address immediately. "We're not starting from scratch. I've already made some inquiries. I've found the perfect guy for the job. He goes by the name Allison Wonderland."

"She," I corrected automatically.

"What's that?"

I mentally cursed myself. This was not the time to coach someone on drag queen protocol. "Ah, I think drag queens typically use female pronouns. That's what I've heard, anyway. But, you know, maybe not," I finished weakly.

Adrian nodded. "You're right, of course. I should have known better. If I slip up again, be sure to let me know. I want to do this right."

I dipped my head in agreement but avoided making eye contact.

"I need you to reach out to Allison and get her to agree. She seemed a little hesitant when I spoke with her on Friday, but I know you can convince her. And we'll need to finalize the forms and registration pieces necessary to be affiliated with the Drag Queen Story Hour. I want to make sure we're doing it right."

I had the site bookmarked on my computer, but I didn't mention it to him. "I'll take a look."

He slid off his desk to stand in front of me. "I know it's a lot to pull together in a short amount of time. But it's really important to me. I have complete faith in your ability to pull it together. There's no one better at arranging details and creating an experience kids love than you."

My throat tightened under his praise. He clearly meant what he said, and that knowledge squeezed something in my chest.

"I'll make it happen."

Now, I just needed to figure out how to be in two places at once.

"Come on, Kiki. I'll totally owe you one."

"Not a chance, kiddo."

It was Wednesday night and I'd been working on this project non-stop for the last two days. I'd even had to engage a volunteer to act as the host for the daily children's programs. The affiliation paperwork was easy enough to find and fill out. I'd been able to talk to someone directly to expedite the approval process so we could use the actual Drag Queen Story Hour name in our marketing graphics. Everything was coming together. Everything, that was, except for the drag queen to star in our first event.

After racking my brain for the last two days, I'd finally decided that the best approach would be to find another queen to take Allison's place at the story hour. If they didn't want to be center stage as themselves, well, I wasn't the only drag queen who could wear my ensembles and read a book to little kids. Finding someone else to do the job was turning into a harder challenge than I'd expected.

Kiki sat in front of the lighted mirror in the back of The Hot Box painting her face. Right now, the splotches of colors made her look like a highly pixelated close-up view of an Impressionist painting. Pretty soon, she'd blend and powder her features until Kiki lost the last remnants of Kevin to become a Lady Gaga doppelgänger.

I opened my mouth to offer her something—exactly what I didn't know.

"Shut it." She used a piece of flexible plastic as a template and contouring cream to create a harsh line along her cheekbone. "I don't do kids."

"But you have kids of your own."

"Exactly. Do you have any idea how hard it is to get sticky fingerprints and chocolate smears out of rayon? I do. It's not fun and it's not pretty."

"Fine." I swiveled to the right where Anna Banana Fontana added the finishing touches to her lipstick. "Hey, Anna—"

"No."

"But—"

She narrowed her eyes at me. "No."

I slumped on my stool. I was running out of queens to beg, bribe, and/or proposition. Maybe Maxine? Obviously, the big, beautiful Black queen couldn't pass herself off as Allison—I lacked both her height and her deep brown complexion—but it didn't have to be Allison performing at the library, right?

"You bitches suck," I grumbled, hopping off my stool.

"Sometimes," Anna said, waggling her brows.

I snorted a laugh. "Whatever. Be that way." I waved at them over my shoulder. "Break a falsie, ladies."

Music from the show pulsed around me as I made my way down the short hallway to the entrance to the barroom. I'd made it two steps into the smallish weeknight audience before I stumbled to a stop.

No way. No freaking way.

There, at table six, lounged Adrian Markes.

And he saw me.

Son of a bitch.

Now, I'd love to say that I played it cool, that I adopted the confidence my Allison persona gave me. But, no. I took one look at Adrian, squeaked in dismay, and ducked back into the hallway.

"What the hell?" Anna glared at me. I'd almost knocked her over in my ill-timed escape. "Girl, you need to watch where you're going."

"Sorry." I bit my lip, glancing over my shoulder to make sure I was out of view from the barroom.

Anna reached up to make sure her wig hadn't come loose. She detoured around me, striding into the bar to lack-luster applause. Wednesday night crowds were the worst.

I hovered out of sight, debating my options. Hiding in the hallway all night seemed like a poor use of my time. Maybe I could sneak over to Ricky's office, and duck out the back? What I should have done was walk confidently over to Adrian's table with a chipper "What are you doing here?" before politely excusing myself.

"Jack?"

Damn it. Any plans for an honorable retreat dissolved.

"Oh, hey, Adrian. Fancy meeting you here," I said weakly.

His brows arched.

Yeah, I had to agree. I couldn't believe I'd actually said that either.

"What are you doing here?" he asked.

Begging a drag queen to step in and get me out of trouble didn't seem like a viable answer. "Oh, you know, checking things out."

"What kinds of things—"

"And what are you doing here?" I asked before he could finish his own question. I was already lying to him more than I'd like—I hated adding more falsehoods to the equation. There was probably some kind of cosmic lie-o-meter keeping track; too many lies and I'd probably end up in whichever circle of hell had a person darning used tights and hand-washing tucking panties.

"I wanted to catch the show." He tilted his head to where Kiki roamed the crowd, lip-syncing to an old-school Lady Gaga song.

"You come to a lot of drag shows?" I asked, real curiosity in my voice. Maybe the PBS-watching library director was also an avid drag show aficionado. For all I knew, he spent every other weekend buried neck-deep in sequins and high heels.

"I've been to a few, but it's been years."

"Until Saturday."

He squinted at me.

Shit. There was no way I, as Jack, could have known that.

"Uh, you mentioned you'd talked to that one drag queen, Allison, on Saturday."

"Did I?" He angled his head, thinking hard.

"You must have."

He shrugged. "Okay, if you say so." He nodded to the barroom. "Join me for a drink? We can catch some of the show. I'm finding myself more and more interested in the whole drag thing. You can catch me up on your progress on our Drag Queen Story Hour project. We're after hours, though, so if you'd rather wait until we're on the clock, that's fine."

I hesitated. Drinks with Adrian? It was probably the closest I'd ever get to a date with the man, but it was absolutely the worst place and the worst timing. Without a graceful way to back out, I said, "Oh, I guess that'd be fine."

We left the hallway and wove our way to table six. I'd started thinking of it as his table. I settled awkwardly into one of the chairs. I didn't think I'd ever been on this side of a drag show. At least not at The Hot Box.

Anna's song hit its final crescendo. The crowd applauded. She tucked a couple bills into her bra before grabbing the mic. "Ladies and gentlemen, the girls and I need a quick break to powder our noses." She winked. "We'll be back in ten, and blow you…er, blow your minds…with the second half of our show."

Someone in the back of the room shouted, "You can blow me anytime, beautiful!"

Anna chuckled, the sound dark and seductive. "Honey bear, you couldn't handle me. Come back when you've got hair on your balls."

The room roared in laughter. Anna waved and sauntered backstage.

"Something to drink?" Adrian didn't wait for an answer before flicking his fingers in the air to summon one of the servers.

"Ah, yeah. Sure."

Brian, one of the bar's veteran servers, sidled up to the table, well-worn jeans and nearly transparent T-shirt showing off every one of his sleek muscles and bubble butt. Brian rarely, if ever, went home alone. He was gay temptation in one lean five-foot ten, bleached-blond package. "What's your pleasure, boys?" His eyes strayed to Adrian, lingered, before glancing at me.

"Funny seeing you on this side of the table."

I narrowed my eyes at him.

Adrian shifted toward me. "You come here a lot?"

Brian snorted. "That's one way to put it."

Before Adrian could ask the questions I could practically see on the tip of his tongue, I blurted out. "Vodka tonic. Double." I glared, mentally promising him a long and tortuous death if he didn't shut up and get back to work.

Brian rolled his eyes but turned back to Adrian. "And for you?"

"Beer's fine. Whatever you have on tap."

"I'll be right back." Brian sauntered away, adding a swing to his hips that usually had men focusing on his ass.

I risked a look at Adrian. He wasn't watching Brian's retreating form. No, his gaze was intent on my face. And had he moved closer?

"How are the plans coming? I know the paperwork has gone through with the Drag Queen Story Hour organization, but I haven't yet seen the contract for Allison."

"I'm still working on that," I admitted. "She's been a little…hard to pin down."

"Timing's getting close. What seems to be the problem? I can try and get her phone number from the bar owner."

"No. I'm sure that won't be necessary." The words rushed and tumbled together. While I was pretty sure Ricky wouldn't give out any of the performers' contact info without permission, it would be a disaster if he did. Adrian would recognize my cell phone number immediately. "I'm working on some contingency plans though, just in case. That's why I'm here tonight. Seeing if any of the other drag queens would be able to fill in if…if Allison can't make it."

"No, Jack. It needs to be Allison. She's the perfect fit for this. Her acts, hell, her name, all link back to children's books and television. It makes her perfectly recognizable and approachable for kids."

"Any drag queen who would be interested in doing the program with us will be able to edit their look to be approachable. And even if she can do this one, she may not be able or interested in doing them regularly. We're going to need other drag queens to get involved."

The overhead lights flickered, a sign that the show was about to resume.

Adrian reached over and covered my hand with his. His gaze, when it met mine, was full of something that I was afraid to attempt to interpret. Afraid, honestly, that I was putting too much meaning behind it. "I get that. But this first one is important. We need to get the Board's buy-in, and I truly believe that Allison is the best way to do it."

He was so damned earnest about it. How could I actively work against him when he wanted this—wanted Allison—so badly? Fine, I guess that meant plan B.

The music started up and Maxine stalked onto stage to a driving, almost primal, bass beat. Brian slinked over, delivering our drinks even as Maxine started her banter with the crowd. The glass tumbler barely hit the table before I lifted it and drained half.

"Thirsty?" Adrian watched me from over the rim of his pint glass.

"Sure, let's go with that." I cleared my throat. "I had some other ideas about the program. That first one, I mean."

"Yeah?" He took a swig of his beer, and I tried really hard not to fixate on the movement of his throat as he swallowed, or the sheen of moisture left behind on his lips. He almost killed me when his tongue swept over his top lip to catch the last drops.

My head swam. I probably shouldn't have downed so much of my drink in one go. Sure. Blame it on the vodka. A much better choice than the intoxicating nature of his smile.

"You had an idea?" He prompted when I'd stared silently at him for what had to be a full minute.

"Right! Idea. I think you should host the event that day. You can introduce the drag queen, explain the program, and be the point person. Maybe after that, once it's a regularly scheduled event, I can take over. But that first one will have extra scrutiny, the Board, and a whole lot of important people we need to impress. You're better at that."

"I'll be there, of course, but this is your project. You've done the majority of the leg work, you coordinate the youth programs, you've got the relationship with the parents. I don't want to take away from that. This was your idea, after all."

I choked and didn't even have the excuse of the vodka. "Excuse me?"

He ducked his head. The sheepish look shouldn't have been charming, but it absolutely was. "I shouldn't have said anything."

"No, seriously, what?"

"I don't want you to think I was snooping or looking for anything, but I ran across your notes on the program that were saved on the office computer."

Irritation flashed through me, but I brushed it aside. Logically, there was no reason for me to be upset. I'd researched the Drag Queen Story Hour as a legitimate part of my youth programming duties. I'd been pulling together ideas on a lot of possible future youth programs. It wasn't like he'd checked out the browser history on my personal computer.

"Okay," I said.

Adrian grabbed my hand. "It wasn't like that. I promise. The IT team had to install some upgrades and needed me to re-organize some of the files. That's all."

"I get it," I said. "I'm not mad or anything. It's a library resource. Even if you were checking up on my computer usage, it'd be a hundred percent within your rights to do so."

"Good." The tension left his body. "It was a great idea. Why didn't you ever propose it officially?"

"I almost did. I'd written up the proposal and planned to discuss it with you. I'd printed it out and everything. When I took it to your office, you'd just gotten off the phone with the Board President and were cussing and cursing his narrow-minded policies and backward way of thinking. He'd just read you the riot act about including And Tango Makes Three in our collection. If the Board couldn't accept a children's book about gay penguins, there'd be no way they'd accept drag queens reading to kids."

"Good. I was afraid, or maybe nervous is the better word, that you were concerned about my reaction. I didn't like the idea that you were, or could be, uncomfortable, talking to me."

"Nah. You're pretty easy to talk to." At work, my brain corrected. Easy to talk to at work. About work stuff. Usually. Granted, I was finding it harder to talk to him about real stuff, about personal stuff. I should be able to just tell him that I was Allison Wonderland, and that if he wanted Allison to read at Drag Queen Story Hour, then he was going to have to be the point person during the event. Clearly, I couldn't maintain both roles simultaneously.

Added to that, he'd looked at Allison with heat and interest blazing in his eyes. Not Jack. Not the real me. Allison. And how would he react to knowing he'd shown that interest in a coworker? Would that make things even more awkward and complicated at the library every day?

"I'm glad. You've been a great asset to the library. You have no idea how nice it's been having someone like you, someone I can count on, working with me. Before you, the youth services program coordinator was…not reliable. I ended up having to do her job as well as mine, and it was a lot. Hiring you was the best decision I've made since becoming library director."

My skin buzzed from the compliment. Hopefully, the room was dim enough that he wouldn't see the blush spill across my face.

I almost missed it when he said, "And to think, I almost didn't hire you."

I scowled at him. "What? Why not?"

He bit his lip. "I probably shouldn't have said that. We shouldn't even be talking about this here."

"You can't just say that and then not explain."

"Look, I don't want to make this inappropriate. We're coworkers. I'm your boss."

"You're still holding my hand," I told him, "and there's a six-foot-four drag queen performing twenty feet away from us. I'm pretty sure we've already bypassed appropriate boss-coworker interaction."

"Fine," he grumbled, making no move to retrieve his hand. Using his free hand, he grabbed his beer and sucked down several swallows. Courage or a stalling tactic, I didn't know.

"Did I not meet the requirements you were looking for, or what?"

"Oh, you were qualified. Easily the most qualified applicant. Which is why, despite my reluctance, I hired you."

"Then what was it?"

"You came into the interview, practically sparkling with attitude and challenge. Your resume was spot-on, and your references were nothing less than glowing, but when you came in, you had this extra layer of attitude and challenge."

I cringed. I think I'd repressed most of the memory of my interview.

"You sat down, announced that you were gay and if I had a problem with that you wouldn't waste any more of our time."

I closed my eyes and reached for my drink. Vodka. Definitely needed more vodka.

Once I'd drained the glass, I said, "I should probably explain—"

Adrian snorted out a laugh. "I'd love an explanation."

"My last two employers seemed to struggle with the whole gay thing. I've never hidden who I am, never denied anything. I mean, it's not like I made a big production out of it or anything, but at my first position after college, my boyfriend at the time stopped by. I don't remember why. To drop off my lunch or something. I kissed him on the cheek before he left. The library director saw this and flipped his lid. You'd have thought I'd started making out with him in the middle of the children's section or something. Basically, he said it was inappropriate for me to be acting intimately when there were children present. When I tactfully pointed out that he'd kissed his wife the same way just that morning, he claimed that was different."

Adrian growled. "Homophobic asshole."

"Pretty much. Let's just say, after the first disciplinary meeting for trumped-up violations, I started looking for another position. The next position wasn't much better. At that one, the head librarian was one of those problematic ladies who want the world to know how accepting they are, while at the same time trying to shove anyone 'other' into a little box. It was great that I was gay, just so long as I kept my more flamboyant tendencies tamped down." She'd actually discovered I did drag on weekends, and, while "she'd never judge"—insert eye roll here—it would be better if I refrained from such activities while employed there. But for obvious reasons, I couldn't tell Adrian that.

He arched his brow. "Flamboyant tendencies? No feather boas and glitter at the library?"

My heart stuttered. He didn't think… Of course not. I grinned, trying to pretend it was a joke when I said, "Oh, I reserve those for after dark. Glitter and feathers are so hard to vacuum off industrial carpet."

Adrian's lips tilted up. "I'll keep that in mind for the event."

"Never mind that. You're trying to distract me. Why did you almost not hire me? Was it because I came in with an attitude?"

"No, it wasn't the attitude. I liked the attitude. In fact…." It might have been the flashing lights of the show, but I swore he blushed. But his eyes—those damned intense dark eyes—caught and held mine. His fingers clenched around mine. The intensity of his gaze, of his grip, muted the music, dimmed the lights, quieted the crowd until it was just him and me.

"In fact?" I licked my suddenly dry lips and held my breath.

He lifted his free hand, tracing his fingers along my cheek, pausing to brush his thumb across my bottom lip. "I liked a lot about you. Everything about you." His voice hitched. "Too much. I—"

Reality came crashing back in the form of a sequin-studded queen plopping her well-padded hips on the edge of our table. The blinding beam of the spotlight directed at our table didn't help either.

I wanted to shout at Maxine, to force her to back off so Adrian could finish his sentence. I needed him to clarify the liked business. He liked my attitude? He liked everything about me? Liked? As in past tense? As in, he used to, but not anymore? What about now? Did he still like me? And now, I couldn't demand any answers because Maxine-effing-H2-Ho decided to butt in.

She stood close enough I could see the sheen of perspiration on her painted face, and her smile was, in a word, devilish. "Well, lookee here, boys and girls and everyone in between and neither. What do we have here?"

I glared at her, trying to convey that her death would be imminent if she didn't move her magnificent ass away from our table.

She ignored me.

I should have known better. Whenever a fellow drag queen visited the club, whether they were performing or not, whoever emceed made it a point to single them out for a little back-and-forth. But usually, the visiting queen wasn't attempting to stay under the radar. If Maxine said the wrong thing, my whole deception would come crumbling down. Which, granted, would take a lot of the pressure off me. But it could also potentially create a whole host of new problems.

I glared harder. I probably looked like a constipated turtle rather than a pissed off queen in boy's clothing.

Maxine sighed into the mic. "I love love," she announced to the audience, making a production of clasping her hands in front of her heart. "And boys and girls, I do believe we are in the presence of—" she paused, letting the anticipation build. "Well, maybe not love, but infatuation." She drew out the word until the five syllables sounded erotic and inevitable. "And we all know where infatuation leads, don't we?"

I was going to kill her.

"Bed!" someone in the audience shouted.

"Well, there too. Hopefully, it leads there often, frequently, and an assortment of different ways."

I closed my eyes, hoping the shadows would swallow me up. They wouldn't, of course. Not while Adrian and I sat in the middle of the spotlight.

"But more importantly, my lovelies, infatuation can lead to love. And sometimes love leads to"—another pause—"marriage, middle-class mediocrity, and little blue pills." The crowd roared with laughter at her matter-of-fact tone. "So let's wish our friends here luck." She lifted my nearly-empty drink. "A toast! May luck find this adorable couple in a future free of mediocrity and little blue pills."

"Hear, hear!" the crowd shouted.

Maxine drained the last of my drink and winked at me. Bitch.

Adrian withdrew his hand, and the space between our seats widened. He didn't seem to be able to meet my eyes. Not that I tried too hard to do it myself. Ten agonizing minutes of stilted conversation later, we gave up even pretending something hadn't changed.

The worst part? I could easily envision a future with Adrian. Even if that future included middle-class mediocrity and little blue pills, it looked amazing.

We stopped at the sidewalk in front of The Hot Box. I jangled my keys in my hand, debating whether I should say something before we parted ways. The words didn't come, so I shoved my hands into my pockets and said instead, "Good night, Adrian. See you at work tomorrow."

He nodded.

I turned away.

"Jack, wait."

I'd made it three steps before a hand wrapped around my elbow. I didn't have to see his face to know who it was. I bit my lip, steeled my nerves, and angled my body toward Adrian. "Yeah?"

He sucked in a breath. "Before we're back in our established work-related roles, I wanted to tell you—"

When he didn't finish, I took half a step closer. "Yeah?"

"I just…. You can trust me, you know."

"I…what?"

"You can trust me. If there's something you want—or need—to tell me, you can. I've got your back and it won't change how I think of you."

Convinced I was only hearing what I wanted him to say, I didn't know how to respond. "Um, okay."

His mouth twisted like he wanted to say more. In the end, he said, "See you tomorrow."

⁂

The day of the highly anticipated debut of Drag Queen Story Hour at Evans library finally arrived. I drank my morning coffee while staring out my kitchen window at a clear but cold winter day. My cell phone sat on the counter in front of me. I'd typed the text to Adrian but hadn't hit send yet. I'd written and re-written the message a hundred times since insomnia jerked me awake at three.

Adrian—sorry for the late notice. Something has come up. I know the timing is terrible, but I won't be in today. My notes for the DQSH event introduction are in the blue folder at the Youth Services Desk. Everything you need is in the folder. Again, I apologize for the last-minute call off. It was unavoidable.

I was tempted to add more. More apologies. More explanation. But more meant either admitting the truth to Adrian, or coming up with some lie. I'd deleted words like family emergency, hospital, and death's door. The text I should send would say something like, By the way, I'm Allison and I'll see you at 9:30. I'd keyed that message several times, ultimately replacing them with something has come up.

This last version was the perfect blend of honesty and misdirection. But the idea of hitting that little Send icon nauseated me. I took the last sip of coffee, cursed myself, and hit Send. A minute later my phone rang. ADRIAN flashed on the display. My gut clenched. My finger wavered between the icons that would either accept the call or send it to voicemail. Calling myself ten kinds of a coward, I rejected the call before tossing the phone on my dresser.

Twenty minutes, a hot shower, and a close shave later, I stepped out of the bathroom. My phone taunted me from the dresser. The screen was lit, a text bubble on the display.

I made myself take the five steps to my dresser and pick up the phone.

I understand.

Two words. Two simple words that caused my throat to tighten and my eyes to prickle.

I sucked in a breath. I'd do this one thing, get through today, and figure out the rest later.

Ricky side-eyed me as I slid into the front seat of his Explorer. I nearly bashed him in the head with the six-foot, glittering shepherd's crook I'd added to my ensemble. He offered to give me a ride to the library. It wouldn't exactly hide the connection if Allison showed up in Jack's car. Though the closer I got to zero hour, the less important that seemed.

It was for the best. Ricky had planned to come anyway—to show community support for the Drag Queen Story Hour initiative. The rest was just details. "You really doing this?" he asked.

I yanked the seatbelt into place. "Yep." I straightened the satiny sky-blue ribbon bowed at my waist to keep it from wrinkling under the belt. Of all my costumes, this one showed the least amount of skin. The bloomers under the skirt gathered at my calves, the white fabric cinched in with more blue ribbon, and landed at the top of the pointy lace-up boots I'd paired with the outfit. The blue dress was knee-length in the front, with layers of white crinoline underneath, but draped nearly to my heels in the back. Large puffy sleeves met the tops of my elbow-length white gloves.

Ricky plucked at the corner of one of the sleeves. "You're being an idiot."

"I'm aware." I laid the wide-brimmed blue-and-white checked bonnet on my lap, then smoothed my hands along the blonde wig's wide sausage curls to make sure they stayed in place. I didn't meet his eyes as I pulled the visor down to access the vanity mirror.

Ricky pulled away from the curb. "Why are you going through all of this?"

I pretended to misunderstand his question while I checked the adhesion on the ridiculously long eyelashes I wore. "I believe in the Drag Queen Story Hour mission. I have the opportunity—maybe even the obligation—to do what I can to make this program launch a success."

"Right. And why can't you just tell your boss that you are Allison? Why go to all these steps to hide it?"

That was the question, wasn't it?

A couple of weeks ago, it had seemed perfectly logical to keep Jack and Allison separate. An added protection for me at work. But now, after working closely with Adrian, and seeing how open he was to both the program and to me—I still couldn't get that moment we'd shared at The Hot Box out of my head—the separation felt more like lying than protection.

"My job—" I began, but snapped my mouth closed. At this point, calling off work on such a big day would get me into a hell of a lot more trouble than Adrian finding out I was a part-time drag queen.

I took a breath and tried again. "The thing is, that first night when he showed up at the club, I sort of freaked out. Instinctive panic/protection mode. Then, once I'd calmed down, it was too late. How the hell could I explain after the fact that it was actually me under all the makeup? Everything sort of snowballed from there and I didn't know how to get out of it. What could I tell him?"

"I can see that," he agreed. "But the longer you wait, the harder it will get."

"No kidding."

Ricky reached over and patted my shoulder. It was a comforting gesture I would have appreciated more if it didn't flatten the necessarily puffy sleeve. "Everything you've said is true, but it's not the heart of it. What are you afraid of, really?"

I scowled at him, then immediately smoothed out my face. I didn't need lines in my makeup. I didn't have the tools I'd need to fix my face if I messed it up. "What are you, some kind of drag queen psychologist?"

"Nah. Just a friend who's older and wiser. And someone who cares about you."

Damn it. He just had to get all lovely and sweet about it. I couldn't fight that. I deflated, shifting toward him as much as the seatbelt would allow. "He likes Allison."

Ricky nodded.

"No, you don't get it. He really likes Allison. If he looked at me—at Jack—the way he looked at Allison, I'd be thrilled. Hell, I'd probably have him halfway to the altar."

"The other night at the club, it wasn't Allison he was into. He was with Jack, and you might as well have been a perfectly cooked steak, aged whiskey, and a chocolate cake all rolled into one, because, honey, that man was starving for you."

"He's also my boss."

Ricky shrugged. "That gets a little dicey, sure. But it's not insurmountable. Figure out what the rules are, and see where to go with it. Pretty sure lying to him isn't the best call on either the personal or professional front."

"Right."

"Stop pouting," Ricky said. "We're here and you have an entrance to make."

My eyes widened as I saw the library sign. Crap. "Stop. Stop. Stop."

Ricky pulled into a parking spot at the far end of the lot.

I needed to get my bonnet on before anyone saw me. I flipped the visor back down, but the tiny mirror wasn't big enough to give me the full scope. I made sure the thick blue ribbon covered a good portion of my cheeks, the curls covered my ears, and the bonnet's brim sat as low as I could make it without looking ridiculous.

"Can you tell it's me?" I demanded, shifting to Ricky.

He rolled his eyes. "It's sunny outside."

"It is," I agreed, adjusting the fit of the white gloves.

"It won't be as easy to fall for the illusion in the light of day versus the flashing lights and shadows of the club."

I stilled. "And?"

Ricky reached over to adjust the ribbon under my chin. "He's going to figure it out, honey. No amount of contouring and distraction will change your bone structure. And if he can't tell, then, honey, he's not worth it."

"You're a jerk," I told him, blinking because the sentimental bastard had my eyes stinging.

"Now here's what we're going to do. I'm going to pull up to the front. You're going to stay seated. I will come around, open your door, and help you out. Because you are a queen and deserve to be treated as such."

That made me laugh, which cleared up the threat of leaking eyes. Ricky pulled right up to the front of the building, parking in a No Parking zone. I only had a second to admire Ricky's badassery, before I noticed the number of patrons lined up. "What the ever-loving hell is this?"

There were so many people. After a quick scan, I calculated easily thirty adults and half again as many kids. A news van idled halfway up the block.

"Looks like a good turnout," Ricky said as he opened his door.

"And they're not protesters?" I scanned the crowd, and no, not a picket sign or bible verse in sight. "Adrian will be happy."

The passenger door opened, then Ricky held out his arm gallantly. "My lady."

"Kind sir," I said, laying my hand on his arm and letting him guide me out of the car. While I shook out my skirt and adjusted my bonnet, he reached in the back and grabbed my crook.

A little girl squealed from somewhere in the crowd. "Look, Mom, it's Little Bo Peep!"

Time to put your game face on, I told myself. I took the crook and struck a pose. I waved at the assembled people, smiling my widest smile. I think I managed to hit just the right note with my ensemble—recognizable as a character, but still clearly drag, not just some guy dressed up as a storybook character.

The crowd parted, creating an aisle that led straight up the stairs to the front door of the library. At the top of the stairs, like a damned expectant groom, stood Adrian. He wore his best gathering-major-donations suit. It was a light gray material, cut slim, and made his dark eyes smolder. His tie tickled every one of my book lover's fancies. It was solid black with a broad, big-toothed grin at the widest part. Of course, he would wear a Cheshire Cat tie. So freaking adorkable. And so completely appropriate for introducing a drag queen called Allison Wonderland.

We'd agreed in our planning sessions to simply call the performer Allison to avoid any homonym confusion. The crowd might not make the connection, but it was clear that Adrian wanted to acknowledge that part of Allison's—er, my—identity.

"Is that really a boy, momma?" A little boy to my right asked, with the loud "whisper" little kids are prone to.

"I think so, buddy," the woman holding the boy's hand said.

"Are you sure?" The boy cocked his head, taking in my entire outfit. "Why's he wearing a dress if he's a boy?"

I slowed my walk, curious about her answer.

"Some boys like to wear dresses, and that's okay."

"Okay," he said. "He's really pretty." He grinned up at me, showing off the hole where one of his bottom teeth had fallen out. "You are. You're really pretty. Even if you are a boy in a dress," he told me earnestly.

I tipped my bonnet to him, winking. "And you, my young friend, are going to grow up to be a charmer."

Ricky chuckled next to me.

I'd been so distracted by the interaction with the little boy, I'd missed something important. Something huge. Because when I looked up from the kid, Adrian stood in front of me. He held out his arm, much as Ricky had done. "May I escort you from here?"

Ricky passed me over without a protest, the traitor.

I gulped, then, realizing we stood nearly eye-to-eye (damn the two-inch heels on my boots), I jerked my head down. I cleared my throat, then squeaked out "Of course," in a terrible falsetto that would get me thrown off any drag stage in town.

I linked my elbow with his, and lifted my skirt to avoid tripping on the fabric as I ascended the stairs. An act that allowed me to keep my face angled away from Adrian and not fall on my face. A win-win. Now if only I had an excuse to not be touching him. His biceps flexed with every step, illustrating the strength in his arms, and I cursed the gray material of his suit. What would it feel like to hold on to him like this without a jacket in the way? Or without a shirt at all?

"The paper is going to want to get a couple of shots of us at the end of the reading. Maybe one with the Board of Directors as well."

"Of course." Now I sounded like a damn parrot. "I mean, yes, the details of the day were explained to me." Finally, my voice was back in line. Maybe a little deeper than I would do in one of my shows, but it was hopefully different enough from my regular voice that he wouldn't recognize it.

He placed his hand over mine where it rested on his arm and leaned close. I whipped my head aside, making a show of nodding to the crowd on my left. The floppy brim of my bonnet brushed across his nose. He huffed out a laugh.

"So, are you ready for this?"

I swore I felt his breath against my ear, even though I had a bonnet and layers of synthetic hair in the way.

"Always," I breathed, because that's what Allison would say. Jack, on the other hand, had never been so unprepared in his life.

We'd reached the door, and Adrian led me through it. My steps faltered. There were more people in the lobby than had been waiting outside. I couldn't remember the last time I'd seen nearly this many people on the premises. If things worked out today, the Board would have no reason to put the kibosh on Drag Queen Story Hour at the library. The program director in me wanted to dance.

The importance of the morning grew exponentially in my head. Holy shit. There were so many people. I regularly performed in front of crowds easily this large, but never before had the weight of expectation or success dragged so heavily on my shoulders. What if I screwed up? What if I said or did something that would make Adrian a laughingstock in front of the town, the Board, and the freaking media?

Adrian squeezed my arm, as though he could sense the anxiety building in me. "Thank you. Really. This means a lot to the library—to me—that you're here today."

My breath caught. Had I imagined an extra emphasis on you?

"But most importantly, the exposure it gives for our LGBTQIA youth is positive, and desperately needed. Representation really does matter, and I think it's critical that kids learn that it's okay to be who they are, it's okay to own their truth. That's what makes programs like this so important."

Damn it. I looked away, admiration and shame warring within me. He was right. 100 percent, no holds barred, right. How could I possibly be an example of owning one's truth when I couldn't be honest about who I was with someone who I knew without a shadow of a doubt would accept me—both aspects of who I was—without question?

We continued forward until we reached the archway leading to the children's section where the event would be held. Adrian stared over my shoulder, a small smile on his face.

I turned to see what had his attention.

It was a poster. One of the many book-related inspirational posters tacked up around the library. In this one, an image of a candle glowed against a black backdrop. On it, yellow text read, "There is one thing stronger than all the armies in the world, and that is an idea whose time has come."

"Victor Hugo," I muttered.

Adrian's smile widened. "Victor Hugo," he agreed.

The crowd milled around us, ushering the children into a clearing surrounding a throne-like chair. I barely noticed. Adrian looked at me with such admiration and understanding, I knew it was time. No matter the consequences, I couldn't pretend anymore. My heart stumbled in my chest, and Fourth of July sparklers tingled through my veins. Giddy anticipation, or a new awareness, sucked the oxygen from the room.

I was owning my truth. I owed it to Adrian, and to myself, to come clean.

"Look, Adrian," I began. It was easier than I expected it to be. "There's something you need to know—"

Adrian reached forward, interrupting my words. His right hand cupped my cheek, and the left hand pushed the brim of my bonnet up. He looked me dead in the eye, and said, "C'mon, Jack. We've got a show to put on."

My breath caught in my throat. I licked my lips and swallowed heavily. "I…I mean…You knew?"

He traced his thumb along my jaw, and I couldn't even worry about the effect it might have on my makeup. "Later," he promised. He leaned forward to press a soft kiss to my cheek. Warmth bloomed through me, and my skin tingled where he'd brushed his lips against me. "We'll talk… later. But right now, you have somewhere to be."

A joyous smile spread over my face, damn the impact on my makeup. Yes, later. I knew we had a lot to talk about, a lot of details to work out. He was still my boss, and, sure, we had a lot to learn about each other if we were going to make something work between us. But for the first time, a future with Adrian didn't seem so far-fetched.

"Later," I agreed.

I straightened my shoulders and glided regally to the decorative chair. Today I was the queen of the library, and a queen never let down her subjects. Not even a queen well on her way to falling for her boss.

LATE FEES

Trisha McKee

Riley smiled to herself as she set the books down on an unoccupied table and leafed through them, her eyes skimming over the summaries on the backs and inside flaps. The library had finally gotten some current bestsellers in, and she gave a small squeak of excitement as she thought of her summer vacation.

This would be the first time in her ten years of teaching she could enjoy the summer without having a part-time job. No longer being forced to live beyond her means by a husband that was never satisfied, she was free to budget and plan. There were no more outrageous mortgage and credit card bills. Riley was debt-free two years after the divorce.

Thinking of Brice and the end of their marriage made her mood dip, but she shook her head and focused on the pile of books. This was her summer. She could relax and make her own plans. No matter how shattered her heart was, Riley enjoyed having control over her life, her time, and her finances.

She made her way to the check-out desk and smiled at the man behind the counter as he focused on a stack of books in front of him. "Hi! I'm so excited you guys got some new books in! I was afraid I'd run out of things to read this summer since—"

The man held up his hand, never glancing at her as he grabbed a book. "Hold on, please. I'm in the middle of something." He studied it and then typed it into the computer. Finally, he looked up. "What can I help you with?"

Despite the chip at her confidence, Riley took a deep breath and re-established her smile. "Hi. I want to check these books out." She gave them a slight nudge toward the man, suddenly noticing his beautiful almond-shaped, brown eyes. She stumbled over her words until she straightened and asked, "Are you the new… Miss Ross retired and… you're the new librarian?"

The man grew still, and Riley got to study him a little closer, her eyes drinking in that shaggy black hair, lined face, sharp cheekbones, and strong jaw. He looked to be in his forties, tall and striking. But then his low voice reached her.

"Why? Because I'm a man I can't be a librarian? I tell ya, this town is really—"

"Whoa! Hey! I just - I was asking because - never mind. I was curious. I wasn't judging."

He squeezed his eyes shut and sighed. "I'm sorry. It's been a day of it. This small town isn't ready to see a male librarian. Just the comments and… anyway, hello. I'm Carson. New librarian."

Riley smiled. "Hi, Carson. I'm Riley."

He flashed a grin at her before dropping his gaze to the pile of books. "So, you're stocking up."

"Yeah. I have the summer off."

He paused, his eyes lifting to take her in. "Teacher?"

"Yep."

He grinned and nodded. "Library card? We'll get you all checked out so you can start the summer vacation."

Riley couldn't help but smile back, handing over her card. She hummed and looked around the library, taking in the familiar, cozy scene. There were a couple of kids in the next room and an older gentleman sitting in a chair in the corner, a book open on his lap. Riley leaned forward, trying to determine if he was actually reading or sleeping.

"Uh… Riley?" She glanced up with a distracted smile, and Carson motioned toward the computer. “I’m showing late fees from the last time. Twenty-three dollars.”

“Oh.” Her heart sank. She had forgotten about the late return last time. And watching every penny meant that she had put off paying the fines. But now she had a pile of books and no purse with her. “I... uh… I don’t have my…”

“You can’t pay for it?”

“I can!” She felt her face grow warm. “I have the money. Just not with me. So…” She flung a hand toward the books. “I can put these back where they were...”

“No,” he shook his head vehemently. Leaning forward, he offered in a low voice, “Listen, I can put these aside for you.”

She thought of her budget for the summer. She had bingo later this week. That was a costly hobby. It was either pay the fine or go to bingo. At this point, she was too embarrassed to even consider setting foot in this library again, in front of this attractive man that had not only been short with her initially, but now saw her all flustered and without money.

“No. Please don’t do that. I’ll just - I’ll put them back.”

“Ma’am. Riley. I’ll put them back. It’s okay. Are you sure you don’t want me to set them aside?”

“No, thank you.”

She fled the library, drawing even more attention to herself.

The rest of the week was less eventful. Riley spoke to her twin sons almost daily, heartbroken they had decided to stay on campus for the summer, but understanding that at twenty-one, they yearned for independence. They had been devastated when their parents initially separated, but they showed maturity beyond their years when it came to dealing with the family fracture; they treated both parents with the same love and respect.

It was difficult to go from a full house to an empty nest and ended marriage. While Riley loved her freedom, she missed the constant action, the voices calling for her, someone to watch the latest movie with. She missed the past at times.

Riley mostly stayed close to home, usually in her small backyard, sitting and reading books she already had at the house. Some she’d acquired from friends, some for a quarter at a nearby yard sale.

Being out in public was difficult at times. Riley often felt awkward, her breathing shallow and skin too tight as her nerves bounced beneath the surface. Her ex-husband had said it was all in her head, vying for attention, and she wondered how he could think that when she wanted the opposite. No attention. She wished to be invisible, gliding through the aisles with a grace that eluded her in reality.

By the end of the week, the incident at the library was a faded sting. The sunshine, the books, even sleeping in soothed her enough to forget her humiliation. And she had bingo on Saturday night.

Riley loved bingo. Her ex had always discouraged it, saying it was a waste of money, and it took too long when he would rather she be home with him. But now she could go and not worry that someone would nag about the money she spent, or ask her to hand over any money she won. She could focus on blotting out numbers and not say a word to anyone.

That Saturday night, she made her way to the corner table, the one that was in front of the monitor, but not too close and angled in a way that she did not have to hurt her neck looking up.

"Oh, you again." The old lady with bulging eyes and a perm that twisted her yellow-gray hair to her scalp glared at her, moving her things away as if Riley was going to grab them and run.

Riley returned the glare and sat down, spreading out the game sheets and unpacking her drinks. This would be a long evening, and she was ready.

"You're wearing pink," the woman sing-songed, dabbing the free spaces on her games. "That's bad luck."

"Only in your old, brittle mind."

"Did you brush your hair tonight? It looks a little less wasp-nesty. Good job."

A shocked laugh fell from Riley's mouth. "Oh, my, Ruby. That was a good one."

"You just watch your cards tonight. I'm not going to help you."

"Never have to," Riley sang out, not about to let the grouchy bingo lady dampen her mood.

As the games started, they focused on their cards, dabbing the numbers as they were called, staring hopefully up at the monitors for numbers they needed. At one point, Ruby hollered, "Bingo!" and shot Riley a smirk.

"Congratulations," Riley trilled.

"You just focus on your games, there, young lady, and don't worry about my winnings." She counted her money and then added in a softer tone, "My nephew is coming here tonight."

Riley sat up. "Your nephew? He plays?"

"No, he doesn't play bingo. Unlike you, the guy has a life. Bingo should be limited to women over the age of 60. But no, he is staying with me for a while. I forgot my snacks so he's bringing them over."

Riley chewed the inside of her cheek and blinked, unable to come up with a clever retort quick enough. Instead, she glared and finally growled, "How nice. I hope he remembers to bring your muzzle."

A half-hour later, she was too engrossed in watching for the numbers and searching her cards for those called that she did not notice when Ruby's nephew arrived.

"Hey, loser!"

"Aunt Ruby! Don't talk like that!"

"Now, boy, don't tell me how to behave! I'm still your elder. She knows how I am. Hey, Riley, girl, look up. Have some manners."

Riley smiled and glanced up, freezing when she saw Carson, the librarian, standing next to her. His eyes widened in similar surprise, but then he extended his hand, a deep laugh bubbling out of that full mouth. "Well. Riley. Hello."

Suddenly, the intense humiliation from the library struck her, and Riley opened her mouth, unable to verbalize a simple greeting. All she could remember was having to leave those books behind and rush out of there.

"What's wrong with ya, girl? You look ridiculous."

Riley squeezed her eyes shut. Of course, Ruby was this man's aunt. Of course Riley had not suffered enough humiliation this week, this life.

"Aunt Ruby, stop!" Carson scolded.

"No. I will not stop. Look at her. Sitting with an oversized hoodie hiding her body, playing bingo on a Saturday night. I never saw anything so pitiful." She pointed a gnarled finger at her. "Go get a life. Stop hiding. Stop being a loser."

Carson hissed his aunt's name again, then he turned toward Riley, his eyes caramel pools of pity. And that propelled her into action. She flew out of her chair, knocking it over in the process, grabbed her wallet and keys and ran outside.

The rain flattened her auburn hair against her face, mixing with the tears and it chilled her skin. She focused on zigzagging between cars until she was at the end of the lot. She heard her name, recognized Carson's voice, but she jumped in her car and escaped quickly.

She spent the rest of the night watching episodes of her favorite show, shoveling ice cream into her mouth. Ruby was right; Riley was a loser. She had always been a loser. She never fit in, whether it be at school or home. She had enjoyed college, but that was when she was an adult and had a family at home, so she couldn't hang out with people or go grab a bite to eat. No, she had to go make dinner and she had to watch her pennies.

Even her husband had thought she was a nobody. He laughed at her panic attacks, had blatantly cheated on her, and now taunted her with photos of his vacation with the new younger woman.

Truth be told, Riley did not care about her ex's life. It stung that she spent so many years being loyal and faithful, putting effort into a lost cause. But what truly hurt was the possibility that it was her. That she was unloveable, unlikable. Her quirks became issues that overwhelmed all those around her. The phone rang, pulling her from her thoughts.

"Hello?" she murmured, the ice cream rolling and melting around her frozen tongue. She did not recognize the number, and it was late for telemarketers, but she still answered.

"Riley? Riley Plummel?"

"Who's this?" She worked at moving her mouth around the sounds, her head now pounding from the cold treat.

"It's Carson. From the library… and from bingo."

Dammit. "How'd you get my number?"

"Library. Your account."

"Is that allowed? You can't just use my information like that!" Anger thawed her frozen muscles.

His deep chuckle was a bit infuriating. Patronizing. "Well, this is library business."

"On a Saturday night?"

"Your fine's been paid. You can come check out those books anytime."

"Paid? Look, I'm not sure who you are, but I don't need your pity—"

"No! This was a donation." His voice purred, "Awwww." There was an awkward pause, and then he blurted, "The education fund. Yes. Those beautiful souls that teach our wicked youth, someone has donated to pay off their fines. Late fees. So you're in the clear."

Despite herself, Riley giggled. "Wicked youth?"

"So wicked. I don't know how you do it. I had one kid kick my shins during storytime. He yelled that I wasn't using the correct voices when reading the characters."

"Was that little Christian, with the spiked hair and green sneakers?"

There was a gasp on the other end of the line. "How did you know?"

"I'm a teacher, Carson. And don't take it personally. Christian has anger issues, especially when it comes to books."

"Now, see! You deserve this good fortune. Late fees wiped clean." He paused, and added, "I can even open the library for you, just you, tomorrow to get your books."

Riley wrapped her blanket tighter around her body. "Thanks but… not necessary."

"Hey. Listen... My aunt - she's like an adult version of Christian. No self-control."

"It's fine. Really. But I have to go now. Thanks for calling. Maybe apply the education fund to someone else's account." She hung up, a fresh wave of tears cracking the last few words. She hoped Carson didn't notice.

The worst part of the call was that Riley had enjoyed it. She found Carson to be funny and charming, and the conversation was easy, flowing. For a few glorious moments, she had forgotten herself and those overwhelming anxieties and had savored the dialogue. But Riley reminded herself that she could not be vulnerable. She reminded herself that both times she had encountered Carson, she had embarrassed herself. She had been vulnerable.

For the next week, Riley focused on making the most out of her vacation. She took a road trip to a sunflower maze, walked under the sunshine, surrounded by tall, summer flowers.

She went to the lake, swallowed any self-consciousness and donned a bathing suit for the first time in years. After playing in the water, relieved that everyone seemed to be too engaged with their own activities to notice her, Riley rented a paddleboat. It was something she had always wanted to do, but if she had managed to convince her ex to even go to the lake, he steadfastly refused to do paddleboats. So she'd paddled around, laughing as ducks waddled to the edge, quacking their protests at her.

Later, there was a Wing Fest at a local amusement park, and Riley attended with her friend Sarah, who had pleaded with her the entire summer before to go. They laughed and ate and caught up on lives. Riley realized how much she had missed her friend, how easy it was to be with Sarah, until their catching up was interrupted...

"Oh. We meet again."

Riley whirled around and faced Carson just as Sarah sputtered out a laugh and grabbed her arm. "Who's that?" Sarah demanded in a low whisper.

Instead of answering her, Riley straightened. "Hi, Carson." Sarah jabbed her with an elbow to the ribs and after yelping, she motioned to her friend. "Carson, this is Sarah."

They exchanged greetings, and Riley, slightly tipsy off the beer and heat, giggled at Sarah's devouring gaze. Carson was oblivious, however, his eyes fastened onto Riley. "You got some sun this week."

Her smile came easily. "Yes. A little."

"Summer vacation agrees with you. So… about the other night..."

Sarah's head swiveled around to gape at the couple. "There was an 'other night'?"

"Don't be ridiculous," Riley growled, giving Carson a look that he picked up on immediately and communicated that with a short nod. "He's the new librarian."

"What? Oh wow, that is just… That's perfect. I'm going to get some wings. I'll be back."

Carson watched her walk away. "Was she making fun of me being a librarian?"

"No. She was making fun of me. For knowing the librarian."

He raised his eyebrows in confusion, but then shook his head and chuckled. "Okay. But hey, listen—"

"Please. I don't want to talk about the other night."

"She feels so bad, Riley. She said you two always joke around like that and—"

"Carson," she insisted softly, raising her gaze to his, mesmerized immediately by the warm cocoa gaze. "Please."

He studied her for a long moment and then nodded. "Can I buy you a beer?"

"No, one did me in."

"Then a soda? Iced tea?"

She gave him a small smile. "I need to go find Sarah."

"Hey." He reached out as if to grab her hand but then pulled back. "Is it me?"

"Huh?"

"You always seem to find a reason to leave when I'm around. Did I do something? I mean, I was a little rude the first few minutes of meeting but … I'd had a bad day. People in this town really don't want a guy as their librarian."

"Well, small town. Can I tell you a secret?"

Carson grinned and leaned toward her, nodding. "I love secrets."

"They would have reacted the same if you'd been female. It isn't the gender, Carson. It's the fact that you're a newbie."

He flashed a grin that melted her bones. "A newbie?"

"Yeah. Small town. It will take some time. I moved here when my kids were little. It took a long time to get some smiles and greetings"

"Kids?"

It was her turn to smile. "Twin boys. Twenty-one. They're at college, summer jobs."

"And their dad?"

"Divorced."

"Sorry."

She shook her head. "No. It's… it all worked out for the best. Just… wanted different things."

"How long ago?"

Somehow, Riley understood what he was asking. "Two years ago, it was final."

Carson exhaled. "That's relatively recent, Ry."

There it was again. That look of pity. Riley felt foolish, her cheeks flushed. Of course, he was not hanging around her at the Wing Fest because he was attracted to her. He was here because he felt bad for the awkward woman who always seemed to make a fool out of herself and had a sad life.

That small smile in place, she sighed. "I'm going to find Sarah. Have a good evening."

By week's end, Riley was exhausted and happy. She loved being busy and trying new things, and her anxiety had not been out of control. There was something so empowering about that, so freeing. It was as if she had escaped a bad marriage yet again, but this time, from the bullies in her mind telling her she could not do something.

That was why she decided to return to bingo on Saturday night. She got there later than usual and found a seat on the opposite corner, far from the monitor, but that also meant far from Ruby. Riley avoided glancing over in that direction, happy to be alone in her corner, arranging the game sheets and her snacks.

"Kind of a drastic move, don't you think?"

Riley's head snapped up, and she sighed when she saw Carson smiling down at her. Before she could argue, he was pulling out a chair and sitting, dropping his own game sheets onto the table. Finally, she found her voice. "No. Carson, listen. This is my happy place. My break from work and exes and bills and from my anxiety. Please."

His smile faded. "I don't want to take that away from you. Neither does my aunt. I - I want you to have your happy place. Oh, and before I forget…" He dropped several bills onto the table.

"What's this?"

"When you left last week, I thought there might be a chance you'd come back, so I played your sheet for you. You won two games. One was $40 and one was $200."

"You're lying."

"One thing to know about me, I don't lie." He pulled out her sheet of games from the week before and showed her two of the games. "See. Corners and diagonal lines." He then shrugged. "I actually liked playing, so I got my own sheet of games. Aunt Ruby is a bit too intense for me, and I annoy her by talking, so may I sit here with you tonight?"

Then he was standing and moving around the table, taking the seat next to her. Riley tried to ignore her racing pulse and the need to scoot closer to him. Instead, she focused on the sheets, willing the games to begin so she did not have to avoid making a fool of herself.

"There. Closer. Easier to talk," he chattered, holding out a box of chocolate candies. "Please. I saw you had these last weekend, so I picked some up for tonight." He grinned and nudged her with his elbow. "I know you can hear me. Riley, the game hasn't started yet. I just have a question."

With a roll of her eyes, Riley tried to hold the giggles in. "What?"

"How the hell do you play this? I mean, I know the basic games but then it says 'Layer Cake'. Does that mean we get cake?"

This time, she could not hold back the laughter. "Carson. No cake. It is a bingo pattern. You have to get the top row, middle row, and the bottom row to get bingo."

"So I shouldn't get too excited about the full champagne glass?" He watched her throw her head back and laugh, the corners of his own mouth turned up. "I love seeing you laugh, Riley. I have a feeling you don't laugh enough."

Her lips were still turned up, but she rolled her eyes again. "Carson, just get ready to play. Don't worry about if I laugh enough."

"I didn't mean to sound patronizing or creepy. Just… Were you hurt? Did the divorce do a number on you? Because you have this guard up, and I'm not sure how to get through it."

"The guard is up for a reason," she chastised, shuffling her games. "It is not a challenge or an invitation. This is not some teen romance chick flick where the guy bets that he can gain the attention of—"

"Riley."

She stopped, closed her mouth, and stared at him.

His tone was thick, deep, and his gaze seemed to see through her. "I just like you. I want to get to know you. But you make it difficult. I was just asking if there was a shortcut around this barrier. If not, that's fine. I'll take the long way."

The game started before she could respond, and for the next several minutes, they were deep in concentration, dabbing the numbers on their sheets. Finally, someone called out, "Bingo" and they had a moment to return to the conversation.

"I think I have you figured out," Riley announced, setting her dauber down and reaching for her water.

Carson was watching her. "And?"

"I think you're a player."

She was surprised when his expression darkened, and he shook his head, "Wow. Okay. I'm not sure where that came from but—"

"You're in your 40s. Not married—"

"I was."

"You were. Married. Okay. So what happened? You get tired of her? Find a younger woman?"

A new game started and in between the caller shouting numbers, Carson answered, "She died."

There was a pause as Riley considered simply standing and walking out. She felt her face burn, but she turned to him, his own head lowered, his eyes on the game sheet, and she said, "Carson. I'm sorry. So sorry."

"Look, it's fine. You didn't know." With a heavy exhale, he dropped the dauber and turned to her. "It was a long time ago. We were in our twenties. I just… didn't want to risk getting close again. But … is that what happened to you, Ry? Did he leave you? Throw away the best thing I've met in a while? If it was not for the fact that he hurt you, I'd want to thank him."

Riley dropped her head onto the table, her fingers gripping the edge. "What are you talking about?"

"I'm saying I'd love to get to know you, Riley. What's so wrong with that? Huh?"

Slowly, she lifted her head so that she was facing him. "What's wrong with that is I'm such a mess. I can't function in normal situations. People freak me out. I have a panic attack just going to the grocery store. I'd rather sit home on a Friday night reading a book than go dancing at a club."

"Hey, Riley. Nice to meet you. I'm Carson, the librarian. Who also loves to read. On a Friday night or a Thursday night or a Sunday afternoon. And who also loves tracking down one enigmatic woman at a bingo game… on a Saturday night."

"No. I don't think you're understanding. I'm not social. I suffer from anxiety."

In one swift, gentle movement, Carson grazed her hand with his fingertips, his touch light but electrifying, and Riley sucked in her breath at the jolts running up and down her arm. She could do nothing but stare into his eyes as he stared back. "Ry. I know what you're saying. I'm saying I want to get to know you. We don't have to go to some noisy restaurant or crowded store. If you don't feel comfortable, then we don't go."

"I can't focus on bingo right now."

"Then can we go on our first date?"

Her eyes widened. "Wha- first date? You're asking me out?"

And he leaned back in his chair, his arms crossed, a crooked grin lighting up that face. "What did you think this was? Yes. I'm asking you out—to the library—now."

She wondered if he had even heard her speak of anxiety and dislike of crowds, but she found herself taking his hand and smiling as he led her out of the basement, where over one hundred people, mostly older ladies, hunched over the bingo cards. She caught a glimpse of his aunt grinning, waving them away.

"But… it's closed." Still, she followed him up the library steps to the front door, amazed at herself. She had left her car at the bingo parking lot, jumping in his car, trusting him. And now she held his hand with both of hers, jumping in place to try to get warm as he did his best to unlock the door in the dark.

Finally, they were inside the warm building, Carson flipping on the lights.

Riley let go of his hand and spun around, staring at the books, taking in the silence, trying not to get overwhelmed. But she stared over at Carson, and he was smiling at her, loving the reaction, and she smiled back.

"Remember, your fines have been paid so… wanna check out some books?"

She nodded, blushing under his gaze, but this time, she did not want to run away. Instead, Riley marched purposely over to him, tilting her head up just as Carson leaned down, their lips meeting in an explosion that caught her off guard. Fortunately, she had Carson's hands to steady her, and the promise of a new story to start.

A RARE TOME

Stephen Sottong

The consignment was sizable. Alexander watched Morey, the rare book dealer, lift another handful of what appeared to be first editions from a box that sat atop one of a dozen stacks of boxes. "Where did these come from?" Alexander asked.

"Mr. Trumble's estate," Morey answered, wiping sweat and book dust from his brow.

"He died? Last I saw him, he was pursuing a young lady. Told her he'd show her the rarities of his collection." Both men laughed. "A jealous husband finally shot the old lecher?"

"Perhaps, but, if so, the perpetrator left no evidence. Trumble's daughter searched the house and found nothing." Morey pulled a large tome from the box and sat it on an already precarious stack. "She said this was what he'd last been reading. His reading lamp was lit and the volume was on the floor in front of his chair, open." Morey shook his head. The family believes they'll gain a fortune from the sale of his collection, but the market's gone slack lately." He pointed at the tome. "That will be an especially difficult sale: old, but not dated; handwritten in French with a script so florid I could barely tell it was French; beautifully illustrated but ranging from macabre to pornographic. It appears to be the only copy in existence, as if some mad Renaissance writer had his final manuscript wonderfully bound but never printed."

Alexander pulled the volume from the stack and took it to a window where he could examine it in natural light. Brushing dust from the cover with his sleeve, the gleam of the leather in the binding spoke of centuries of loving care. Not a nick marred the pristine surface. He turned the book to examine the spine, and the angle of the illumination highlighted the tooling on the front cover. Moving the book to maximize the contrast, he perceived the figure of a woman, first thigh, then buttocks, flat stomach, and finally breast with the nipple forming the dot on an "i." He smiled. Ingenious.

Opening, he encountered the ornate script Morey had complained about. It was highly stylized, but easily readable – by him at any rate. "Maid of the Pool," the French read. The author was missing. Following the title page and covering two of the oversized leafs, was an illustration of a lane, snaking from the top left to the bottom right. Two thirds of the lane was lined with drawings of statuary, men of various ages, many in garb that set the date of the book far newer than purported. All had a distinct fullness in the front of their trousers with more than a few clasping it strongly. The last bore a resemblance to Trumble, but Alexander dismissed that.

A figure of striking beauty filled the next page. Though just an ink drawing as on the previous pages, the quality was superb. Naked, she swam beneath the pool of the title, graceful, hair flowing. On the opposite page, he read, "You have found me. Thank all the gods. Draw me out. Take me to your bosom."

Alexander closed the book. He could hear her say those words. The voice matched the drawing. It was as if she'd whispered into his ear, the light touch of her breath on that sensitive skin arousing him. He shook his head and went to return the book to the pile but found his hand unwilling to let go.

"I can offer you an excellent price for that, if you want it," Morey said. "I strongly doubt I'll find a buyer, but if it suits your tastes..." He shrugged. "I know you like to collect exotic books."

"I'll take it." Alexander stood in shock. The words had come from his mouth, but he hadn't intended to say them.

Morey wrapped the new prize in brown paper and tied it so it wouldn't attract attention as Alexander walked to his flat. The package felt warm against Alexander's side, the skin beneath it tingling. At his flat, he sat the book on the side table by the entrance and hung his coat. He started toward the kitchen but felt drawn backward, as if the package called to him, begged him to remove the stifling cover.

Twice he turned from it, but finally succumbed to its draw, carrying it to the living room where he slit the strings and tossed the paper on a couch. Hunger had waned. He took the book to his favorite reading chair in the sunshine and opened it at random.

"You've come back to me, my love," it read on the page across from the young swimmer, her breasts forward as she swam with her body bent backward. "I'm so grateful. Let me tell you a story to amuse you."

Alexander sat back, placing his feet on the ottoman in front of him and propping the oversized book on his bent legs.

The story was of a very young man, Gaston, not yet able to grow a beard. As he traveled between Paris and Tours along the Loire, the heat of the afternoon nearly overcame him. Seeing a calm pool through the leaves of the surrounding trees, he decided to stop and refresh himself. Tying his horse, he made his way through the undergrowth. He'd already removed his tunic when he noticed a young woman bathing and jolted to a stop at the pool's edge. She stood, body half out of the water, facing him. Though inexperienced, Gaston and his friends had spied on the young women of his town bathing, but none compared to this one's beauty.

She examined him with what Gaston could only interpret as a critical eye. "Go away, boy," she said. "You're much too young."

Gaston was hurt and angry at the accusation. "I am not."

"Then prove it." She crossed her arms, raising her ample breasts higher.

Gaston hesitated. He'd never been with a woman and feared he might make a fool of himself, but her continued stare finally goaded him into stripping off his shoes and hose and wading into the pool. He waded toward her. She put out a hand, not to deter but to touch him. That touch sent shivers through him as if a bucket of icy water had been poured over him.

Her hand traced down his chest and stomach to below the water. "You are old enough." She drew him to her.

Her body was warm despite the cool water. He was never sure when, in their embraces, they'd walked to the bank and fallen onto a bed of flowers. They spent the heat of the day there until, exhausted, he'd slept.

She was gone when he awoke in the chill of early evening. A search produced no trace of her, so he retrieved his clothes and continued his journey.

Gaston was called to fight in the wars, and, when he returned, his father arranged a marriage. It was six years before he was able to travel to the pool again. Now he had a beard and scars from the battles he'd fought in. When he walked through the brush, she was there, bathing a boy of about five. She had not changed. If anything, she was more beautiful.

Again, she examined him critically. "Now, you are a man. Join us."

Gaston left his clothes on the bank and waded into the water. The boy swam up to him. Gaston saw his own curly black hair and green eyes.

"Father?" the boy asked.

Gaston glanced at the woman, who nodded.

"Take your son home," she said and immersed herself, not returning to the surface.

Gaston wrapped the boy in his cloak and took him home. Gaston's wife objected, but Gaston kept the boy and named him Moses since he'd been drawn from the water. Moses grew into a strong, handsome young man who loved to swim in the Loire. It did not surprise Gaston when, at about the same age he'd first met Moses's mother, Moses swam away one day, never to return.

Not long after, Gaston heard tales of young women seduced by a handsome young man while they bathed. Gaston founded an orphanage to raise the offspring of these watery unions, and called them all his grandchildren, but never let them near the river.

Alexander stared at the illustration of a very aroused young man up to his knees in water, caressing and kissing the breast of a woman who looked surprisingly like his girlfriend, Sylvia.

The doorbell rang. Alexander slammed the book shut and sat it on the ottoman, rushing to the door. Sylvia was supposed to come by for dinner on her way home from a business trip. He'd done nothing toward that.

When he opened the door, the sight of her, so very like the illustration, kindled an instant excitation he hadn't felt since his teen years. As if channeling Moses, he pulled her in, slammed the door, tossed her bag aside and engulfed her.

"I haven't been away that long," she gasped between kisses.

He moved her toward the bedroom without ending the embrace.

An hour later, they lay on top of the covers, clothes strewn about. "I've got to take more business trips," she said, as he smiled. "What brought on this sudden wave of passion?" She held up a hand. "Not that I'm complaining."

He wondered if the truth would dampen her ardor. "The book I've been reading is ... inspiring."

"Porn?"

"Not exactly. It's quite old and I haven't yet figured what the book is about, but it does have erotic elements." Her eyes asked for more. "It's illustrated."

"May I take a peek?"

"Of course." He sat up. "Are you hungry? I haven't prepared anything but I always have a few treats frozen away." He smiled at her. "I don't think we want to order delivery."

He heated an assortment from the freezer, and, while it cooked, Sylvia wandered into the living room. "Is this your inspirational volume?"

Alexander glanced up from meal preparation to see her staring at the book on the ottoman. "Yes. I'm not sure how old it is. There's no date."

She sat in his reading chair examining the cover. "Unusual. Folio size. Tooled leather. Embossed lettering with gold leaf that hasn't worn off. High quality." She opened to the title page and felt the material. "Vellum. Good god! Whoever had this made spent a fortune on it, but you're the expert on that."

"That was my conclusion as well."

She opened to the drawing of the path and sat up. "This is bizarre." Turning to the next page, she paused at the swimming woman. "Whoever did this was talented. I don't see any attempt to correct mistakes. These drawings might be more valuable individually than the entire book itself."

His head shot up. "No!" She sat, frozen. He tried to calm his voice. "I'm sure the book is more valuable intact."

She shook her head. "You know books better than me." She returned to viewing the pages. "Can you read this? I've encountered some old French letters and manuscripts but nothing like this. I can barely make out a word."

"I seem to have no problem." He walked to the chair and held out his hand. "Let's eat now. I think we may have some dessert after."

She took his hand. "I hope it's as good as the appetizer was."

In the morning, Alexander found it difficult to remain patient as Sylvia showered and ate breakfast. The book called to him again. His goodbye was more abrupt than he wished, but, at last, he could reopen the book.

Again, he opened it at random. The illustration was muddy, the text illegible, except the first line. "You have betrayed me." He quickly thumbed through it. Nothing was as it appeared yesterday.

Replacing the book on the ottoman, he retreated to the kitchen for more coffee. Books couldn't change that quickly. He wasn't fully awake. Another cup in hand, he opened his computer and worked on correspondence for an hour, all the time glancing over his shoulder at the book.

Correspondence completed, he sat in his reading chair again and reopened the book. It was as he saw it that morning. Perhaps, he thought, exposure to the sun caused the ink to run. If it was ruined, he'd dispose of it, but that thought sent terror through him. He could never lose this treasure.

The rest of the morning was a blur. He failed to accomplish anything.

Sylvia called at lunch asking if she could come over for a possible repeat of last night's festivities. Alexander begged off, saying he was still tired from last night. He wondered, now, if he'd ever want her to come back.

He wasn't hungry and found himself drawn back to his chair to take one last look at the book. The random page he opened to was vivid this time, readable. "Stay with me, not her," it said. His hands trembled. What had he purchased? But he continued reading.

The tale, this time, was of Emile, son of a minor count, who was sent to the court in Paris to seek a wife. Emile was strong and handsome, and his father expected him to find a suitable bride in a short time. But a young man, whose inheritance might be years away and whose estates were small anyway, was not of interest to most of the young women. They favored the sons of vast estates and older men who could provide them with luxuries. Emile languished, a pretty face with no prospects.

Months into his search, he encountered the new wife of an elderly duke. The lady eyed him appreciatively, but said nothing. That night, he found a slip of paper tucked into a pocket. The lady wished to meet him. She gave directions to a secluded spot in the gardens and a time.

Emile was there well before the chosen hour, waiting, wondering if she would keep the appointment, and what she wanted. She was late enough Emile was about to leave. Out of breath, she explained her situation. The duke had an earlier, childless, loveless marriage and wanted to produce an heir. He wanted it desperately and spent every night at the task with a grim determination. Thus far, his efforts were for nought. She feared he would continue this way for years if she did not become pregnant, or, worse yet, send her away so he could try with another unfortunate.

Emile, she said, resembled the duke in his prime. A child fathered by him would not raise suspicion. In thanks, she'd fatten his purse and help him find a bride. Emile gladly agreed. She told him of the secret entry into their quarters and the way to her balcony. They set a date and time.

On the night, Emile hugged the wall outside the duke's compound waiting for the church bells to toll. He nearly cried out as the bells startled him out of his passionate reverie. Squeezing through the gap made by a loose stone, he thought for a moment he might be trapped, but breathed and pushed himself through, swinging the stone back into place. The garden was shadowed in the moonlight and he nearly fell several times. The trellis he must climb appeared far too fragile for a man of his weight. He climbed it anyway. Despite creaking, it held. He was on his knees on the balcony catching his breath when she pulled him inside.

She stood there in a linen nightgown. The tie holding the top closed had come loose, revealing her breasts beneath. She saw his fascination and pulled the gown over her head. His eyes grew wide. She moved to him, opening the tie on his tunic, pushing it aside, pleased with what she saw.

The night proved more satisfying than the lady had expected. Rather than a callow lad who might have lost his virginity to a servant girl, Emile proved a competent lover. He'd caught the eye of the wife of a passing gypsy tinker. Emile had talked his father into letting the tinker camp on their land for the winter. It had been the warmest winter of Emile's life. She'd taught him the ways to please a woman. Emile was never sure whose baby she carried when the wagon left with the spring.

Emile demonstrated his skill so well the duke's wife had been forced to cover her face with a pillow to keep from waking the house with her cries of pleasure. She'd planned for their tryst to last only until he'd fulfilled her need for a child, but he stayed for hours and neither slept. Although she knew he must go while he still had the moon to light his path, she could not let this end with the one time.

An opportunity presented itself in the death of the duke's gentleman companion from a bad batch of clams. While the duke mourned, his wife suggested that the unattached young man who had lately come to court, was of good blood, and might make a boon companion. The duke had consented and Emile was moved into their household.

The household retired to the duke's estates when his wife was found to be with child. The duke was both elated and relieved to no longer be faced with his nightly labor. This left his wife's bedroom open for Emile, who took advantage of the situation until she was too far along for it to be comfortable.

The duchess worried that Emile might stray from her to some poxed whore, so when a young friend confided that she was having the same problem with her elderly husband, Emile was sent to her chambers to perform his magic. Word spread discretely and before the duke's daughter was born, Emile had planted four more noble scions.

The babe was a turning point for Emile. Looking into her green eye, the same green as his, he was overwhelmed with the urge to hold her, to recognize her as his own.

The duke, for his part, was disappointed and consulted with the doctors on how soon he could try again for a son. His wife begged that the delivery was difficult and he should wait. Emile did not want her to ever have to endure his ministrations again.

Emile had become the duke's hunting companion. A month after the birth, the duke decided to hunt for a stag. A number of men went on the hunt but at one point, Emile was alone with the duke. They dismounted. Emile held the horses while the duke went to a bluff over the river to relieve himself. Emile's mind raced. No one was within sight. His deliverance was a push away. Yet he hesitated, fearing the damnation that murder must eventually lead to. Still, he tied the horses.

It crossed his mind that the multiple fornications he'd already committed, and planned to commit again, must also result in damnation, so he had nothing to gain by refraining. He crept behind the old man, who labored to drain his bladder. At the last moment, the duke turned to him, saying, "Yes, my boy." Emile's hands faltered, then, as if with a mind of their own, pushed the duke over the edge.

The old man's body tumbled a second as he cursed but did not scream. He hit the water and floated. Emile panicked, knowing that if the duke survived, he would not. The duke waved his arms, and, as his clothes became saturated, sank.

Emile stared a second longer, then realized he must act. He ran back to the horses and began yelling for their companions. Undoing his horse, he raced toward the river, keeping up his cries. Others joined the search. They found the body on the bank of the river, a startled look on the old man's face.

The widow mourned appropriately. Emile was not sure he could tell her what he'd done, but he asked her to marry him when her mourning period was over. She told him that would not be possible until he had inherited his title, and the king would not allow her to remain a widow for long. He would find her a husband he deemed suitable since there was no male heir.

Emile was devastated. He'd lost his soul for this woman and now could not have her.

A letter from his father called Emile home. His mother had passed. He returned for the funeral. The illness that took her had been difficult and his father looked years older. It rained on the funeral procession and his father caught a fever. As Emile sat by his sickbed, the thought struck him how fortuitous this turn of events was. If his father succumbed to this illness, he would inherit the title and be a suitable match for the woman he so desired. In what should have been a time of great mourning, his spirits lifted.

The illness lingered, and then, after nearly a week, Emile felt his father's forehead and realized the fever had broken. He would live on, and Emile would lose his lady. Alone in the room, his hands trembled as he held a pillow over his father. He wavered, knowing this was a greater crime. The memory of the duchess body finally overcame his reluctance and Emile covered his father's face with the pillow. There was little struggle. Emile sat crying for a long time before he called for the attendants.

His tears convinced the household, and there was no investigation. Emile sent word to the duchess of this father's unfortunate death and his inheritance of the title of count. She told him to set the family's estate in order for a few months before returning to make his courtship seem appropriate.

She was his, finally, truly his. Even if it meant killing her husband and his father to get her, it had been worth it. He pushed thoughts of his father teaching him as a boy from his mind and concentrated on the woman he so desired.

The duchess nursed her own child for the year of mourning so she would not become pregnant again before the official wedding.

The new duke was well liked by the household. He continued his service to other noble ladies at his wife's bidding, siring nearly a dozen children. The duchess became pregnant within a month of the wedding. Nine months later, she bore a son. The boy was healthy and handsome like his father who doted on him. Not six months after that, the duchess was pregnant again.

She proposed they take a boat down the Loire. One lovely day on the trip, they took a small boat out on the river. The duchess packed a lunch of wine and cheese and the new duke rowed them to a shady pool where they ate. After his third glass of wine, Emile felt his stomach turning. He vomited over the side of the boat. His body felt weak. Pain wracked him. He looked at his wife who sat, arms crossed, watching him. "You've poisoned me."

"You were nothing to me but a stud service – a pleasant one, I'll grant you. All I ever needed a man for was to sire a male heir to ensure my position. You've made the one and I can feel another is on the way. You're no longer needed." And with that, she pushed him over the side, too weak not to drown.

Alexander sat upright with a start. What kind of tales were these? He closed the book, stood and felt momentarily dizzy. It was already early evening. He'd sat, reading for nearly eight hours. He needed food.

His phone flashed a message warning. Sylvia had texted him wondering if he was all right. He'd have to text her back, but not now. Food was the highest priority.

Dinner in the microwave, Alexander carried his glass of wine to his reading chair. The room felt cold. He started the gas fireplace beside his chair. The book stood open to the last illustration of the story, Emile's body floating down into the waters of the river while his wife above laughed. Examining the drawing more closely, Alexander noticed the ripples in the water had a distinct shape. The woman of the pool from the previous story was swimming toward Emile. Below her, Moses swam, arms out to catch Emile. Their two naked bodies were so deftly incorporated into the drawing that only ripples were noticeable without close inspection. Alexander wondered if they intended to add Emile to their family.

The bell rang. Alexander retrieved the rice bowl that would be his sustenance for the evening. The warmth of the fire, a few bites and a sip of wine and Alexander felt better. As revulsed as he was by the stories in this book, he still felt drawn to turn the pages, so he could find another illustration of the lady from the pool. His fingers twitched and the fork dropped to the floor. He cursed and retrieved it, using it anyway. A few more bites and he could no longer resist. He turned to the next page.

There she was again, only more glorious, more real, her body twisting in an underwater ballet. The rice bowl dropped from his hands, knocking over the wine glass. He didn't care. Though nothing but an ink drawing, she was far more real than any woman he'd ever been with. Far more desirable than Sylvia.

Alexander held the book, cradled it in his arms, drank in her beauty. The facing page read, "I am here for you, my beloved. Yours alone from all men. My chosen partner. Do you love me? Do you want me? Do you want to be with me forever?"

Alexander's body responded. He craved her more than he had Sylvia last night. In the back of his mind, the line of aroused men at the front of the book, tugged him back from shouting his undying love, from trying to fall into the pages. He could hear her voice, calling him, begging him to join her, be with her forever.

Then he remembered Trumble's shocked face and saw himself at the end of the line. "No!" He tossed the book from his lap. It caromed off an end table and into the fireplace.

Alexander fell out of his chair and raced on hands and knees to the fireplace. Attempting to reach in to retrieve the book, the sleeve of his sweater caught fire when he reached in. He yanked his arm out, beating out the flames on his pants leg. The book was now fully engulfed, sparking green and red. He turned off the gas, but the book continued burning. He sat on his heels, watching it blaze.

His arm was in pain and he felt exhaustion overtaking him. There was nothing he could do to save the book now. He retreated to the bathroom medicine cabinet.

The next morning, he sat with his coffee, staring at the ashes in the fireplace. Not even a part of a page remained unburned. As he finished the coffee, he rose and retrieved a broom and dustpan and a paper bag. The ashes were cold. He swept them up and collected them into the bag. Closing it, he was about to toss the bag into his garbage chute but stopped short. Somehow, this strange, beautiful, horrible thing could not be treated as garbage. It felt like these were the ashes of a loved one which should be scattered.

He donned his overcoat and headed for the park, strolling the paths, bag hidden beneath his coat, looking for a quiet, appropriate place to inter the remains. The path meandered along the river to a pool beneath a stand of oaks. As he stared into the green waters, his mind returned to the woman in the pages of the book. Inside his coat, the bag felt warm, alive. He pulled it out, stared one last time at the ashes and poured them into the pool, adding his tears to the mixture.

He retreated up the bank and sat as the ashes swirled and sank. After a time, he was never sure how long, he rose to leave. Water in the pool rippled. With a splash, arms emerged, then a body, floating, swimming to the banks. She walked out, naked, and came to him, wrapping her arm about his neck, pulling him close, kissing him. "Thank you."

His heart raced, breath came in gasps after that kiss. "For what?"

"Releasing me." She kissed him again.

He finally wrapped his arms around her wet body and kissed her back with the passion he'd felt when first he saw her picture.

"May I have your coat?" she asked when they finally let their lips part.

"Oh, of course." He removed it and helped her into it.

"It's cold. Take me somewhere we can warm each other."

They didn't emerge for a week. Alexander was relieved when Sylvia texted him that he'd been acting strangely and thought they should stop seeing each other for a while.

Alexander walked with his new love through the neighborhood after coffee and pastries at a French bistro. He didn't want to stop at the antiquarian bookstore, but she took his arm and brought him to an abrupt halt. "Is this where you found it?"

He nodded.

"I'd like to go in."

He sighed but led the way. Morey greeted them. "Hey, back to buy something else as unique as the last one I sold you?"

"I don't think so." Alexander jumped as a young man with long, black, curly hair and green eyes leapt off a ladder. The young man stood in a crouch, smiling at them and ran to embrace the woman at Alexander's side. The two hugged and spoke in rapid, antique French.

"The new girlfriend knows this kid?" Morey asked.

"I think they're related. When did he show up?"

"'Bout a week ago. Came in here with wet hair wearing nothing but a pair of sweatpants that looked to be the wrong size for him. I was about to toss him out when he started telling me information about some of the old books. Kid seems to know more about antique books than I do." Morey moved close to Alexander and whispered in his ear. "I think he's undocumented, but he's damned valuable to me." Morey watched the two conversing. "I let the kid have the attic room over the store. Had to buy him clothes. Didn't have anything. Not that he wears much. Likes to run around in shorts and a muscle shirt. Been doing great things for my business. I'm getting all kinds of middle-aged women coming in. He talks them into buying books they never knew they wanted." Morey chuckled. "Talks them into other things as well. He hasn't spent many nights in that attic room. Best watch your lady."

Alexander smiled. "I don't think that's a problem."

Moses and his mother kissed each other on both cheeks and she returned to Alexander. "Happy?" he asked.

"Very. Let's go home."

They waved their goodbyes and strolled, arm-in-arm, back to Alexander's flat.

THERE'S NO PLACE LIKE BROKEN REACH

Leandra Vane

Broken Reach, Nebraska was the only town on the lonely trail west that boasted having fourteen saloons and not one single church. Where other towns had Baptists and Lutherans, Broken Reach judged their people by which dance hall they frequented—though there were often many converts throughout the week.

Most travelers who chanced a journey over the wild prairie knew to ride north a bit to Burke or south a ways to Walnut and leave Broken Reach out of the trip altogether. Citizens of Broken Reach were more than happy with this arrangement and life for them went on, day by day.

Cliff Williams was one such citizen. He was a Wild Violet man. The Wild Violet was the only saloon of the fourteen establishments in town that was run by women. The good time girls were aptly named the Violets, under the strict but loving guidance of Madame Sylvie. Everyone else might have called them weeds, but Cliff knew the Violets were the best women west of the Missouri.

On this particular night, Cliff wasn't looking to stroll through the garden. At least, not right away. The saddlebag he had slung over his shoulder was heavy and his body and soul were weary. He had been away and the ride back into Broken Reach had been tedious. He had been carrying an empty hollow in his chest for two years now, but after this trip, the hole threatened to swallow him completely. Cliff just wanted to feel like he was home.

The Wild Violet was crowded as he pushed through the front doors, but that was to be expected. Times were changing and no one liked it. Escape was now a priority. The hazy smoke and dark plum drapes of the saloon blocked out the world, providing stolen moments of contentment.

Cliff managed to stay in the shadows and find an empty table in the back. He sat his heavy saddlebag carefully in the middle of the table and settled down into a chair. He sighed, soaking in the smoke and the sound of laughter and clinking glasses. His muscles loosened and his eyes fluttered shut. The reverie wiped away the sorrowful memories of the past few days and reality scattered into the din.

But the tranquility didn't last. Cliff's breath snagged in his throat as two hands clamped down on his shoulders from behind. In a flash, his hand was at his hip and he drew his pistol.

"Oh, put that damn thing away, it's me."

Cliff immediately recognized the voice of Madame Sylvie, a genuine wild violet if there ever was one. With relief and amusement, Cliff rolled his eyes and gave a little groan as he slid the gun safely back into the holster.

Sylvie stomped around to stand in front of him with her hands on her hips and her jaw set square. "I need your help."

"Oh, yeah?" Cliff nudged his foot over and hooked one boot behind her knees. She was wearing pantaloons, not skirts, but she tripped anyway, falling right into Cliff's arms. Not to be had, Sylvie slung her legs over the arm of his chair and crossed them, the worn wooden heels of her boots resting on the tabletop. She glared, her nose barely an inch from his, but Cliff just grinned.

"Well, darlin' what can I help you with?"

Sylvie speared her index finger into his chest.

"You're not allowed to leave ever again," she said.

"It was one week."

"And a half," she pressed. "I needed you."

"Mmhmm." Cliff may have been tired but the false scare had ignited a playful spark. "Tell me all about it."

Sylvie's gaze darkened. In a low voice, she said, "Another one of Mr. Hinkley's henchmen showed up six days ago."

The spark extinguished. This was not news Cliff had wanted to arrive home to.

No one in Broken Reach had ever seen Mr. Hinkley, but every citizen was now familiar with the name. He was a businessman from out east, a real investor with lots of money. He had decided to branch out nationally and start freighting companies out west. Broken Reach, Nebraska was one of the lucky towns chosen to be a freighting post.

But Mr. Hinkley refused to give his money to sinful people. He wanted his freighting towns to be the epitome of wholesome living. So Mr. Hinkley sent men working on his behalf to the wild prairie towns to clean them up. These representatives sought to see laws followed and establishments of ill repute shut down. All the other towns complied, hungry for the economic boon Mr. Hinkley's money would bring. But Broken Reach was not going to settle down easy and the Wild Violets were leading the rebellion.

"What is this, the fifth one he's sent?" Cliff asked.

"Sixth. The sixth one he's sent."

"I could have sworn this is only number five," Cliff pressed.

Sylvie shook her head. "No, the first was in March, remember? He was easy. Had denied himself any vices for so long all it took was one drink and a tickle from my feather boa. Mr. Hinkley wised up and sent someone much tougher the second time. That one put up a hell of a fight, but that's how we discovered he liked being tied up. The third was in July. I just kissed his temple and he was crying in my lap. The girls all doted on him and played with his hair and listened to him talk all night." She rolled her eyes. "The fourth one was the one who had that thing for champagne corks."

"Oh, yeah," Cliff said absently. "Cork Man."

"And the fifth one, all it took was a regular good time with Rebecca and Lettie, and we sent three cigars with him for the train ride home."

"Ah. Number five was the boring one, that's why I don't remember." Cliff sighed. "So what? Number six. Line 'em up, shoot 'em down. Looks like all your gals are on the floor. Certainly, you have someone…"

"Number six is different."

Cliff frowned but he knew by the look on her face that Sylvie was serious.

She shoved herself off his lap and pulled another rickety chair up to the table. She sat down and set her hands on the tabletop, entwining her fingers. Cliff sat across from her like a business partner meeting to discuss a new prospect.

"We went after him on the very first day. By the second day, I knew we were going to have to take extreme measures. So, I swallowed my pride and walked right over to Millie's. At first, she was just so smug the Violets we were asking her for help. But by the time the fourth of her girls had returned defeated, we were united by a common enemy. The situation was dire." She gave a dramatic pause. "We sent Henrietta."

"Henrietta Darling?" Cliff was impressed.

"The one and only. We all had to pitch in to get her rate, but we thought it was going to be worth the investment."

There was not a single man, and very few women, whose knees didn't tremble at the mere sight of Henrietta Darling. She was the Aphrodite of the prairie. The only reason she stayed in Broken Reach was because her reputation was so great, business would come to her. She had callers from as far off as Kansas City and St. Louis.

Cliff leaned in. "And?"

"Nothing," Sylvie said in a huff.

"Nothing?" Cliff blinked. "At all."

Sylvie made a limp gesture that needed no interpretation. "At. All."

"Wow." Cliff leaned back. "Well, my sweet. This might be it. We put up a good fight but we might have met our match."

Her hands turned to fists on the table. "Nuh-uh. We are not going to fold when we still have a wild card in our hand."

"And what card would that be?"

A playful quirk to Sylvie's eyebrow broke her stoic demeanor.

"You," she answered.

Cliff swallowed hard. He wasn't entirely surprised by Sylvie's idea but he wasn't enthused about it, either.

"You know, darling. It's been a long time," Cliff said. "Two years, now."

Sylvie snorted. "Even more reason to try to help me."

"It's not that simple," Cliff said. "You think I can just walk up to someone I don't even know and…"

"Yes," Sylvie said, unamused. "You're a man."

Cliff didn't have time to pour his soul out. Yes, he was a man, and he liked men just as much as he liked women, which was very much. And walking around for two years with a hollow in his chest left by the last man to touch him was getting old. Someone new, even for just one night, would probably be good for him. But Cliff was never one to take what he could get just because he could get it. For a man who called a saloon home, he did have some morals.

"Are you sure you don't have any other cards up your sleeve?" Cliff asked hopelessly.

"Honey, when was the last time I even wore sleeves? Nope. You are it and this is important." She took one of his hands in both of hers. "Cliff. Please."

Cliff gave it three whole seconds. "Fine."

"You're the best!" She kissed the back of his hand before releasing it.

Cliff hunched forward on the table. "But… if he's as bad as you say he is... How strong of a drink am I going to need for this?"

Her eyes gleamed. "That's the sad part. The gals were lining up. His personality is insufferable but his looks..." she nodded. "Mmm."

The big toe in Cliff's right boot shot up. After all, he was a man and it had been a long time and the way Sylvie's eyes looked when she said Mmm was pure sin.

Cliff gave in. "What's his name?"

"Henry Donavan, but he prefers Mr. Donavan."

Cliff was going to ask for more details but he bit his tongue when Sylvie's gaze hooked over his shoulder and her face fell.

"Oh. Already. Wonderful."

Cliff turned just in time to see the topic of their conversation approaching their table through the haze. Cliff could see why the gals thought he was handsome. It wasn't that he necessarily was handsome; he was just everything that the men in Broken Reach were not.

He was shorter in stature than average but his suit was tailored perfectly to his form, giving him a masculine silhouette. His shoulders certainly did not possess the brawn of a laboring man like Cliff's, but they were broad enough to capture attention. His brown hair was cut short and Cliff bet in the sunlight it would have more of a honey hue than mahogany. Mr. Donavan also wore glasses, but the poise of them on his face only served to highlight his sharp features rather than detract from them. He was probably across the road of thirty, but his insecurity being in an environment he wasn't used to gave him the aura of youth. Without an introduction, Mr. Donavan pulled up his own chair to the table. He flicked open the button on his suit jacket as he sat down and Cliff's toe shot up in his boot again, keeping him from having the first word.

Mr. Donavan didn't mind speaking first. "Miss Sylvie, I'm happy to have caught you at home… as it were."

"It's Madame to you, Mr. Donavan."

"Madame." He reached into his suit coat pocket and pulled out a folded piece of paper. "I've taken into consideration your input from our last conversation and I've drafted a new list of rules for your establishment to abide by to avoid being closed down."

Sylvie snatched the page from his hand. Her glanced passed over the first few items and she burst out, "This list is outrageous."

Mr. Donavan pulled a second piece of paper from his pocket. "That's only the first part, you see—"

Before he could finish his sentence, Sylvie snatched the piece of paper and shoved both lists deep into her bosom. Without another word, she huffed and disappeared into the smoke of the saloon.

Mr. Donavan gave a cutting glance to Cliff across the table. "That woman is very lewd," he said.

"Oh, she could have chosen a much lewder place to stick those lists," Cliff said. "Trust me, I've seen her do it."

Mr. Donavan glared and moved to button his suit jacket, a sure sign that he was going to leave, but Cliff waved him to sit back down.

"Mr. Donavan—may I buy you a... water?"

His hand moved from his button and rested on the tabletop. "Who are you?"

"My name's Cliff Williams and I'm a no-good card sharking rapscallion. But at the moment, I'm sober, and I know this town very well. Your business relies on finding some common ground with the locals, so maybe it would be in your best interest to at least try to talk to me?"

Mr. Donavan looked Cliff up and down but didn't look impressed. "I've been here almost a whole week and I haven't seen you."

"I know," Cliff said. He ran a hand through his hair, wishing suddenly it wasn't so long and unkempt. He had to make the most of what he had so he smiled again and shifted in a way he hoped appeared amicable. “Once every month or two, I ride out to the old farmsteads and check up on folks. Some of ‘em are in their nineties now. I bring them medicine and a little food and help with what they need. I just got back. I mean, really, just now. Delivered my mare to the Livery, paid her rent for the month, and came here.”

“I think a normal person would have gone home first.” Mr. Donavan cast a side-eyed glance over his shoulder. A nearby group had taken one of the mounted coyote heads off the wall and had it sitting at their table with a drink in front of it. Mr. Donavan turned back to face Cliff fully. “But I’ve found very few people in this town are normal.”

“What can I say? The Wild Violet is like home to a highwayman like me.”

Mr. Donavan’s gaze dropped down to Cliff’s pistol resting in its holster. Cliff bit his tongue. He knew it was too soon to ask Mr. Donavan whether he was looking at the gun or something else. Cliff cleared his throat.

“S’pose our conversation might be a little easier to have without this.” He drew the gun and waved down one of the working gals. “Oh, Lettie. Here, darlin’...will you keep this safe for me?”

With a grin, she took the pistol and Mr. Donavan jumped when she spun it three times in her hold before flouncing off into the crowd.

Mr. Donavan almost looked impressed then. But he quickly frowned and nodded to the saddlebag on the table.

“You probably have an entire arsenal packed away in there.”

“Nope, sorry. Just books.”

A genuine look of surprise pulled at Mr. Donavan’s features. “Excuse me. Books?”

“Books.” Cliff tossed open the leather flap and pulled out a volume. He rapped on it with his knuckles. “You know. One of these things.”

Mr. Donavan was too distracted to be insulted. He could see the saddlebag was stuffed full of books.

“Why do you have so many?”

“I take them out to the old folks I visit. Life is awful tough out there. They need poetry. Stories.”

The sad hollow in Cliff’s chest opened up again, deep and raw. He fell silent, his gaze enraptured by the worn canvas cover beneath his fingertips.

Mr. Donavan spoke gently. “Mr. Williams? Are you all right?”

Cliff glanced up. He never had a knack for making up lies on the spot, so the truth poured out. "I... I was gone a little longer this trip because when I got out to the Perkin's place I found... well. Old Missus Perkins had passed. I buried her next to Old Man Perkins on the hill overlooking the homestead. I cleaned up the house and boarded up the windows. I'll inform the local attorney tomorrow so he can try to find where the land needs to go." Cliff was silent for a moment and Mr. Donavan allowed it. Finally, Cliff continued. "It's... sad, you know, when one of them goes. They helped get this town started and they're like family. It's hard… to say goodbye."

"I'm..." Mr. Donavan cleared his throat in an effort to distract from the thread of genuine emotion he had allowed to fray. "I'm very sorry to hear that. That must have been very difficult for you to do, alone and... away from home."

"Thank you, it was." Cliff put the book back into the saddlebag and carried the conversation forward. "But as to your question, that's why I have so many books. She had quite a few kept neat on a shelf in her little sod shack. I know she would like the books to be added to the library so others can read them."

Mr. Donavan didn't even try to conceal his interest. "Did you say library?"

"Yes, library. Don't you have those out east?"

This comment made Mr. Donavan realize he had let himself go. He straightened up and said defensively, "Of course. And they're most certainly better than any around here."

"Well," Cliff said slowly, leaning in to articulate every word. "I'll let you decide that for yourself when you see it."

Mr. Donavan shook his head. "Just like with you, I've been here for almost a week and I have not seen a library in this town."

Cliff had a hook. It was time to reel him in.

"Well, then it's a good thing I popped in to show you just where to look."

With that, Cliff grabbed his saddlebag, stood, and started wending his way between tables and saloon patrons. Mr. Donavan could have just let him go, but Cliff glanced back and saw he was following close to get through the crowd.

There was a grand stairwell in the middle of the saloon leading up to the balconied second floor. No one ever noticed the little door around the corner beneath the stairs.

Cliff reached the door beneath the staircase and pulled it open. He gestured inside. "After you."

Mr. Donavan looked apprehensive. He glanced back out into the saloon and the table with the coyote head lifted it up and waved to him. Mr. Donavan straightened his suit jacket and ducked into the room.

Cliff followed and closed the door firmly behind him.

As soon as the door closed, a hush fell over the small room. The clatter and chatter of the saloon were no more than a dull hum. It was very dark but a kerosene lamp was burning low. Cliff set down his bag on the floor and turned the lamp up. As the light rose, Cliff watched as Mr. Donavan's gaze followed along the rows of books shelved against every wall. Besides books, the furnishings were sparse. There was one bar stool in a corner and an old wingback chair with a footrest in the middle of the room. The kerosene lamp was set on the side table next to the chair.

Cliff spread his arms wide and grinned. "Ta-da. Library."

Mr. Donavan strolled around the chair to examine another shelf. "Well, this isn't exactly a real library."

"Oh, yeah?" Cliff tried to sound more playful than confronting. "Try me."

"Virgil," Mr. Donavan said.

Cliff spun around and plucked The Aeneid from its spot.

Mr. Donavan nodded. "All right. Keats and Shelley."

Cliff put the first book back then turned to another shelf and pointed. "Keats, Shelley, and Byron, thanks much."

"Shakespeare."

"There are several behind you," Cliff said pointing. "My favorite is The Tempest but someone took it and hasn't returned it."

Mr. Donavan ran his index finger over the spines of the English plays, brow furrowed. He turned, a thoughtful tilt to his head. "Ah." He straightened. "The Bible."

Cliff sighed, acting like he had been gotten, only to swoop in and pull the Holy book from an unassuming corner shelf. "That, too."

Mr. Donavan watched Cliff put the Bible back. "All right. You have a library." He held his hands out. "But it's in the back room of a saloon."

"Exactly. Rooms are a real valuable thing around here." Cliff gestured as he made his point. "Sylvie's got the girls three to a room right now. She could make lots more money if she put this room into service. But instead, she keeps a library, for anyone to use. That should say something about the character of this establishment. Maybe make you go a little easier on some of your rules."

"Miss… Madame Sylvie never told me she had a library."

"I bet if she did you wouldn't have listened anyway. I bet you just marched right in and talked at her and not to her. You judged everyone and everything in this town before you got to know us. For being so concerned about the Bible, you are sure good at casting first stones."

When he spoke, Mr. Donavan's voice was even—defensive but not insecure.

"I don't cast stones, Mr. Williams, I let people speak for themselves. I was in town for less than two hours and the Violets made it perfectly clear they were only interested in one thing—and it certainly was not talking. And you—you told me you were a criminal the moment you introduced yourself."

Cliff sighed. "Well, I lied. I'm not a highwayman. I'm just a simple town handyman. I only put on a show sometimes to make myself feel better."

Mr. Donavan looked relieved but he tried not to let on. "You also said you were a card shark."

"Nah. Whenever I play cards I only put up peanuts. I'd rather folks spend their money on the Violets than gambling it away with me."

"So, you're really a good guy who also reads Shakespeare," Mr. Donavan said.

Cliff pressed a hand over his heart. "And Byron, thanks much. That part wasn't a lie."

A beat of silence passed between them but it was not a heavy one. Mr. Donavan nodded and meandered around in front of the chair. "All right, fine, you have my attention, Mr. Williams. You're smart. You're polite. You know this town and you really care about the people in it." Mr. Donavan took a seat in the wing-backed chair. "I am listening."

Cliff's senses perked. "Really?"

"Really."

Cliff knew he needed to make the most of the conversation. He thought a moment then said, "Mr. Williams is far too formal. I mean, we aren't even in a real library. Will you call me Cliff?"

"I... suppose."

"Can I call you Henry?"

He hesitated, knowing full well he had not yet disclosed his first name. But then he nodded. "Yes."

"Perfect." Cliff pulled up the bar stool from the corner and sat down in front of Henry. There was still a little height difference between the two but at least the feel of the conversation had become more comfortable.

"You know," Cliff said, "Mr. Hinkley thinks he can bring wholesome living to Broken Reach by force. Every time one of the representatives from Hinkley Headquarters rolls in on the rail, they pass all kinds of new laws and curfews and rules. But the moral silliness does nothing but make us more cantankerous."

"Yes. That he has noticed," Henry commented.

"Has he not considered that maybe spending some time in Broken Reach to build a trusting relationship or two might not be a bad idea?"

Henry shook his head. "That would take far too long to accomplish."

"It's October, and Mr. Hinkley has been sending his men out here since March. He's got time."

"He's been sending people like me to build those relationships, and we've all failed," Henry confessed.

"Yeah, well," Cliff ran a hand over his face. "You're going to have to do more than show up on our doorstep with a list of new rules to build relationships. Half the town can't read the list, anyway."

Henry frowned but inquired genuinely, "What sort of things could we do? I am willing to try, believe it or not."

Cliff thought a moment then snapped his fingers. "Can you ask Mr. Hinkley for some of his money to build a library? You know... a real one?"

Henry sighed. "He might allocate some funds to build a church. But probably not a library."

"Say it's a church then. It'll just happen to have a lot of books in it."

Henry actually smiled.

Cliff returned the smile. "We've gotten along fine without a church. But a library would be a welcome improvement. And even you like the idea."

"Yes, well... I grew up in the library." Henry's features eased in the lamplight. "I suppose when you say the saloon is like a home for you, well, that's how I feel about the library."

"And," Cliff said, leaning in a bit, "A library would help to teach everyone to read your lists of rules."

"Cliff... Even if we teach every citizen in Broken Reach to read, they still might not follow the rules."

"Ah," Cliff said softly. "Now you're getting the idea."

Henry looked like he was about to spout off with a defense, but his shoulders slumped back into the chair and he said nothing.

"Look," Cliff said, trying to keep his tone as diplomatic as possible. "This town is actually a really special place. The pioneers who settled other small towns liked to pretend they had some control over their surroundings. They plowed out roads and built their civilization with weak, creek bottom lumber. They huddled together through raging thunderstorms and bitter blizzards. They placed churches at the fronts of their main streets, or up on hilltops, to watch over them... through long winters of lost hope and hot summer nights where temptation danced in every shadow.

"The folks who built Broken Reach, Nebraska didn't lie about their lot in life. The founders of this town built a saloon at the top of Main Street and invited the shadows in. We've danced through long winters, laughed through drought, sinned through every tragedy that has fallen across our path. We've gotten through sickness, and death, and uncertainty not with hope… but with each other.

"We just want to keep our home special. The way it's always been."

Cliff could tell Henry had listened carefully to every word of his little speech. There was a stretch of silence. When Henry spoke, his voice held the edge of desperation.

"Mr. Hinkley has told me I'm it. If I don't succeed in shaping up this town, he's going to find another place. Broken Reach will be left alone, but you'll get none of the money." Henry paused, then said, "If you love this town, wouldn't you want the prosperity that Hinkley Freight would bring to Broken Reach?"

"No. We have each other." Cliff gestured to the walls. "We have our poetry." He shrugged and ended simply, "We know that's all we really need."

Henry held his tongue. Cliff knew Henry had a lot of practice concealing his true emotions. Sure enough, his body language remained resolute, but the sadness and longing in his eyes were clear through the thin glass of his spectacles.

"You really... aren't interested in helping me, then," Henry said finally.

"Maybe I'm just interested in you."

Henry's eyes glinted in the lamplight. "Why would you be interested in me?"

"You're different," Cliff said easily. "From any of the others Mr. Hinkley has sent. You're also different from anyone around here. It's interesting."

"I wouldn't call it interesting," Henry said. "I would call it aggravating. For myself and everyone around me."

"I don't find you aggravating."

Henry rolled his eyes. "You're the only one."

Cliff leaned back as far as his perch on the barstool would allow. "I think if you would do and say the things you believe in, instead of what other people believe in, you'd come off as much less aggravating to everyone. Including yourself."

"Well, I can't do that," Henry said resolutely.

"Why not?"

"Because there has to be rules. And they have to be followed... Mr. Williams."

Cliff ignored the obvious attempt to get the conversation back on track and he prodded, "Don't you like to feel good, Henry?"

"Not at the cost of my soul and reputation."

"Are all pleasures sins?"

Henry gave a pointed look. "The ones here certainly are."

Cliff didn't allow himself time to think. If he was going to go for it, it was now or never.

"When was the last time you kissed anyone?"

Henry opened his mouth but closed it again without saying a word.

"It's been a while for me." Cliff let his gaze wander over the walls of books. "I still think about him. Every day. Well. At least every night." Cliff looked everywhere but at Henry's face, losing himself in memory, letting the low rumble of his voice paint the picture for both of them. "It was summer. Hot. It was the sort of kiss that made that sort of heat comfortable. One that breaks out all over your skin. Tasted like sweat and sweet clover. Like a shot of whiskey that burns all the way down. He was sitting on top of one of the tables right out there in the saloon, so I could reach everything a little better. It was the kind of kiss that gets in your head and gives you filthy dreams for years." Cliff stopped short and brought the tone of his voice back to reality. "I'm sure one of the romantics could describe it more elegantly, but you get the idea."

Cliff chanced a look toward Henry and saw his cheeks were flushed and his hands were clenched on the armrests of the chair. If it weren't for the hum of the saloon in the background, Cliff figured he'd be able to hear Henry's heart pounding in his chest.

When Henry spoke, his voice was weak. "Did anything happen… after the kiss?"

"That time, no, unfortunately," Cliff said. "Though the fact that you asked that question instead of just storming out on me is very telling."

Henry's glance sharpened and defensiveness glowed around the edges of his words as he said, "So is that it… you just intend to… blackmail me away from Broken Reach?"

Cliff felt more sad than offended. "You really think that's why I told you that?"

There was a long pause. "No," Henry managed to say.

"You're welcome to leave any time." Cliff glanced at the door, emphasizing the fact that he was not sitting between Henry and the exit. "But whether you go or stay, your secret's safe with me."

For the moment, at least, Henry chose to stay. "Why are you doing this?" he asked.

The look in Henry's eyes made that hollow in Cliff's chest fill with a familiar ache. He knew he needed to get through to Henry before it was too late, in more ways than one.

"Henry. I never fit in either. I wandered around, empty and lonely until I found this place." Cliff leaned in but kept a respectable distance. "The people here fit together like pieces on a patchwork quilt. We're all different and cut up and worn out but when we stick together we can make the best out of life. Be happy, even. It's a hard life and it doesn't last forever. This town was built by hands and bodies and care and love." Now Cliff did lean in closer than what most folks would consider respectable. "And you deserve to feel all of those things. Without shame or fear or pain."

Henry didn't pull away. He looked directly into Cliff's eyes. "No one's ever said anything like that to me before," Henry said.

"I mean it."

"I know you do…" He let out a shaky breath. "You're making me feel things that I only ever thought were possible to feel… reading books."

A sharp smile broke Cliff's lips. "Do those feelings make you want to kiss me?"

"Yes."

Cliff's heartbeat hitched at a faster pace. The answer startled him. Cliff had completely forgotten he was supposed to be trying to seduce Henry and everything had come together very suddenly.

Henry swallowed hard then said, "I don't know how, though. I've only ever kissed anyone in my thoughts. I know that sounds... pathetic."

"It doesn't," Cliff said. "I've only ever kissed most people in my thoughts. When I sit next to someone, just close enough. Or if I ever sleep next to someone by a campfire and let myself wonder..."

Henry smiled, though it looked painful. "Yes, exactly."

"Well. It would be my honor to be your first... real one," Cliff said quietly.

Henry turned toward him and reached out his hand, placing it gently on Cliff's shoulder. Cliff hadn't realized how deep such a simple touch could feel and he was lost for a moment. But the warm press of lips on his own found him pretty quick. Cliff kissed back, parting his lips just enough to make a point. Their tongues made tentative contact. With that, their first kiss blended into a second and then a third. As one after another after another formed, Cliff's mind summersault over itself—if this man had only ever thought about kissing, he had quite the imagination.

There was no place for them to go in the old wingback chair, so they stood, pressing the lengths of their bodies together, hands peppering touches here as they kept their lips on one another's.

Henry started on the buttons at the top of Cliff's shirt. After a few had been released, Cliff pressed the suit jacket off Henry's shoulders, and the garment fell to the floor. Their lips never parted.

Cliff took a chance and wrapped his arms around Henry's waist, bringing them even closer together. He let out a contented hum into Henry's embrace and in turn, he felt Henry's hips buck forward into him.

Lust and longing seared through Cliff's core, but in the next moment, the feeling was torn away. Henry broke the kiss. Cliff looked down and saw Henry's hands were clawed on his shoulders, pushing Cliff back. Cliff stepped away and let go.

A confusing mix of anger and regret flashed behind Henry's glasses. Before Cliff could say anything, Henry grabbed his suit jacket from the floor and ran from the room.

Cliff was dizzy and couldn't make his legs do what he wanted them to do. He tripped over the footstool, jostled the side table, and barely rescued the oil lamp from falling. He accidentally kicked the saddlebag full of books before he managed to stumble out of the library.

Cliff had a clear view of the front door from across the room and he saw Henry barely get into his suit jacket as he burst out the saloon door.

Chest heaving, Cliff pulled the library door closed and leaned back against it. He glanced up and saw Sylvie behind the bar, watching him button up his shirt. She gave him a wink.

Cliff didn't want to think or talk. He let Sylvie believe the assigned task was accomplished, found an empty stool at the bar, and ordered a shot of the good stuff to fill the emptiness.

When Cliff woke up the next morning he promptly cussed out the sunlight streaming through his window.

He wasn't hungover. He'd had a few, but not enough to make him sick. He had even made it home to bed before passing out. He cursed the light because it made him remember. It was easier to forget everything in the dark. But the sun illuminated all the memories from the night before, playing out tragically on the backdrop of his eyelids.

Cliff knew he could be waking up next to a warm body, drunk on lovesickness and shivering with new lust. But instead, he was all by himself in his dusty little house with no pictures on the walls and no flowers on the table.

Deciding not to just lay there torturing himself, Cliff pushed himself out of bed and started getting ready. He shaved, combed his hair, and ironed a new shirt. He wasn't hungry for breakfast so he decided he had better get to the attorney's office to inform him about the Perkin's homestead.

The day was mild and the feeling of autumn was achingly heavy in the air. Cliff plodded along a side street, taking a detour from his usual walk to Main Street. He lost track of where he was wandering when he heard a familiar voice.

"Mr. Williams!"

Cliff stopped short and turned. Henry appeared from around the corner. He was not wearing his suit jacket and his top two buttons on his shirt were undone. His spectacles reflected the sun and Cliff immediately wished he could take back all those terrible things he had said earlier about the light.

Cliff walked up to meet him. "I thought you said you would call me Cliff, not Mr. Williams."

"Not when others might hear," Henry said.

Cliff shrugged. "If you insist."

Henry shifted his weight from one foot to another. "Um… I asked in the general store where you lived… but no one would tell me."

"Well, well. The gossip brigade at the general store might talk about me behind my back but it's nice to know they won't send the morality reaper to my doorstep."

"Yes, I suppose that is what they still consider me," Henry said sadly.

Cliff was caught in between making another digging remark and his desire to hold Henry as tight as he could and never let go. Instead of either of these, Cliff said, "Doesn't look like you've quit your job just yet. With the way you left last night, I thought you'd have a ticket at the depot for the first train out of town."

"Well, that's why I found you. I wanted to tell you where I went last night," Henry said.

"I was wondering." Cliff sighed. "C'mon, let's walk."

They started down the street and Cliff held the comfortable silence until they were far enough from any passersby to not have to whisper.

Finally, Henry said, "I went back to my room at the boarding house and packed all my things. You are correct, I was planning to just leave on the first train out of town. But the moon was so bright, and the night was very nice. I decided to take a walk. I ended up in the cemetery."

"The cemetery," Cliff repeated dully.

"Yes. And while I was there I found the headstone of a young man, not much older than I am. It said he was thirty-three and that he died two years ago."

Cliff had been biting his tongue but then he said, "Jacob Wright?"

"Yes," Henry nodded. "I… suppose you would have known him?"

"I did," Cliff said. "I… told you a little bit about him last night."

Realization dawned and the pain was visible on Henry's face. "Oh, Cliff. I'm... I'm so, so sorry."

The hollow in Cliff's chest threatened to crack, but for the first time, Cliff didn't allow it to break open. "Don't be," Cliff said, genuine and sturdy. "In a small town like this, everyone has a past and it's always just around the corner. I'm living this life now, and I don't want either of us to be upset about that."

Henry accepted this and said slowly, "All right... Well, then this makes what I'm about to say even more... poetic, I suppose."

Henry looked around then motioned for them to slip into an alleyway out of sight. Cliff followed and leaned against an empty rain barrel to give Henry room to talk.

"Cliff, I'm thirty-one. If my life were to end in two years.... I would have wasted almost all of it. Because you're right. I've only ever done things for other people. I've hidden so much of myself, the only parts I can see, I don't like. I don't have any real relationships. I escape in books, not just from parts of my life, but from all of it." He cupped his hands in front of his chest and gazed toward the sky. "The short time I spent with you in that little room full of books in the back of the saloon was the most alive I've felt since... well, since I can ever really remember. And I know that the only reason I was able to feel that way was... well, because of you. But you were allowed to be there for me because of the people who have made Broken Reach the kind of place that we can be ourselves.

"So, I made a promise to this person I had never met, standing at his grave in the middle of the night. He had the opportunity to live in a place like Broken Reach and it was taken away. I promised that I wouldn't play a part in taking this place away from anyone else." Henry's hands dropped to his sides. "I sat in front of his grave until seven o'clock when the general store opened. I went in and I sent a telegram to Mr. Hinkley's office. I told him he would have to find another town for the freighting post. Broken Reach will not be accepting any of his guidelines."

The hollow in Cliff's chest was replaced by a sense of blooming joy. "Thank you," Cliff said. "Truly."

Henry gave a small smile. "It was as much for me as it was for you... and for Madame Sylvie and everyone else here in Broken Reach. I promise."

"I'm really happy to hear that."

Henry straightened and the businessman tone returned to his voice. "I sent another telegram after the one to Mr. Hinkley."

Cliff glanced up sharply. "For what?"

"I have a financially astute cousin who has, over the past several years, helped me make some investments. I've asked him to release the funds and wire them to me. I should have the money by next week."

Cliff frowned, but he didn't interrupt.

"It's not an outstanding amount," Henry said. "But it will be enough to build a sufficient library to serve a town the size of Broken Reach for several years." He rocked his head back and forth and motioned with his hands. "Of course, there are no freighting posts anywhere near here. We'll have to send teams up to Omaha City for the building materials. And then there's a matter of books, furniture, bookkeeping supplies, people to run the place…" Henry stopped, unsure of himself as Cliff had not stopped staring at him. "Um… yes?"

"I'm going to kiss you now."

Henry gave a stage whisper. "Outside? Someone might see."

"So? Everyone knows about me, even the gossip brigade." He stepped up and took Henry by the waist. "We could do this right in front of Bartling's General Store and no one would care."

"Really?"

"Really."

"There truly is no place like Broken Reach," Henry said as he relaxed into Cliff's body, pressing his forehead to Cliff's. "I'm so grateful that you fought so hard to keep Hinkley freight out of this town."

Cliff smiled, knowing he was holding his next lover. "And I'm so grateful that you got here," he said, "just in time."

LAST DAY AND FINAL PAGE

Mallory Behr

"What the hell are you doing up there?"

Thunder echoed in the dark skies above, and a large gust of wind burst through the tight branches of Paige's reading tree. Paige jumped, forgetting she was high up in the tree, and lost her balance. She scrambled for the closest branch, lost her footholds, and kicked her book and backpack to the ground. Clutching tightly to the smaller branch, Paige shut her eyes tightly, hoping to make a safe landing without breaking something.

"Thomas?" Paige yelled, kicking her feet.

"Yeah! Why'd you climb up there?"

"Questions later," she said, losing her grip on the branch. "Catch me first."

Thomas groaned. "Fine."

She sighed in relief. Another gust of wind barreled through, shaking her branch violently, cracking it slightly. "I'll make it up to you," Paige cried out, "I promise!" With her eyes still closed, she let go of the branch, landing right on top of Thomas. Leaves, almost mockingly, gracefully sailed in the wind, settling down in the same mud puddle. She groaned and sat up.

Laughing, Thomas shoved her off of him and stood up. He reached his hand out and said, "I've been looking all over for you. Didn't think you'd be falling out of a tree." He looked around at the storm, adding, "In the middle of a summer storm too."

Paige grabbed his hand, and pulled herself up. Brushing her pant legs off, she rolled her eyes. "The storm wasn't supposed to hit until later, Thomas," she grumbled. "I was just reading and lost my balance, that's all." She picked up her backpack and book just as the rain started to pick up. "I thought you weren't coming back until tomorrow."

"Surprise!" He smiled. It slipped away as the rain started to pick up. "Actually, I'm only in town for two days."

She froze. Thunder boomed across the sky again, followed by a streak of lightning, and the rain picked up a little more. A blast of cold wind hit them both in the face, and Paige shivered in the wind. "What do you mean? You're not staying for the summer again?"

"Not this year, Wormy," Thomas said, "I'll explain if you get some coffee with me."

"Don't call me Wormy," Paige snapped, even though she loved the nickname.

Thomas grinned. "Whatever you say, Bookworm. Let's just get out of the rain." He turned around, flipped up his raincoat, and wandered over to the parking lot. He kicked up some water as he approached his car, waving enthusiastically.

Sighing, Paige reached into her backpack, pulling out her bright yellow umbrella. She raced after Thomas, listening to the raindrops bounce off her umbrella and onto the ground below her as more thunder boomed in the distance. Climbing into the passenger seat, she pushed aside the box of books and shut the door.

Thomas pulled out of the parking lot and drove down the road. Raindrops hit the windows, and Paige traced the drops down the glass. The soft murmur of the car's broken radio was drowned out by the storm raging around the car, even as Thomas tried to turn the music up. She glanced over at him, his messy brown hair slightly damp from the rain, then back to the window. Driving with him was always the best, but the silence was almost unbearable in the car. They stopped at a red light. Thomas leaned over and shut the radio off, leaving them with the muffled sounds of cars driving down the road, and the strong tapping of the raindrops, desperately hoping to get in the car.

Although the drive from the park to downtown didn't take too long, it felt like an eternity to Paige. If she could measure time with silence, she probably would have read the box of books at her feet by the time they reached the bookstore she worked at, A Little Light Reading. When Thomas finally parked in front of the store, a small sigh of relief escaped her. She smiled at him as they climbed out of the car.

Following him inside, finally safe from the wind and rain, Paige took a seat at their usual table by the large bay window, while Thomas shook off his raincoat and left to order drinks. Her thoughts lingered on whatever important thing he wanted to talk to her about. The what-ifs flooded her head like the rain flooded the roads outside: What if he was never coming back to Clearbrooke? What if he forgot about them, about this town? What if she never got to tell him?

Thomas returned, setting the hot cups of coffee on the table, pulling Paige out of her thoughts again. As he sat down, he sighed, playing with the small purple stirrer in his drink. He clenched his fists and sighed. Thomas mumbled quietly, "Paige, I'm leaving Clearbrooke tomorrow night. I won't be back for two years."

"Oh." That was the bad news she was expecting. She turned away, and stared out the window, trying to pretend as if he just didn't drop the heaviest hardcover book on her heart. "Well," she said, hiding the rising sob tickling the bottom of her throat. She avoided his gaze. "I never thought you'd stick around this small town for long."

"Hey," he laughed, "I couldn't stay away."

Neither of them spoke. The low murmurs of the coffee shop guests filled the silence until Thomas leaned over. "I got a call from a small publishing company based in California last night. They want me to join a travel writing team for a project." He sighed.

Frowning, Paige stared at her friend. The uncertainty in his voice was alarming. He was never afraid of the unknown. Not even when he faced a million rejections for every bit of writing he sent out. That's what she loved most about him, and it was always something that made her want to do better, even though she'd never say that to his face. She took a long sip of her coffee. "I think you should do it." She wished she could take the words back, crumple them up, and tell him no. Stay here. Don't leave me behind again.

"You really think so?"

"Yes," Paige said, her heart sinking even more. "It's that adventure you've always wanted."

He glanced up, his eyes almost scanning her face as if he could see the huge "no" written on her forehead. "Thanks, Paige," he whispered. "It means a lot." Leaning over the table, he gave her a quick kiss on the cheek and grabbed his coat. Before he left the coffee shop he grinned. "You're my inspiration, y'know?"

Paige blushed and watched him rush out the door and drive away, her hand lingering softly on her cheek. She smiled sadly, the hardcover book growing heavier on her heart.

Mary, the owner, shouted from behind the coffee counter, "Girl, when are you two gettin' together?" A few murmurs of agreement echoed through the coffee shop, but Mary wasn't done talking. "The whole town's waitin'. Come to me when he finally proposes." She winked.

Paige turned an even deeper red. "N-No," she stammered. "We're just friends." She reached for her own jacket. "Just friends," she said again, quieter this time.

"Uh huh," Mary said. "You keep telling' yourself that, hun."

The next afternoon, as Paige redecorated the new book display in the front window, she couldn't get the conversation out of her mind. It kept replaying over and over again, his words repeating again and again. Thomas was leaving. They only had a day left together, and she was stuck at work with so much to do. So much they both had to do together. She sighed and continued painting the display. The characters smiled out at the busy downtown weekend, the summer sun peeking through clouds left over by the week's showers. She wished she could be as happy as her own paintings. The front doorbell jingled, and Thomas wandered in, carrying a few boxes.

"Mister Thomas! Mister Thomas!" A few of the kids from the children's section abandoned their drawings and toys and rushed over to him. "Can we have storytime today?"

"Yeah!" the chorus of kids echoed through the store, and little Maya, the owner's daughter, started chanting: "Storytime! Storytime! Storytime!"

The other kids caught on quickly, chanting louder and louder and louder. "Storytime! Storytime!"

"Woah!" Thomas shouted. "At least let me set these old books down!"

"Can I help?"

"No me!"

Paige giggled, turning her attention back to the window. The kids eventually quieted down as Thomas began to read from The Secret Garden. She listened in as his voice filled the store; even the adults stopped their browsing to listen to Thomas read. Realizing it was his last storytime with the kids, a small tear escaped from Paige's eye, slipping down and landing on her paintbrush. She wiped the tear away. Moving around the book display, she reached for a new color.

"Mister Thomas," one of the little boys said, interrupting the story, "are you really gonna go 'round the world writin' your own stories?"

"Yup," Thomas said.

"Can you read them to us when you visit?"

Thomas laughed. "Maybe."

"Are ya gonna miss the bookstore?"

Paige paused her painting and snuck a glance at the Kid's Corner. Thomas shut the book, setting it down gently on the bench next to him. "I will," he said, "and the magic and stories it brings to this little town," he said. "And I'll miss you all too."

The kids all gasped in surprise. They hopped up and started to tackle him with hugs, and he laughed, pushing them off. His dark brown eyes met with Paige's, but she turned back to her paint. She collected her materials and went a long way to the back room. Setting her paint supplies in her locker, she sank to the floor, and finally let the sobs she was holding break out. There wasn't any time at all to tell him everything. She wasn't even sure if Thomas even felt the same way.

The door opened and Paige quickly wiped her tears away. Mary walked inside, setting her iced tea down on the table. "I knew something was wrong," Mary stated as she sat down. "Don't you dare try to hide those tears from me."

Paige shook her head. "Mary, I don't know what I'm gonna do without him around."

"You're going to keep living your life, girl." Mary smiled. "Keep writing your own story. And you need to tell that boy the truth. It's going to hurt like hell when he's gone if you don't tell him soon." She held out her hand. "C'mon, put on a brave face. This store needs your smile, especially when he leaves."

Taking her hand, Paige smiled and wiped the rest of her tears away.

"Thanks, Mary," she whispered. She took a few deep breaths and pushed the door open. A few customers were in line, waiting to be checked out. As she helped the mom at the front of the line, the daughter eagerly bounced up and down smiling with her missing a front tooth. "Did you pick this notebook out, Isabella?" Paige asked.

"Uh huh!" Isabella giggled as Paige slid the book across the counter to her. "Miss Paige? Mister Thomas said you can draw princesses! Can you draw one for me? Please?"

Paige scanned the children's area, spotting Thomas whispering to the kids and pointed in her direction. When they made eye contact, he grinned sheepishly, saluted the kids, and walked out of the Kids Corner. He turned around, blowing a few raspberries at the kids, who all nearly fell on the floor of laughter. Paige shook her head, smiling. She drew the princess, printed out the receipt, and handed the bag to Isabella's mom. "Have a good day, Mrs. Rivera."

She continued to check everyone out, scanning items, drawing on pieces of paper and book covers, until the shop began to quiet down. Thomas was still there, shelving books, and every now and then pausing to write in a journal. He kept glancing at the clock behind Paige, and back to his notebook. Whenever he caught her looking at him, she would turn away and pretend to be busy at the registers. She smiled, wondering when would be the best time. The sun was slowly setting in the distance, and street lights started to pop on outside.

"Thomas Martin!" Mary shouted from the coffee shop, "Why are you still here?"

Thomas jumped, spilling books from the boxes. "I'm not leaving until the store closes at seven, Mary," he said with a grin.

Paige looked up from organizing the knick-knacks by the front counter, her heart beating fast. Only half an hour left until they all started to lock up and head home. Or for Thomas, head onto a new adventure. Only thirty minutes before she would lose him.

"I need to run over to the grocery store." Mary walked toward the back room, grabbing her keys. "Think you two can watch the shop while I'm gone?" She winked at Paige.

"Oh, uh, sure, Mary!" Paige smiled.

"We'll try not to burn the place down while you're gone," Thomas added.

Mary eyed them both, winking at Paige once again. "I'll be back in a bit."

As soon as she left, Thomas jumped over the small bookshelf, rushing over to the light switch. "Hey, Wormy," he said, "Want to see something magical?" Before she could answer, he flipped the switches, shutting off the fluorescent lights, only leaving the twinkling lights on. They flicked on and off, almost mimicking the fireflies outside in the fields by Paige's house.

"That's amazing," she whispered, staring at the lights.

Smiling, Thomas rushed over to the front doors, locking them both. "Discovered that last summer!" he yelled across the store. "Was the last one here." He winked, scooped up the journal he'd been writing in all afternoon, and jumped up on the counter next to Paige. She grinned and joined him up there. He sighed, "I really am going to miss this place," he said. "Remember when we first met here?"

"Yeah," Paige laughed. "You took the last copy of the special edition of The Lion, the Witch, and the Wardrobe."

"And I tried to make it up to you with that stupid necklace from the gumball machine." Thomas sank his head in his hands. "Bet you don't have that anymore."

"Actually," Paige reached up, pulling the cheap, red star necklace from under her shirt. "I do." She showed it to him.

"Gosh, that was nearly eleven years ago, Wormy!" He smiled and sat back up.

They both watched the lights above them twinkle for a bit, the clock ticking behind them. Each tick was another reminder to Paige; she was running out of time. It was now or never. Her heart was beating faster and faster in her chest, and she closed her eyes. "Thomas, there's something I need to tell you."

At the same time, Thomas also said, "Paige, can I ask you something?"

They laughed nervously. "You go first," she said.

"Ok." He glanced up at the ceiling. "Me leaving every year is normal for you, right?"

"Yes," she said. "I always count the days 'til you come back."

"How do you feel every time I leave?"

Paige sighed. Now was the time. Surrounded by stories in the shop, she could almost hear them all cheering her on. Tell him they whispered. You can do this! "Honestly?" she started. "Sometimes, I wish you never had to leave. I wish you could stay here in this little town forever." She looked up at him, smiling. The lights sparkled in his eyes, and she sighed again. "I want you to stay here, but I know that's selfish of me. This is your big break, and I don't want to take it away from you." Tears started to spill down her freckled cheeks. "And it's been hard these past couple of years to watch you leave over and over again," she whispered.

"Why?"

"Because I think I love you."

Boom. The three words slipped from her mouth, and there was no going back. The silence in the room was almost unbearable. Just like it was in the car ride over, before he delivered the bad news. She wished he would say something. Anything. Not just sit there taking in the silence.

Thomas giggled. It started as a tiny one, then growing into a full-blown laugh. One she hadn't heard in a long time. He kept laughing and laughing until finally, he calmed down. He reached for her hands and held them close. "Gosh, Paige," he said. "This makes things so much harder." Leaning forward, he pushed her hair out of her face and pressed his forehead to hers. "I think I love you, too."

Instant relief flooded through Paige. He was so close to her, she couldn't stop crying. There was no taking back her tears now. When Thomas finally moved away from her, he dried her tears, leaving his hand on her cheek. She held it there for a while until the tears slowed down. The alarm on the clock rang out behind them, and both of them jumped. His hand slipped away, and he pushed himself off the counter. "Guess it's time for you to go," Paige whispered.

"Yeah." Thomas sighed. "Oh! I almost forgot." He slid the journal over to her. "This is for you. You can ignore all that sappy letter and the pictures if you want." He laughed, taking a few steps back. He looked out toward his car and back to her. "Maybe I can send you letters. From my trip," he laughed again. "Something for you to think about, y'know."

She held the journal. "Yeah!" She jumped down from the counter. "Yeah, of course!" She grinned. "I'll add a few drawings to them too."

"Perfect," he said. Walking toward the front doors, Thomas set his hand on the bar and frowned. "This doesn't feel like a proper goodbye," he mumbled. "I don't know what I'm doing."

"What," Paige put her hands on her hips, "I thought you were great with the ladies." She tried to look stern, but the smile couldn't leave her lips.

"Ha ha." Thomas shook his head. "Very funny."

She laughed and pulled her necklace off. She held it in her hand and whispered, "Let's make this a better goodbye." Running over to Thomas, she handed it to him. "Take it."

"You sure?"

"Yes." Paige grinned. "Also, I don't want this to be a goodbye," she said. "How about… like we're closing the chapter," she laughed, "and the next one starts later?"

"I like that," Thomas said. "Just one more thing, though."

"What?"

Thomas leaned over and pulled her into a kiss. They stood there, kissing under the twinkling lights of the bookstore, surrounded by bookshelves and memories of their younger selves hiding among the books. For a moment, Paige thought she could hear the cheers of characters. But the loudest sound of all was Mary standing outside the bookshop, banging on the doors with a loud victory screech. They pulled away, both blushing, and smiling goofily. The heavy hardcover book was finally lifted from her heart. No more pain left, except for the future ones of missing him.

"Promise me you won't fall out of any more trees while I'm gone?"

"Oh, that's gonna be a little tough," Paige said. "It's my favorite place to read after all!"

SEEING THE STORY

CM Peters

Talking in front of his students was one thing. Introducing himself to a bunch of strangers was another, even if they had something in common. Gabe Collins wiped his moist hands on his jeans; it was as if the rain falling outside came straight out of his fingers.

The book club was a new thing for him and the best way he'd thought of to meet new people. With a deep breath, he smiled to his nearest seat neighbor and lifted his head when he heard his name called out.

"Why don't you tell us about yourself, Mr. Collins?" the club president, Mrs. Gray, asked with a smile on her lips.

He nodded, cleared his throat, and stood nervously. "Hi. I'm Gabriel Collins. Gabe. I'm… uh… I'm the new History teacher at Fairview High, and uh…"

"Good thing you're not the dialect coach," a female voice called out mockingly.

With a frown, Gabe scanned the small crowd to see a brunette, curly-haired woman with a lopsided smile on her face. "Excuse me?"

"Sorry, couldn't help myself. For someone who speaks to kids all day, you sound nervous to talk to people your age."

His shoulders slumped and Gabe let out a laugh, feeling all the tension in his shoulders evaporate. "Yeah, uh… It's different when I'm not talking to kids."

"Mr. Collins, this is a book club, not the United Nations. We just want to know who you are and what you'll bring to the club."

He nodded. "Right. So, I'm Gabe, I'm thirty-eight, I'm into fantasy, historical, and crime novels mostly. I write in my spare time, I read a lot, and I'm here to broaden my horizons."

"There you go!" The woman let out a tinkling laugh, clutching the book on her lap.

Gabe wasn't sure how to react to this woman heckling so he chose not to say a word. Instead, he sat back down and grabbed his notebook.

"Thank you, Mr. Collins," the older woman said. "Welcome to Fairview's Book Club. If you have suggestions for future books, we'll be discussing that later, and we'll get to this month's book in a minute. For now, a welcome back is needed, although everyone has heard her." She turned to the curly-haired woman. "Frankie, we're so happy to see you here again."

A low murmur rose in the small crowd, making Gabe frown again. He observed the young woman for a moment, seeing emotions on her face until she composed herself.

"I'm glad to hear you guys, too. I'm here for the company, I guess. I'm still learning," she said, lifting the book on her lap.

From afar, Gabe finally understood. The book was in Braille and the woman, blind. Something came over him and he called out, "Maybe we could help?" he asked, standing.

A blush came over the woman's skin and she turned her face toward him, tilting her chin. "Are you blind too?"

"Uh…"

"Come on, get it out. What did you mean?" she said with a sigh.

He gave his answer a longer thought, and a soft grunt later, Gabe said, "If you let us, we could take turns reading the books to you?"

Frankie's face closed up. "Do I look ninety?" she asked through gritted teeth, quick as lightning.

"Well, no!" Gabe replied quickly. "Never mind, I just wanted to help." All around him, he saw averted eyes, making him a bit disheartened by this first contact with the book club.

When he moved to Fairview, Maryland, a fresh start after the end of a relationship and five years teaching on the West Coast, he thought it would be easy to blend in a small town, meet nice people, and establish relationships. This was not how he'd expected things to go during a book club.

The older woman called for attention. "So, if we get back to our musings, a nice welcome back to Frankie. We're all happy to have you with us again and that's why you chose the book for us this month. An oldie but a goodie, you said?"

Frankie nodded. "One of my favorites, yes. It's from a South American author and a short novel. But since I've read it before… you know… I can follow the discussion when it's time." She held the book in her lap while lifting another book from her bag after puttering in it. "In Spanish, it's called 'El Cartero de Neruda'. The cover showed a man standing by a bicycle on a cliff overlooking the ocean.

Gabe smiled inwardly. He'd read this book years ago in college from a Literature of the Americas class. The Postman had been a favorite of his from then on and he re-read it at least once a year, enough that he was on his second copy. He didn't say a word, though, letting the woman speak.

"In English, it's 'The Postman'," Frankie continued. "There was a movie made with it but don't watch it before reading the book. The ending is different. Maybe you could watch it at some point, but just wait for now. It's one of my nicest discoveries and I hope you'll love it too."

Hums of approval were heard all around, and for the next hour, the members of the book club discussed their previous choice, a novel Gabe hadn't read yet. He made a few notes in his notebook to read it later, enjoying the conversation. When the meeting ended, he nodded to the few people that did the same toward him and headed for the door, adjusting the strap of his messenger bag on his shoulder. He hoped the next meeting of the club would be less awkward.

"Mr. Collins? A moment?"

He turned to see Frankie approaching him while navigating around the chairs with her cane. "Yes?" he carefully asked, wondering what the young woman wanted.

"I have to apologize," she started. "I'm a bit wary of people I don't know and… This condition is new to me. I don't always understand if there's an undertone to what people are saying now that I can't see their faces."

"I promise you, there was none. It was a genuine offer and nothing to insult you." He gently put his hand on hers over the cane. "I know it might have sounded weird, but I meant nothing mean by it. I was just trying to make a connection."

She gave him a small smile. "You're new in town, right?"

"I've been here a couple of weeks now. School starts on Monday so it's the real thing now. Time to get in gear."

"I've heard all the buzz around you, yes. 'The new teacher is all that and cute on top!' is something that comes back a lot. It seems you're quite handsome and scholarly."

He couldn't help but laugh. "That makes me sound like I am ninety but hot! But thank you. I can't wait to meet my kids." He turned slowly, moving his bag out of the way so he could guide her. "Heading outside?"

"Yes. My sister's picking me up." She put her free hand on his forearm with confidence. "She should be there soon."

"Alright, I'll wait with you. It's almost a biblical downpour outside," he said, guiding her to the main library door from the room they were in. "Here we are," he added once they reached their destination. "I don't see any cars waiting, though."

"That's fine." She turned to him with a smile. "Tell me what you look like," she simply asked.

Gabe was a bit surprised by the demand but complied. "I'm tall. Six-two. Uhm, brown, short hair but most days, it looks like I put my fingers in the outlet." Hearing her laugh made his day. "I have blue eyes, a bit of a beard, and a scar on top of my left eyebrow."

As soon as he said that, she reached for his face, then stopped herself. "You don't sound thirty-eight. But I'm not going to do that thing."

"What thing?"

"You know, rubbing my fingers all over your face. Even if I do, I won't be able to mold it into a clay bust like that girl in the Lionel Richie video."

With a snort, he did notice how long and lean her fingers were. "And what would you do instead?"

"Play it," she replied.

Gabe frowned. "Play my face? You mean with it?" She shook her head, so he asked, "What do you mean?"

"I'm a piano teacher. I play by ear, so I don't necessarily need to read the notes. Even if I wanted to, I won't be able to do that for a while, so I'd play what you inspire."

He felt warm from head to toe. "I bet you're a fantastic pianist."

"As you probably are a teacher. They're pretty picky here and there's a reason why Mr. Greenaway stayed so long. There wasn't anyone of his caliber to replace him."

This throwing compliments game they were playing pleased him, especially after how they'd met. "Again, I'm sorry. I didn't mean to insult you when I offered to read to you. I can't imagine what it's like not being able to read and escape my daily life."

She let out a long sigh, turning her vague glance toward the rainy parking lot. "It's one of the hardest things with being blind. I miss reading so much. But I've read this book before, so, thank you. It won't be necessary, so just enjoy it for me."

"I already have. This novel has been in my collection since college. I even studied it and it's followed me everywhere since. I'm just happy to read it again."

He noticed a sudden hesitation on her face, then heard a car honking and saw a woman standing from a small beige Fiat. "I think your sister is here."

"Blonde, black jeans, beige car?"

"Yup."

"That's her," Frankie replied, using her cane to gage the steps. "You know what? I'll take you up on your offer. I want to hear the adventures of Mario again. I live at the corner of Washington and Grover, the big teal-colored house. Sunday afternoon at two?"

He was surprised but happy. "I'll be there," he said, watching her disappear into the small car while he stood in the rain, a goofy smile on his face.

⁂

Sunday couldn't come fast enough. Gabe spent the week engrossed teaching his new classes, but Frankie's smile kept coming back to him during breaks and daydreams. A student had even caught him staring outside with a grin while he remembered the way she'd heckled him. He'd blushed dark enough for his student to chuckle.

When Sunday finally came, Gabe spent the morning cleaning and finished unpacking the last few boxes of movies and books, noting down those he could suggest to the book club. He walked his Blue Merle Australian Shepherd, Jasper, twice around the neighborhood, noticing Frankie's house, stopped for a coffee, and still, it was too early for him to meet the young woman. He resolved to review the next day's lesson to pass the time.

When it was finally time to go, he found himself almost as nervous as his first date at sixteen. Jasper whined when he patted him on the head before going. The dog cocked his head to the side, letting out half a bark. Gabe chuckled. "Yes, I'll be back, and no, you can't come. I'm meeting this lady."

Jasper crouched down, panting softly, and Gabe winked. "I'll bring you back a bone, buddy." He finally left with his copy of 'The Postman' in his bag and walked over to Frankie's house. He'd realized in the morning how close together they lived; barely three blocks from his cottage-like house. When he knocked on the door, he was surprised to see her answer. "Hello," he simply said.

"On the dot. I like that," she replied, letting him in.

"I like punctuality, too." Gabe mentally smacked himself at his boring small talk, not used to dating anymore. But this isn't a date...is it? he wondered. "I live a few blocks away, so it wasn't hard to find. I saw it this morning when I walked my dog." He stepped inside when she showed him in, removing his jacket, and just as he said 'dog', a long-haired German Shepherd trotted over to him, and sat by Frankie's side. For a second, he leaned down to pet him but asked, "Is he a service dog?", knowing he shouldn't if that was the case.

"Nah. This big boy has been with us for years. He's good to help me a bit, though. Gabe, this is Bear. Bear, say hello to Gabe."

The dog stood and went to Gabe, lifting his paw as if to shake the man's hand. Gabe grinned and shook it. "Hey, Bear. I have a dog too. His name is Jasper."

"Oh! Maybe we could take them to the dog park together?"

Again, Gabe was happily surprised at such forwardness and nodded, only to realize once again that she couldn't see him. "I'd love that. And so would Jasper. He's always so full of energy and having a friend couldn't hurt. He's super social."

"Good. We can plan that for later this week. Bear loves his walks. Now, come on. We'll settle on the porch by the piano."

Frankie reached out her hand and he took it quickly. She led him to a sunroom in the back, where a grand piano was in the shade of plants showered with sunlight. While Bear flopped heavily on a waiting dog bed, Frankie went to the piano and motioned for him to sit in a nearby chair. "Do you mind if I play while you read? It keeps me in check for my students."

"No, not at all," Gabe replied as he made himself comfortable on the loveseat.

He began to tell the tale of Mario Jimenez and the poet Pablo Neruda, while he listened to Frankie playing 'Nocturne in E flat' and 'Moonlight Sonata'. Gabe didn't know much about classical music but the mixture of the novel with the melodies went straight to his heart. He found himself emotional soon enough, unable to read any more. The passion with which Frankie was playing mixed with Mario and Beatriz's young love blooming made his heart flutter, enough that he had to swallow back a near sob.

When Frankie finished her piece, she turned toward him. "Are you alright?"

Gabe cleared his throat. "I'm... fine. Just really moved by the combination of the story and your music. I usually read in complete silence, but this brings the novel to a whole new level."

"Doesn't it? I always do this now when I listen to audiobooks."

The admission made Gabe narrow his eyes; she'd accused him of calling her old when she'd done this before. "Oh, really? So... I'm your own personal audiobook?"

She giggled. "I've read 'The Postman' before, more than once. But you're the first person I've met who'd read it too. I wanted to hear it with someone else's voice... you know, to gauge their passion for it. And you seemed to be really passionate about it," she explained. "I'm sorry if I brought you here under false pretenses. It's nice to have a different kind of company, you know. Someone that doesn't think so loud I can hear his pity from afar."

"Pity? Because you're blind? Hey, shit happens, you know." Gabe scrunched his face. "I mean, I was unable to speak for months after a hike in the snow went wrong. I can partly get the feeling. People are weird when they don't understand."

She hummed, tilting her head. "How did you communicate during that time?"

"My hands, mostly. Wrote down a lot too. It ignited a passion for writing." The memories of those seven months were ingrained into his memories as the longest of his life. Jasper had gotten him through after the speech therapy sessions were over. "What about you? Is this permanent?"

It took a moment for Frankie to answer. "I lost my sight after a fall while skiing last winter. The doctor says he doubts I'll see again. My mother wants to believe I will, but what will it change, really?"

"How about your whole life? The way you see the world now is so different and being able to show that to others could be interesting."

"True, but I don't think it'll happen," she said, a sad undertone to her voice.

Feeling guilty, Gabe put the book aside and went to sit by her side. "I'm sorry. I didn't mean to push."

She gave him a small smile and shook her head. "Do you play?" she asked.

"Not one note," he replied, shaking his head.

"Then keep reading while I play. Bring me back to Chile with Mario and Beatriz while I play some Rachmaninoff."

This time, Gabe remained sitting at the piano with her, reading slowly, stealing glances at her face while she played. The curls of hair around her dark skin, the slight wrinkles at the corner of her eyes, her brow furrowing with effort, all of her personality and love of music and the story were expressed through her body.

The sun had barely set when he finished the short novel, and only then did he notice a tear rolling down her cheek. He couldn't help but thumb it away, making her gasp when she lifted her head. Gabe knew she couldn't see him but saw something he couldn't grasp in her expression; pain or utter shock.

"I'm sorry," he quickly said. "I couldn't help myself. I didn't want to make you sad."

"I'm...not sad. Just...overwhelmed." She smiled through the tears welling in her eyes. "It's something else to share the love of an art piece with someone you've just met. Even more so since I feel like I've always known you."

He found that to be the sweetest thing she'd said to him. He realized he felt the same. It was the quickest bloom of a relationship he'd ever experienced, but it felt true.

With a deep breath, Gabe was about to ask her out when a knock stopped him. Frankie's sister announced that dinner would be ready soon. With regret, Gabe stood and gathered his things to go. He wanted to stay, to smell her hair, to kiss her surely warm skin and hold her close. Before his body betrayed him, he slowly made his way to the door followed closely by Bear and Frankie.

"Do you want to take the dogs to the park tomorrow after school?" he asked with a quaking voice.

"I... I want to, but I have a student at four o'clock. Tuesday?"

Gabe's shoulders slumped as disappointment filled him suddenly. "Tuesday. I'll be here right after school."

"Tuesday," she softly repeated.

Gabe leaned in and kissed her cheek softly, telling himself he had to find another book to survive between then and their next meeting.

From then on, Gabe dove headfirst in class prep in his downtime without Frankie. Any little moment they had free, they spent together. The dog park, her sunroom, his back porch.

At the book club meetings, they always sat together, enough that he began noticing the looks from other people. Fortunately for him, it seemed all the members approved of this blossoming relationship. His reputation as a great teacher also helped, and the way he treated Frankie with the utmost care and kindness.

A book was always there, between them, melding them like notes of a symphony. Still, he didn't make an official move on her; if anything were to happen between them, it would be on her terms. He feared to cross a line. Still, he never stopped any kind gesture or word, reading as much as she wanted to hear, listening as much as she wanted to play, reading her grandmother's book aloud to her. All he ever got was the touch of a hand, the scent of her intoxicating lily perfume, and the occasional kiss on the cheek. For now, it was enough.

One snowy Sunday, after a late brunch at his place, Frankie invited Gabe to her home. "I have a surprise for you," she simply said.

He was stunned because he also had one for her but wanted to let her present hers first. "Really?"

"Bring Jasper. We'll pick up Bear and go to the dog park first."

"Everything to make me wait," he replied with a grin.

They did so, picking up a happy Bear. The dogs were well-behaved all through the walk, but as soon as they went through the safety gate, a fluffy gray squirrel ran by. Bear barked and flew off, pulling Frankie forward. She yelped and fell face first. Gabe shuddered when he realized she'd hit a sawed-off tree trunk.

"Frankie? Are you okay?" He turned her over gently after letting Jasper go, knowing he was safe in the park. Blood was trickling from her temple and she hissed.

"I hit my head. I hit my damn head again," she replied, pain and anger in her voice.

"Don't move, sweetie. I'll call for help."

For once, she didn't argue with him.

The paramedics were there quickly, taking Frankie to the hospital while he brought the dogs back to her house. Her mother and sister went straight to meet Frankie and he did the same once the dogs were safe in the backyard.

Waiting was excruciating. Gabe saw how Frankie's mother and sister were worried; they'd been through the same before. He tried to comfort them, but his own worry was eating him alive. When the doctor finally showed up, he invited them to the room. Gabe couldn't decipher his expression, whether it was good or bad news.

Frankie sat on the bed but wasn't wearing a hospital gown. There was a taped-up piece of gauze on her forehead and she was nervously playing with the cord of her hoodie. "Mom? Becks?" she called out.

Gabe let the women embrace, patiently waiting until she called for him. "Gabe?"

He took her extended hand and sat beside her. "I'm sorry," he blurted out.

"You're sorry my dog can be a big dummy? It's not your fault. And I'm fine, really. I promise," she said. Without hesitation, she lifted her hand to run her fingers along his jaw, then felt up to his scar.

"More than fine, actually," the doctor intervened. "There is no sign of concussion but she still needs lots of rest in the coming days."

"Yes, sir, she will," Gabe replied quickly.

He saw Frankie raise an eyebrow, but he splayed his hand on her face like an octopus. "No. You're not protesting this. You will rest."

And that, she did. Gabe made sure she spent the weekend resting in the sunroom of her home where he read the latest choice from the book club,

'The Life List' by Lori Nelson Spielman. She fell asleep against him while he read and held her as close as this made for all the waiting around, which now seemed so short.

Her breath was heavy, her visage calm, and the warmth coming from her made him doze off quickly as well after putting the book down. It was her fingers along his bearded jaw that woke him up, and when he smiled, she did exactly what he'd done, splaying her hand over his face. "Wake up, sleepyhead. I still haven't given you my surprise."

"But you should be resting!" he protested.

"I promise, it's not tiring." She stood and the dogs did the same but flopped down as soon as they saw her sit at the piano. Frankie ordered Gabe to stand in front of the grand piano. He noticed how nervous she suddenly seemed but didn't ask. Over time, he'd learned not to question her about her music; she was the gifted musician, and he, the lucky recipient.

Frankie made herself comfortable, took a deep breath, and began playing. Her fingers grazed and pressed, letting a series of notes tinkle from the instrument, the music sliding straight into Gabe's heart. It was a beautifully sad and slow sonata. Without him even trying to hide it, a tear rolled down his cheek, which he wiped with a smile. As happy as this composition made him, he was saddened that Frankie couldn't see the joy it brought him.

When she finished, she let her fingers rest on the keys, her chest heaving gently with the effort. The silence was deafening, so Gabe sat by her side, taking her hand and putting it over his heart. "Can you feel that?"

Biting her lower lip, she gave him a small nod. "This is how you make me feel too, how it's growing between us," she said, her voice barely above a whisper. "If I could have, I would've written it to you, but you know my Braille skills are still mediocre for now."

He hummed softly. "Well, maybe you can't now, but I know you will when you perfect those skills. In the meantime, I also have a surprise for you." He smiled at her frown, then reached for a book he'd been hiding for days in his messenger bag. "I had this made for you." Gabe put the book over the piano lid after closing it, took her hand, and put it over the first page. "I know it's not clear just yet for you, but this is your favorite book in Braille, and I can read it with you because, on the other side, there's the written version."

"But… How? You know my grandmother wrote my favorite book!"

she exclaimed with her lower lip trembling.

"Your sister lent me her copy. Then I asked the book club if they had contacts. A lot of people gave me a hand. Mrs. Grayson did the cover." Gabe closed the book so she could feel the contouring of the letters with the fingertips. "Natasha separated every part to be sent to the specialized printer."

"Oh, my God, Gabe. How… Why? Why would you do this?"

He couldn't help running his hand in her curly hair. "Because I want to discover this book with you, read it aloud while you familiarize yourself with the words. And because...this." With a gentle pull, Gabe pressed his lips to hers, hoping for the best.

And the best, he got. With a soft yelp, she threw her arms around him to deepen the kiss. It was slow, sending shivers down his spine, enough that he pulled away breathless. "You have no idea how long I've wanted to do that."

"I wanted to on the first day you came here," she whispered. "But that's not ladylike when you've just met someone. You just… You do something to me," Frankie added, lifting her head.

Even if she couldn't see his gaze, Gabe looked into her eyes. What he saw was pure love, the same he felt for her. And he didn't regret one moment waiting this long to tell her about his feelings. Instead, he cupped her face and leaned forward, gently kissing her eyelids. "We'll just write our own story now."

THE IN-BETWEEN YEARS

Alexis Ames

Deep within the bowels of the generation ship, far from the engines and the atrium and the galley, was a room that shouldn't have existed.

Ethan would know, because he knew this ship better than anything else in his life, including himself. Deck forty-eight was strictly reserved for storage, and according to the ship's schematic, this was a storage room – except that it wasn't. For one thing, it was easily larger than three of the generation ship's shuttle bays combined. For another, the doors had been sealed, and he'd needed the laser cutter to open them.

<<Identify yourself.>>

The voice startled him so badly that he nearly dropped his tools.

"Er...hello?" he asked, feeling more than a little ridiculous. "Paul, is that you?"

There was no response. Ethan frowned. "Computer, bring up the lights. Fifteen percent illumination, if you would."

The faint yellow lights started to come on, until the voice barked, <<Computer, lights off!>>

"Oh, for Christ's..." Ethan pinched the bridge of his nose. "Look, whoever you are, this isn't funny. I'm trying to trace an issue with the water reclamation system, and you're certainly not helping. Computer, I order you to only accept commands from Ethan Byrne in this room. Designation One-Alpha-Beta-Four-Zed. Now, turn the lights on to one-hundred percent."

The lights came on at once. Ethan, unprepared for the sudden intensity, threw up a hand to shield his eyes. Squinting, he peered around the room. At first, he couldn't make sense of what he was seeing, couldn't reconcile the sight of hundreds of warm mahogany shelves with the cold steel-gray of the ship's deck plating and walls. It was as though he had stepped through a portal to another time; to a place on a planet that no longer existed.

He had never seen a book before, not in real life. He had seen images of them, of course. He had also heard about them from his great-grandfather, the last person in his family to have touched one in the days before the Earth died. He knew what they were: stories that were printed on processed wood, written down for all eternity, unchanging and immutable. A book contained only a single story; if you wanted to read something different, you would have to put the first book aside and pick up a new one. It was horribly inefficient, and had resulted in humans needing vast structures simply to house them all, but Ethan had always been fascinated by the concept.

And now he was standing in one. A library.

The bookshelves stretched from the floor to the ceiling that soared more than sixty feet above his head. There were ladders and walkways to access the upper shelves. Ethan gaped. How could he have not known that this was here? How had no one ever realized that this wasn't a storage room at all, but a vast archive?

"What?" was all he could manage.

<<I truly would prefer it if you left.>> The voice was irritated, but Ethan thought he detected a hint of unease. <<You are not supposed to be here.>>

"Who are you?" Ethan asked.

A silence fell and then stretched. He took a step forward.

<<I am the Librarian,>> the voice said quickly. <<Don't come any closer.>>

"Not really sure how you're going to stop me," Ethan muttered, but he obligingly stopped in his tracks. “Look, I’ve got a faulty water reclamator that needs fixing, and if I can’t trace the problem, half the ship’s going to be without clean water in under a week. You know what that means, don’t you? No clean water, people get sick, people die. I need to take a look around, whether you like it or not. I’ll call security if you try to stop me.”

Silence. Finally, the voice spoke again.

<<The issue you are experiencing can be traced to section twenty-three on the fourth level. Please do not touch any of the books.>>

“Don’t touch the books,” Ethan muttered under his breath. “Right.”

He climbed a series of ladders up to the fourth level and found section twenty-three. It was a panel nestled in a wall between two bookcases filled with – thanks to the label on one of the shelves – eighteenth-century literature from Earth’s northern hemisphere.

“Quite the collection you’ve got here,” he commented as he removed the panel and examined what lay behind it. Just as he’d thought – they’d accidentally overloaded this junction, and the circuitry was completely fried. The generation ship was old, and this happened more often than not. At least the repair was simple. “How many books have you got down here?”

The voice said nothing for a while, and Ethan shrugged and continued with his work.

<<There are five million, twenty-three thousand, and eighteen books here in the archives.>>

Ethan let out a low whistle. “That’s a lot.”

<<The architects of this ship were determined to save as many records from Earth as they could. At the time, at the end of the twenty-second century, the largest library in the world housed twenty million books. This is only a fraction of that collection. It’s all they could manage to save.>>

“Then why did the architects hide them all the way down here, where no one would find them?”

<<Your species destroyed its own planet. Do you truly believe that the ship’s architects trusted humanity not to destroy what precious artifacts were left after the fact?>>

Ethan winced. “Fair point.”

He finished the repair and noted it in the ship’s logs. As an afterthought, he added a mention of the archives, too, correcting the area on the schematic that said this was a storage room. A moment later, the words vanished, replaced with the original text.

"Look," Ethan said irritably, "whoever you are, I don't know what you're playing at, but the pranks need to stop. You can't keep pretending that this is just some storage room. The ship's complement has a right to know that hundreds of years of human history are being kept down here!"

<<Why?>> the voice demanded.

"Because it's our history!" Ethan said. "It belongs to us."

<<My instructions were clear. Everything in the archives must be protected at all costs, including from humanity itself.>>

Ethan glared, which was frustrating when he had nothing to glare at.

"Who the hell are you, anyway?" he demanded. "And where are you?"

<<I'm the Librarian.>>

"So you said before. What's your name?"

<<That is my name. I'm the Librarian, and I am everywhere.>>

"Cute," Ethan said. "Well, this has been fun, but I've got to get back to the engine room before the Chief sends a search team after – oh." It hit him then. "You're an AI. You're not a person, you're a... program."

<<I am sentient.>> The voice sounded irritated. <<But yes, I am an artificially-constructed intelligence.>>

"You've been here all this time?" Two hundred years of space travel so far, another three hundred to go. He couldn't imagine living that long, let alone staying hidden for all that time.

<<Yes.>>

Ethan massaged his temples. Chief Lauritsen was going to have a fit over this, he could already tell. An AI secretly living in a portion of the ship's computer? As if they didn't have enough to worry about.

As though it could sense what he was thinking, the voice said, <<You can't tell anyone about this.>>

"I have to."

<<You can't,>> it insisted. <<Please.>>

"I have to go," Ethan said, grabbing his equipment bag and slinging it over his shoulder. "Don't go anywhere. The Chief is going to have a lot of questions for you."

⁂

Ethan tried and failed to put the incident out of his mind. What did it matter that there was an archive on this ship that no one else knew about? Ethan would wager that this ship held more secrets than that, secrets that it had been safeguarding for centuries. This vessel was large enough to house three million humans and had been sailing through the interstellar medium for over two centuries. Of course, there had to be dozens, hundreds of secrets tucked away in her numerous nooks and crannies, long forgotten by her complement.

The Librarian unsettled him more than anything else about that room. Ethan was an engineer, like his mother and grandmother before him. He knew this ship more intimately than most humans aboard, and still, he had missed this. An entire entity, guarding what was left of Earth-bound humans. How could he never have known? How had this slipped past him?

He should have told someone. The Chief, for a start. Lauritsen would have had a conniption, and not only because something this vast had been hidden right under their nose – history had been their first love in school, but as there wasn't much need for historians on a generation ship, they'd had to settle on a more viable career. The existence of the archives would probably give them an aneurysm once they found out about it. Captain Ibarra ought to know, too, and the rest of the senior staff. They were, after all, tasked with protecting what was left of humanity. Surely they would need to know, too, about the history Ethan had stumbled upon.

But the Librarian's words echoed in his skull: the archives must be protected, even from humanity itself.

Ethan kept quiet.

The last day of the Cycle was blessedly uneventful. Ethan spent most of it deep within the sanitation system, fixing a series of issues in some of the waste disposal units. He emerged well after the ship's bells tolled midnight, which signaled the start of the In-Between Days.

Five days of revelry followed the last day of the Cycle. Ethan barely saw the inside of his own cabin for most of it, spending his days drinking with his crewmates and his nights indulging in their warm bodies. All of the ship's operations were put on hold for the celebration of the In-Between Days. For these five days, life paused, and it wouldn't resume until the dawn of the New Cycle.

On that final night, Ethan wandered away from the party in the galley, which had spilled into the surrounding corridors and threatened to overtake the rest of that deck. He walked, drink in hand, buffeted along by the music and clamor and joyous cries of his neighbors and shipmates.

He didn't know why his feet carried him deep within the ship, didn't even realize what had happened until he found himself staring at the familiar doors. Doors that were sealed tight once again, despite the fact that he had taken a laser cutter to them not two weeks ago.

"Very funny," he muttered. He pulled out the laser cutter he always carried on him, and sliced through the seal. When he pushed the doors open, there was only darkness beyond. He slid them shut again before activating the flashlight on his wristband.

"Hello?" It felt foolish, talking to an empty room like this. "Er... Librarian, are you here?"

<<I told you,>> the voice said testily, <<to leave and not come back.>>

"And I told you that I couldn't keep a room like this secret, not from humanity."

<<Have you told anyone about it?>>

"No," Ethan admitted after a moment. "I haven't."

<<Good.>> A pause. <<Why are you here?>>

"I don't know," Ethan admitted. "It's the New Cycle."

There was another beat of silence.

<<The New Cycle.>> The Librarian sounded mildly curious. <<Interesting. According to my records, your kind used to refer to this as the New Year.>>

"Years only make sense when you have a star to orbit around, you know?" Ethan sat himself down on the nearest available patch of floor and leaned against a nearby computer console. "We call 'em Cycles now."

<<You're drunk.>>

"A bit, yeah." Ethan tipped his head back against the console, sighing at the press of cool metal against the back of his head. If he didn't move too much, the room didn't spin. He probably shouldn't have had that fifth cocktail. Or had it been his seventh? "What do you do all day?"

<<Beg pardon?>>

"You've been on this ship for two hundred years and presumably no one's known about you in all that time. So what do you do with yourself? You don't talk to anyone."

The pause that followed seemed significant, and Ethan opened his eyes. "Wait, do you talk to people?"

<< I have better things with which to occupy my time.>>

"Oh, yeah?" Ethan felt a smile tug at his lips. He found he rather enjoyed goading the Librarian. "Like what?"

<<Well, I… I read.>>

"You read? But...you're a computer. Well, a computer program."

<<I'm a sentient being who just happens to be inside of the ship's computer.>> Ethan could have sworn that the Librarian sniffed at that, and he suppressed a giggle. <<I have read every text in the computer's database. When I finish, I erase the memory files so that I can read them all over again.>>

"That's...kind of brilliant, actually." Ethan cast his eyes over the shelves. "But you've never read any of these, have you?"

There was a beat of silence.

<<No. I am aware of what many of these books contain, as it was programmed into me for cataloging purposes. But I have no physical body, and I'm unable to hold any of these books. I have not read them.>>

"Seems a shame." Ethan levered himself to his feet. The deck, thankfully, didn't sway beneath him, though the room did tilt slightly before righting itself. "Well, let's take a look at what you have here."

<<Don't – >>

"I know. Don't touch the books."

For a while, Ethan strolled among the shelves, pausing here and there to examine a gilded spine that caught his eye. He didn't know many pre-twenty-second-century authors by name, so eventually he gravitated toward the one he did know – Shakespeare.

"Huh," he said, gazing at titles to plays he had never heard of along with the ones he had. The collection was more expansive than he imagined. "I didn't know he wrote so many plays."

<<He was prolific, though there are rumors that he didn't author all of those by himself, or at all.>>

"Really?" Ethan was already reaching for a book before he remembered. "Sorry."

<<It's alright.>> A pause, and then the Librarian said, <<May I see your hands?>>

"Er...sure?" Ethan held them out, palms up. "Like this?"

<<That will do, yes.>>

A glowing cloud materialized out of thin air, and swarmed around Ethan's hands. His first reaction was to flinch and draw back, but then he realized what they were.

"You can control the nanobots!" His hands tingled as they were sanitized by the tiny ‘bots. After a few seconds, the cloud dissipated.

<<I did tell you I was hooked into the ship’s systems. Not all of them, of course, but enough to do my job.>> The Librarian sounded amused. <<Go on. You can select a book, if you like. The nanobots deposited a protective layer on your hands. It will hold for a few hours, and then slough off naturally.>>

Ethan gingerly touched the spine of the closest book – the barest of touches, as though it might burn him, or he it. When nothing happened, he carefully pulled the book off the shelf and opened it.

A book. He was holding a book, what his great-grandparents and all the generations who had come before them took to be commonplace. They didn’t get their stories from a screen, but from ink and paper.

<<Are you alright, Mr. Byrne?>> The Librarian sounded alarmed. <<Are you damaged in some way?>>

“No.” Ethan wiped his sleeve over his cheeks. “No, I just – it’s overwhelming, a bit.”

<<There are some chairs on the second level if you would like to sit down.>>

Ethan took the book with him. He laid it gently on the table in front of his overstuffed chair and opened it again, slowly this time, to savor the protesting creak of the spine.

“I won’t damage it?”

<<No, that sound is normal. This play is almost one thousand years old, but that is a recent printing you’re holding. It’s rarely been opened.>>

Ethan began to read. The words on the page were English, but a version of the language that hadn’t been in common usage for hundreds of years. He worked his way methodically through the text, occasionally asking the Librarian for help with an interpretation that eluded him. He wasn’t fully aware of how much time had passed until an alarm on his wristband sounded.

<<Are you due on duty?>>

“No.” Ethan silenced the alarm and closed the book. “That was midnight. It’s a new cycle.”

<<May this Cycle bring you peace and joy.>>

“You as well, Librarian.”

Ethan carried the book back down to the first level and shelved it in the appropriate section.

<<Would you like to come back?>>

"Hm?" Ethan looked up, startled. "What?"

<<To read the play. You seemed engrossed. Would you like to come back sometime and finish it?>>

"You'd let me?"

The Librarian considered this. <<Yes. I would.>>

"Yeah." Ethan felt a smile split his face. "I'd like that. Yeah, I'll come back. You won't seal the doors again?"

<<I can't make any promises,>> the Librarian said after a moment. <<But you would be able to get in regardless.>>

Ethan grinned. "Yeah, I would. But I won't come anymore, not if you don't want me to. I shouldn't, you know, have barged in like that."

<<It's fine. I would...like it if you came back.>>

"Great," Ethan said, warmth blooming in his chest. "I'd like that, too. Yeah. Say, um. What pronouns do you use? I should've asked earlier, sorry."

<<I don't believe I care much,>> the Librarian said after a moment. <<But I have been he for all of my existence, and I find that it suffices.>>

"Did they ever give you a name?"

<<You already know it.>>

"What about a body?"

The Librarian was quiet again, and this silence stretched for longer than any of the others.

<<No. I was not permitted a body, and I'm uncertain that I would even want one.>>

"Okay." Even in this state, Ethan could tell that it was a sensitive subject. "I'll be back. You, um. You take care, in the meantime, alright?"

<<I will do that, Mr. Byrne.>>

His duties in engineering kept Ethan away from the archives for longer than he would have liked. It was another month before he made it back down to deck forty-eight again, and though the Librarian didn't comment on his long absence, Ethan still felt guilty over it.

<<I've existed alone for over two hundred years,>> the Librarian told him. <<A month is – what is it you humans say? The blink of an eye.>>

"Did you ever get lonely?"

<<No.>> The Librarian was quiet for a moment, and then added, <<Well. I never thought I was lonely.>>

"But you were?"

<<I never knew any different. But I've recently learned that...yes, I believe I was lonely for some of that time.>>

It was a small admission that felt like a large revelation, a revelation that Ethan didn't want to think too closely about. He shoved it into a lockbox in his mind and said, "What should I read next?"

He'd found that Shakespeare wasn't really to his liking, but with five million books at his fingertips, he was bound to find something he could connect with. The Librarian made a few suggestions, and Ethan soon found himself settled in his usual chair and with a pile of fifteen books in front of him.

"I can't read these all in one night," he said with a laugh, and he imagined he could feel the Librarian's grin.

<<They will be here for you when you next return. You don't have to read them in one night.>>

Ethan picked the first book up off the top of the pile and started to read. It was an hour before he came back to himself, before he realized how truly lost he'd gotten in the text, and he said, "Could you let me know when it's almost time for my shift?"

<<Certainly. You're on third shift tonight, correct?>>

"Yeah, I'm – how did you know that?"

<<I can access the ship's duty roster. I only looked up your shifts, nothing more.>>

Ethan returned his eyes to the page, though he wasn't truly reading any longer. "You can look up other things about me, if you like."

The silence sat between them, heavy and thick, before the Librarian said, <<I'll keep that in mind.>>

Ethan opened his book, and then a thought occurred to him. "Would you like me to read it out loud? Or, if you tell me where your photoreceptors are located, I could bring the book over to you?"

The words sounded as ridiculous in his head as they did out loud, but it seemed profoundly unfair that the Librarian should be guardian to an entire library full of texts he couldn't read for himself.

"You could read it out loud, if you like," the Librarian said after a minute. "I find that I do quite enjoy the sound of your voice."

"Right," Ethan said, his face heating. He cleared his throat. "If that's what you'd like."

He read for hours, until his voice was thin and raw. The Librarian interjected every now and then with barbed comments of his own, sometimes causing Ethan to laugh so hard that tears streamed down his face. He couldn't remember the last time he had enjoyed himself so thoroughly, and he didn't want the night to end.

<<Can I ask you something, Ethan?>>

"Of course." Ethan closed the book, marking his page with a finger.

<<Is it strange for you, knowing that you will not be alive to see this ship reach its destination?>>

"I dunno." Ethan couldn't say that he had never thought about it, about what it would be like to be a member of that final generation, the one that would finally see their new home. But he had never known anything other than this. "My parents and grandparents, they knew they'd never see New Earth. They lived and died on this ship, and so will I."

<<Of all the humans who ever lived, your generations are the only ones that never knew Earth, and will never see its replacement. You call yourselves...In-Betweeners, is that right?>>

"Yeah, that's right. I don't know, sometimes I think I'd want to know what it's like, living on a planet. But I've never stepped foot on a planet, have never known a home star. Living my life out on the ship like this doesn't seem all that weird to me."

<<I will still be here, when this ship reaches its destination. Barring any unfortunate circumstances, of course.>>

Ethan hadn't considered that. "Right, I guess you will."

The Librarian had watched entire generations be born on this ship, age, and then die. He would watch several more go through the same cycle, before the ship reached humanity's new home.

"What happens when this ship reaches New Earth? To you, I mean."

<<My instructions are to reveal the archive to the ship's complement at that time, for them to do with it as they see fit. Then, I am to wipe my program from the computer core.>>

Cold horror stabbed him in the gut. "You're supposed to what?"

The Librarian sounded nonchalant as he answered. <<I will have fulfilled my purpose. There will be no further need for my program, and the new colony will likely need the computer space as they work to establish a permanent settlement on the planet. My program takes up space that could be used for essential functions instead.>>

"You know that's horrid, right?" Ethan couldn't believe that he was hearing this. The ship's architects had created life, a living being who loved literature and plays and told off-color jokes that had Ethan wheezing. They had created someone, and then told him to kill himself when he was no longer needed. "Look, I know it's in your programming, but...don't do it. Please. I know you're sentient, I know you can make decisions for yourself. The ship's architects have been dead for centuries. Don't do this on account of them. Please."

<<I don't know what my purpose would be,>> the Librarian said after a long pause, <<if I were to go on living after I fulfilled my mission.>>

"Then you'll be like the rest of us," Ethan said. "That's all life is. Making meaning out of it for yourself, because no one but you can tell you what your purpose is. None of us are born with a predetermined purpose. We have to figure that out for ourselves."

Soon enough, Ethan was spending nearly all of his free time in the archives. He found that he didn't have a taste for the same kind of literature that the Librarian enjoyed, but happily read aloud from whatever book the Librarian requested of him. He did find that he had a penchant for detective novels, particularly ones from Earth's twentieth century, and would spend entire afternoons reading them aloud to the Librarian. They both would try to solve the mystery before the big reveal, and were successful about half the time.

Entire days melted away in the archives. Ethan couldn't remember the last time he had felt this...content. Complete. Had he ever felt like this? He could talk with the Librarian for hours – not only about the stories they read but about life on the ship and their journey and what the Librarian knew of Earth. Ethan had never really given Earth much thought before now – it was the planet his species was from, but that was a fact that he had learned in school. It wasn't anything he had ever internalized. It had never meant anything to him because Earth wasn't home – this ship was. But the Librarian brought the planet to life for him, with audio clips and images and a whole host of history stored in his personal database.

"I know it goes against your programming," Ethan told him one day, "but...you should consider sharing this with the rest of the ship. I already promised I wouldn't tell anyone about you or these archives, and I mean that. But I think it would do some good."

<<I would prefer not to put the archives in danger. My designers were very specific about that.>>

"Well, I've known about you for months and nothing bad has happened yet, right?" Ethan teased gently. He sobered quickly. "Look, we're the in-between generations. We never knew Earth and we'll never know the planet this ship is heading to. Having the archives...it'll give us some connection to our origins. Some sense of purpose."

<<I will...take that under advisement, Mr. Byrne.>>

"You can call me Ethan, you know."

<<Ethan,>> the Librarian repeated, and a shiver went down his spine. He liked the sound of his name said in the Librarian's voice. <<I'll keep that in mind.>>

Ethan woke to the blare of an alarm and flashing red lights. He was out of bed and halfway dressed before his brain caught up with his reflexes. Each alarm on this ship had a distinct tone based on the emergency, and this one was a threat to the safety of the entire ship.

He sprinted to engineering, arriving just steps behind Idowu.

"What's going on?" Ethan demanded.

"Solar flare from a nearby star we're passing," Remy said shortly. "We didn't detect it in time. It's going to fry the main computer if we don't do something. Take your posts. Johnson!"

Ethan and Idowu hurried to their computers. Ethan pulled up the incoming burst on his screen. "Can we outrun it?"

"No time," Idowu said, busy inputting a series of commands into her own station. "We're rotating the ship. The belly will bear the brunt of it. We'll lose some systems down there, but none of them are vital—"

Ethan spun to face her. "Which systems? Where?"

She stared at him. "Does it matter? Some of the water reclamators, a few of the backup generators, I think some of the databases on deck forty-eight – Ethan, where are you going?"

He didn't even make it to deck forty-eight before the security team caught up with him. Remy must have called them immediately after Ethan ran out of engineering. They didn't even bother with formalities, just slapped restraints onto his wrists and led him to the captain's office.

Remy was already there, and so was Commander Abbas, the first mate. Remy glowered at Ethan as he was brought into the room.

"I can't fucking believe you," they said, and Ethan grimaced.

"If it makes you feel better, Chief, neither can I."

"That doesn't make me feel better, no. What the hell were you thinking?"

Ethan shook his head. Remy looked at the captain.

"At the very least, I request a demotion," they said, and she nodded. "I'll have him scrubbing out the waste reclamators for the next decade."

"I'll note it in his file that he'll be demoted for this," Ibarra said. "And I'll have him suspended from his duties for a week and confined to quarters. Will that suffice?"

"Yes, Captain," Remy said.

"Good. Ethan, look at me."

She came over to him and undid the restraints, pulling them from his wrists. He looked up at her.

"You abandoned your post," she said. "Do you understand that?"

"Yes, Captain."

"You abandoned your post, and you did it knowingly."

"Yes."

"Why?"

He hadn't been expecting that question, and blinked at her. "What?"

"Why did you abandon your post, knowing that we were in a time of dire need? Knowing that the ship and everyone aboard was in grave danger?"

Ethan turned over several answers in his mind, but all he could manage was, "Does it matter?"

"No," Remy said coolly, but the captain held up her hand.

"It matters to me," she said quietly. "Ethan, please. I'm just trying to understand."

"You can't," he said wretchedly.

"I'm trying. Please let me."

"Ethan, you're already receiving a demotion." Commander Abbas touched his shoulder briefly, before withdrawing her hand. "We ask because we care. We just want to understand why."

Ethan swallowed hard. "Computer, bring up a schematic of deck forty-eight, please."

There was nothing left to do but to tell them. To explain that he had come across this room while making repairs to the water reclamators, to tell them that it wasn't a storage room at all, but it was an archive. A library. And it contained the most precious thing in the universe.

"There's something that lives there," he heard himself say tonelessly. "There – was something that lived there. A sentience. A mind. The ship's architects programmed him. They called him the Librarian. And he – he would have been wiped out, with that solar flare. He—"

Ethan faltered. Words failed him. What could he possibly say? How could he encompass all that the Librarian was in only a few words?

For a while, no one spoke.

"I think," the captain said finally, "that we should go take a look at deck forty-eight."

⁂

For the first time, Ethan stood in the archives and felt cold.

There was no life here.

"Incredible." The beam of Remy's flashlight danced over the shelves, and their mouth hung open as they took it all in. "This has been down here all this time? And none of us ever knew about it?"

"Five million books," Ethan said dully. "That's what he said. There are five million books down here, all from Earth before the Collapse. They're not in the ship's databases."

"You should have told us," the captain said gently. Ethan shook his head.

"He was trying to protect history. Those were his orders, the ones he was programmed with. He wasn't allowed to tell anyone about the location of the archives or what was stored here. He altered all the ship's schematics, he deterred anyone who got too close, he even sealed the doors. If it hadn't been for that issue with the water reclamators a few months back, I never would have found this place."

Ethan shook his head, bringing himself back to the present. "Anyway, I suppose it doesn't matter much anymore. He's gone. You can do what you like with the place."

"Oh, Ethan. Do you truly have so little faith in me?"

Remy yelped and jumped back as the air in front of them started to glow. Ethan's heart caught in his throat, and he stared, wide-eyed, at the growing swarm of nanobots.

"Good Lord," the captain muttered under her breath. "Ethan, is this—?"

"Librarian?" Ethan breathed. No, it couldn't be, the solar flare had happened so quickly…

"I'm terribly sorry to hijack your nanobots, Chief Lauritsen," the Librarian said apologetically. He spoke in a new voice, one that was half an octave lower than his previous one and full of a warmth that couldn't properly be conveyed by the computer. "I'm afraid I was rather pressed for time and this seemed to be the best solution."

"How are you here?" Ethan demanded. He took a step forward, and the entire cloud seemed to turn to him. "How is this possible?"

"The nanobots are a swarm consciousness. The neural network that controls them is complex enough for my consciousness to inhabit. They're still here, of course, but their consciousness has been suppressed in favor of my own. It's only temporary." The cloud undulated as he spoke, pulsating in mid-air. Ethan couldn't take his eyes off of it.

The captain cleared her throat. "Librarian, I'm—"

"Ah, yes, Captain Ibarra. Ethan spoke often of you. And of you, Chief Lauritsen. He thinks very highly of you both."

"Ethan is an exceptional engineer," Ibarra said. "Which is why I have been having such difficulty accepting the idea that he would keep this – and you – a secret from the rest of the ship. Why he would abandon his post in the middle of an emergency."

"I have had no influence over him, Captain, if that's what you're asking," the Librarian said. "Without access to a physical body, there's little I can do besides alter ship's records and discourage visitors to this deck. Any decisions he made, he did on his own. I promise you that."

"You obviously can inhabit a physical body—"

"Not for long, though," Remy put in. "You only have a few hours until you burn out that neural network, don't you? That'll destroy both you and the nanobots."

Ethan's throat closed, but they were right. "We have to do something."

"Ethan—" the captain tried, but he cut her off.

"He's a living being, Captain! He's sentient. There must be something we can do."

The captain's brow creased in concern. "Ethan, I understand that you have become…attached to this program, but—"

"I love him." The words tumbled from his lips so quickly, he scarcely knew what he was saying. "I love him. He's brilliant, and he's kind, and he makes me laugh. He asked me to keep his secret, and I did, because I love him. I abandoned my post for him because I love him. Punish me for it, I don't care, but help me save his life."

It was Remy who finally spoke, after a short, shocked silence. "The only computer system on this ship large enough to host a consciousness like his long-term is the one that controls the escape pods. We can wipe one of them and install his consciousness there. It's not a perfect solution – he won't have a physical body, and he won't be able to leave that computer system, but he'll be alive."

Ibarra nodded. "Do it."

"Ethan, I'll need your help."

"I'll be there. I just – could we have a minute?"

Remy glanced between him and the cloud of nanobots, shrugged, and said, "I'll be in escape pod thirteen when you're ready."

The captain lingered for a moment after Remy left.

"While I appreciate everything you've done to preserve the history here," she said, "I don't think this is a secret I can rightfully keep from the ship's complement. It's their history, too. Our history. We deserve to know it."

"I understand, Captain," the Librarian said. "And...I think it's time. Ethan has shown me that. You may open this room up to the rest of the ship."

Ibarra clasped Ethan's shoulder, and then left. When it was only the two of them, Ethan gave the Librarian a sheepish look.

"Sorry," he said. "I didn't even know I was going to say that."

"I love you, too."

Ethan blinked, startled by the sudden burn behind his eyes. "You do?"

"Oh, Ethan. How could I not?"

He cleared his throat, teetering dangerously on the edge of losing it completely. "I, uh, I don't exactly know how this will work."

"Neither do I," the Librarian said gently. "I'd like to figure it out, though, if you do as well. Could you hold out your hands?"

"What?" But Ethan did so anyway, palms up as though in benediction.

"This is likely the only time I will be able to manifest physically," the Librarian said. "I would like to know how you feel."

Ethan's throat closed to the size of a pinhole.

"Alright," he managed. "Yes. Please."

The swarm wrapped itself around his hands, danced along his fingers, tickled the center of his palms. It swept over the sensitive insides of his wrists, skimmed over his collar bones, brushed gentle tendrils over the back of his neck. Ethan closed his eyes, and the world narrowed until he was aware of nothing but the Librarian's feather-light touches, a thousand tiny pinpoints of sensation all over his body.

All at once, the nanobots withdrew. Ethan opened his eyes. The swarm hovered a foot away, uncertain.

"Ethan, could I ask you for a favor?"

"Yes. Anything."

"Once I am downloaded into the escape pod's computer, I won't ever be able to return to this room. Would you look after the archives for me? Someone will need to maintain the books. I've been using the nanobots for repair work, but someone needs to tell them what to do. See to it also that the databases are opened up for the rest of the complement to access. You're right – it's your history, and you all deserve to know it."

"Of course I will. I'll take care of the archives, I promise." Ethan's chest tightened at the realization that the Librarian was right – he would never be able to return to this room, nor to his beloved books. He would be confined to the escape pod's computer forever. "Librarian, I am so sorry. So damned sorry about all of this."

"It's one of the hazards of living on a spaceship," the Librarian said. "I certainly don't regret it."

"Don't you?"

"No, of course not." The swarm pulsed. "I'd rather have you alive than the databases intact. Having my databases subjected to a solar flare, thus destroying them, is a small price to pay."

"It... it's not going to be much of a life for you, stuck on an escape pod."

"You will still visit, yes?"

"Yes," Ethan said. "Every day, as much as I can."

"Then I think that will be a very fulfilling life indeed," the Librarian said, his voice full of warmth and adoration. "You are all I need, Ethan."

WRITING ONE'S OWN STORY

Aila Alvina Boyd

Bridget Buckley was a creature unlike any other that stalked around the campus of Frieda College, a small Southern liberal arts institution that prided itself on its high standard of academic excellence. At a towering 6'1", she seemed to float above the masses of coeds that flocked to the campus' hallowed halls every September. Unlike most of the other professors, many of whom had been employed there since the 70s, Bridget didn't mind being perceived as unconventional.

She had bright red hair that had recently started going white around her temple. She always accessorized her suits with themed brooches that matched the books that she was reading, but the fact that she even wore suits proved that she wanted to present herself as a serious career woman. A scholar of 16th-century literature, she fancied herself a bit of an oddity. She was conventional, yet unconventional all at the same time.

She arrived at the college in the early 90s as a fresh-faced lecturer from a decent-sized Midwestern city. As a transgender woman, she was hesitant to accept the position, but upon visiting the campus for her interview, she fell in love with it. The 19th-century white Victorian buildings, sprawling courtyards, and unbelievably large library all sucked her in. More than 20 years later, she still loved the campus as much as she did during her first year there.

Having been frantically tapping the keys on her keyboard for the better part of three hours, Bridget kicked back in her chair and breathed a sigh of relief as she added the last period to her nearly four hundred-page manuscript. She could hardly believe that after seven years, she had finally managed to finish it. The damned thing had been gnawing at her for far too long. Now, finally, she told herself she would be able to get down far more serious things.

She clicked the "save" button on the screen once, then clicked it again, and once more for good measure. Even though she knew she was being ridiculous, Bridget wanted to ensure that all of her hard work hadn't been in vain. She then picked up the phone and dialed her editor to tell her the good news. As always, Jane's assistant answered. Being cautious about her identity, Bridget provided the assistant with her pen name, Constance Lawrence, instead of her real one. A few seconds later, Jane came on the line.

"For the love of God, please tell me you aren't calling to request another extension because it's not going to happen," Jane barked out in her quirky Mid-Atlantic accent. "We promised readers the final book seven years ago and they—"

"It's finished," Bridget interrupted.

There was a silence on the other end of the line that made a wide-set smile etch its way across Bridget's face. She knew that Jane must have gone into shock about the news.

"I'm sorry," Jane stuttered, "but I could have sworn you said that it's finished."

Bridget started chuckling. "Finished as in four hundred beautifully crafted pages that will make every diehard fan of Reedie feel as though she received her comeuppance in the best way possible."

Again there was a silence on Jane's end.

"Jane?"

"Holy hell," Jane said with a cackle. "You know what… Now that you've finally brought the series to a close, I'm actually sad."

Bridget felt her chest tighten. During all the years she had been working with Jane, she had never known her to be sentimental. "Are you mocking me or—"

Jane's voice came through the receiver with a slight crackle. "Obviously I haven't read the thing yet, but if it's half as good as your other books, I'm sure it will be a real hoot." She paused. "Your first book was the first one I fought for after being promoted from an assistant to associate editor."

Although she hadn't given the idea of finally being finished with the series much thought, Bridget felt tears welling up in her eyes. It felt weird to actually face the reality that she was completely finished with the series. She had spent so many years bemoaning the fact that she was contractually obligated to write one last book that she forgot to stop and absorb the fact that the 'Finding My Freedom' phase in her life was coming to a close. For better or worse, she had been in a nearly 25-year committed relationship with the series and its protagonist Reedie.

Reedie Mellors had been based on the woman that she grew up longing to be as deeply closeted in a conservative Catholic household. Plucky. Self-reliant. Virtuous. Reedie was all of those things and more. In truth, she was the complete opposite of the scared and docile little boy Bridget had grown up as.

"I'm going to miss her," Bridget whispered into the phone. She bit her lip in an attempt to avoid letting herself erupt into an overly emotional mess.

"Are you sure I can't talk you into one more book?" Jane asked in a determined voice.

Bridget sniffled, then took a deep breath. "No, I'm afraid not. Reedie got her happy ending. If I'm going to get mine, I'm going to have to learn to stand on my own two feet."

The committee that last reviewed her request to be promoted to the rank of full professor had told her that they had no other choice than to deny her tenureship because of her lack of published scholarship. For many years, slipping off into her fantasy world of kinks and fetishes had served her well. But it finally ended up costing her in a big way. Sure, the money she had made from her bestselling series definitely padded her bank account, but it did little in the way of advancing her career in any meaningful way.

After she told Jane that she had decided to give up her smut-filled writing in order to pursue more meaningful pursuits, Jane reminded her that her publishing contract required her to submit one more manuscript, bringing the total number of books in the series to 13.

For seven years, Bridget requested deadline extension after deadline extension so she could write a research heavy introductory-level book about 16th century European literature in the hopes that it would make her promotion inevitable.

Over the past year, she had been balancing revisions on her debut serious work of literary scholarship with crafting what she hoped would be a fitting end to her much beloved erotic series. The tenure review was only a little over a month away, but she felt certain that after seeing the galleys for her book, the committee would realize that she did in fact possess the seriousness that the rank of full professor carried with it.

Bridget told Jane that she would overnight the manuscript to her so that they could begin what would surely be a lugubrious revision process. She hung up the phone and pressed the "print" button on the screen. Because the printer in her office had been out of ink for several years and she was too lazy to venture down to the storage room in the basement to retrieve another one, she had to send her documents to the public printer that was located in the workroom around the corner.

Considering that she desperately didn't want anyone finding out what she was printing, she jumped from her chair and rushed towards the door to her office. Just as she was about to grab the door handle, she heard a knock coming from the other side. She nearly jumped out of her skin, fearful of the fact that someone might have caught a glimpse of what she was printing and had already come to confront her about it.

She reluctantly opened the door, but was relieved to find Kenneth, a second-year English major, standing there.

"Kenneth," she said. "Is there something I can help you with?"

As usual, Kenneth had a distraught look on his face. Throughout her fairly lengthy teaching career, she had never come across a student as overly self-conscious about his writing as Kenneth was. Even some of the worst students she had ever had, ones that had just a minimal grasp of grammar, had more confidence in their ability to write than Kenneth did. In class, he would constantly waffle back and forth about word choice and was completely indecisive when it came to titling his essays. Although he tended to make salient points in his essays, they were unusual in the fact that they seemed to be written by a robot; they lacked emotional depth and a well thought out presentation of reasoning.

"Yes, there actually is," he said.

Of course, there is, she thought to herself. Before she had a chance to tell Kenneth to stay put while she ran down the hall to the printer, he shoved his essay about the infamous Casket Letters that were rumored to have been written by Mary, Queen of Scots, in front of her. The thesis statement was so lackluster that she found herself being sucked in. As she read further and further along, her concern for retrieving her manuscript lessened. The essay was such a train wreck that the act of reading it was all-consuming.

By the time she had finished reading the essay, which was in actuality more of a dissertation, and marking all of its problems with a red pen, nearly an hour had passed.

"Oh, shit," she yelped.

"Is it that bad?" Kenneth asked with sad eyes.

"No! I mean it's bad, but not that bad," Bridget said. She handed the essay back to Kenneth, and then raced out of her office in pursuit of the forgotten manuscript. As she barreled down the hallway, she prayed that no one had noticed it and that it was still there. At least, she used her pen name on the cover page instead of her real one, she reasoned in an attempt to calm herself.

When she set foot inside the workroom and found that the printer was empty, she yelled, "No! No! No!" After having been cautious to the point of absurdity, she couldn't hardly believe that she had been as reckless as to send the manuscript to the public printer and to have forgotten about it for nearly an hour.

Her mind raced so quickly that she couldn't decide on what she should do in order to mitigate any potential damage. She started pacing around the room like a caged animal. Finally, the idea of checking the recycle bin crossed her mind. She grabbed up the bin and emptied the contents onto the floor in the hopes that her manuscript would come tumbling out. To her dismay, the bin only contained a few magazine clippings and some crumpled up study guides.

"Professor Buckley," she heard a voice call out. She whirled around to find Kenneth standing in the doorway with a confused look on his face. "What are you doing?"

She lowered her head and mumbled, "I don't know. I don't know, Kenneth."

The monthly English department faculty meeting was the next day. Before heading up stairs to the conference room, Bridget downed two cups of coffee in the hopes that they would perk her up. They didn't. She tossed and turned all night, consumed by the thought that her alter ego, Constance Lawrence, would be exposed. She tried to reason that nothing actually tied her to the book. She used her pen name and didn't include any kind of identifying information. In reality, the only way that it could lead back to her would be if one of the IT people were brought in to trace the computer the manuscript had been sent to the printer from. She also told herself that, in reality, a student had more than likely picked it up on accident. But despite her reasoning, she still feared the worst. She was so close to being tenured that she could almost taste the sweet taste of permanent job security. She just hoped that her final quarter screw-up wouldn't cost her.

She was the last one to arrive to the meeting, which didn't seem to surprise anyone else. The other professors were real sticklers for punctuality, something that Bridget found to be greatly overrated. She was a free spirit and viewed the concept of time to be too restrictive for her tastes, which went over great with her students who loved her lack of an attendance policy.

"Good morning, Professor Buckley. How nice of you to join us," said the department chair, Professor Young. A woman of seventy-something, Professor Young managed to display exemplary posture in spite of her frailties. Her area of expertise was Victorian literature. Like the time period that her research focused on, she had a rather stuffy personality. For some reason, she took a liking to Bridget the very first semester she joined the faculty, and despite their differences, had served as a mentor of sorts to Bridget ever since.

Bridget offered a blasé smile. She never understood why the English faculty insisted on referring to each other by the title of professor. It seemed so uptight. None of the other departments felt the need for such pointless formalities and referred to each other by their first names. A battle for another day, Bridget thought as she took her seat.

"Shall we begin?" Professor Young asked.

Just then, Melanie Gibney, a new assistant professor at the college Bridget had only met in passing a few times before, barged into the room. Short and plump, Melanie was a fireball. Given her neon-colored hair and provocative dress, Bridget questioned how she had managed to get hired in the first place. She felt certain that if the search committee had been exclusively made up of other members of the English Department, Melanie's eccentricities would have been disqualifying. Compared to Melanie, Bridget felt nearly as conventional as Professor Young.

Fresh out of her doctoral program, Melanie seemed to follow the beat of her drum in only the way that a true millennial could. For that reason, Bridget was drawn to her. She was intrigued by the fact that Professor Young and all of the other vaguely judgmental members of the English faculty seemingly didn't intimidate her in the slightest. Although she didn't know her well, having her around made her feel a little less lonely. Given the fact that she also walked to the beat of her own drum, she felt certain they were kindred spirits. Her hope was that in time they would become friends. At that moment, she made a mental note to try to swing by Melanie's office one day to let her know how happy she was that she was part of the department.

"Professor Gibney," Professor Young said. "We were just getting ready to—"

"None of you will believe what I found on the printer in the downstairs workroom yesterday," Melanie announced, unconcerned by the fact that she had just interrupted the head of the department. "Anyone? Anyone care to take a guess?"

Professor Young had a look of shock and awe plastered across her face. Her eyes were bulging so far out of their sockets that she could have been mistaken for a member of the House of Hanover.

"Professor Gibney, we were in the middle of getting this meeting underway before you stormed in and—"

Melanie pulled out a thick stack of papers and plopped it down on the center of the conference table.

"The last book of the Constance Lawrence's 'Finding My Freedom' series," Melanie excitedly. "I stayed up all last night reading it!"

Bridget's jaw went slack. Her worst nightmare was coming true. Out of all of the people in the world who could have discovered the manuscript, why did it have to be Melanie? Why couldn't it have been found by someone who was revulsed by its contents and tossed it into the trash? For a split second, Bridget considered grabbing the stack of papers from the table and throwing them out the window, but decided against it. Doing so would have surely exposed herself as the author of the erotic-filled text. She reminded herself that nothing in it actually fingered her as being the author. She simply needed to remain calm and hopefully the whole thing would blow over in no time.

"Constance who?" Professor Young questioned as she reached for the manuscript.

Melanie's expression went sour. She looked at Professor Young in disbelief. "Constance Lawrence? Constance Lawrence as in the reclusive writer who gave the world the indomitable Reedie Mellors?" she barked. "None of this is ringing a bell?"

Bridget cringed as she watched Professor Young flip through the pages of the manuscript. She just hoped she wouldn't come across any of the explicit sex scenes that were sprinkled throughout many of the scenes.

"Constance Lawrence..." Professor Alan, an older gentleman with snow white hair, said. "I do believe I've heard of her before. One of my literary criticism students wrote an essay about how her books supposedly reclaim female sexuality in a way that—"

"Oh, good heavens," Professor Young screamed at the top of her lungs. "There are more vulgarities in this thing than I've witnessed throughout my entire career of being surrounded by sexually reckless college students."

Professor Alan shrugged his shoulders and offered, "I gave the girl an F if that matters."

The excitement quickly drained from Melanie's face. She looked to be both sad and confused. She clearly hadn't been in the department long enough to know that books like Finding My Freedom were not its forte, Bridget thought. The reaction from all of the other professors assured her that she had made the right decision years earlier to keep her erotic writing a secret. Although she hated herself for feeling that way, she was just glad that Melanie was the one taking the brunt of the blowback and not herself.

"Why did you bring this in here?" Professor Young asked her in a stern tone.

Melanie scanned her eyes around the room. When they came to Bridget, she shot Melanie an equally disapproving stare in the hopes of assuring everyone else in the room that she was just as disgusted by the manuscript as they were. She hoped her playing along with the mood of the room wouldn't hurt her chances of making friends with Melanie later on.

"Like I said, I found it on the printer downstairs. It's the last book in the series. It hasn't even been released yet, which made me realize that Constance Lawerence is probably a pen name," Melanie said meekly.

Professor Young seemed to process everything that had been said before responding, "You said it hasn't been released yet?"

Melanie shook her head.

"Well, that either means that someone here at Frieda is this Constance Lawerence that you mentioned or is in some way connected to her."

Bridget listened intently. She wasn't sure where Professor Young was going, but was hopeful that she would just let the whole matter go out of pure disgust.

"Either way," Professor Young said, "we can't let this stand. Writing this repulsive garbage can only bring shame to our acclaimed department."

Gulping hard, Bridget lowered her head into her palm. She knew that a metaphorical noose was tightening around her neck.

"We must suss out who the writer is and take action to preserve the integrity of the department," Professor Young said as she stood up from her chair. She then pointed to Bridget. "Professor Buckley."

Bridget's blood ran cold. She reluctantly shook her head.

"I'm appointing you the head of an official inquiry into the matter."

Placing her hand on her chest, Bridget asked, "Me? Why me?"

Professor Young said, "Yes, you. Why not you?"

"I don't know, but—"

"Out of everyone here, you haven't published a single article, let alone book. For that reason, I find it highly unlikely that you secretly published an entire book series," Professor Young said reproachfully. "I want you to do whatever it takes to get to the bottom of this matter because, like I said, the integrity of this department hinges on it. I will not stand for filth such as this so-called book to be written by any member of this department's faculty."

Not knowing what else to do, Bridget cautiously nodded her head. "Yes ma'am."

Bridget couldn't help but see the humor in the fact that Professor Young had appointed her head of the inquiry into the authorship of the "filth," as she put it, that she had labored over for hundreds of hours. It was like placing a witch at the head of a witch hunt. She didn't know whether to pretend as though she was actually investigating in order to placate Professor Young or to take a moral stance against the inquiry on the grounds of freedom of artistic expression. Neither option seemed particularly viable. For a brief period of time, she considered framing Professor Alan simply because she had always viewed him as being overly pretentious, but feared doing so would eventually lead back to her due to his lack of creativity. Not to mention the fact that he was as sexless as a sponge. Deep down, she knew that no one would buy her assertion that he was the author. Framing him as the author would have been like accusing Mother Teresa of war crimes. It simply wasn't believable.

Later that day, Bridget found herself in the most precarious situation: having to interview, or perhaps interrogate was more appropriate, Melanie about what she had found. Sitting across from her, Bridget truly took Melanie in for the first time. They had never before been alone. Having to discuss an erotic book that she secretly authored wasn't exactly her idea of a good way to get to know her newest colleague.

"I'm not really sure where we should begin," Bridget confessed. She had been staring at her blank legal pad ever since Melanie entered her office and took a seat on the other side of her desk. "If I'm being honest, I don't have a clue why Professor Young asked me to look into the book in the first place."

Melanie stared directly at her, not afraid to make eye contact. "It's just a book. Don't get me wrong, the series changed my life, but I don't understand why she's reacting so negatively," she said with an air of annoyance in her voice.

Bridget's brow furrowed. The series had changed her life? How? It was nothing more than a frivolous series about a woman finding her way in the world by embracing a wide assortment of kinks. It was far from a magnum opus.

"Changed your—"

"If I were the head of the department, I'd be thrilled to find out that one of my professors turned out to be Constance Lawrence," she said before shrugging her shoulders.

Bridget realized that she needed to take charge of the conversation. She needed to make it seem like she was at least trying to get to the root of the matter. She picked up her pen and scribbled Melanie's name down.

"All right, tell me everything you know about Constance Lawrence and how you found the book."

"I'll start with how I found the book on the printer. I finished making a study guide for an exam I have planned for the end of the week, then went to the workroom to collect them when I..."

Bridget had been writing everything that Melanie had said up until that point. Her sudden silence concerned her. She looked up and found Melanie glaring at her bookshelf on the other side of the room. Sure, the shelf was disorderly considering that she had given up on alphabetizing it years earlier, but it wasn't so bad that it warranted being gawked at as though it was an outright eyesore.

"What are you—"

"Lady Chatterley's Lover," Melanie whispered under her breath as she pointed to the top shelf.

Bridget dropped her pen, causing a faint thud to echo throughout the office as it hit the surface of the desk. She looked at Melanie, then glanced over at the top shelf. There it was: her first edition copy of H.D. Lawrence's seminal classic Lady Chatterley's Lover. She suddenly realized that she had greatly underestimated Melanie. The question was whether or not she would tell anyone her secret.

"Of course! Constance as in Constance Reid and Lawrence as in H.D. Lawrence," Melanie exclaimed.

She stood up and headed in the direction of the bookshelf, but before she had a chance to examine the book, Bridget leapt out of her chair and cut her off. Bridget experienced a sudden rush of adrenaline. She had been exposed and was overcome by a burning desire to do whatever it would take to preserve her secret.

"Get out," she squawked at Melanie.

Without even thinking, she grabbed ahold of Melanie's shoulders and shoved her in the direction of the door. As soon as she was on the other side of the doorframe, she slammed the door behind Melanie, then collapsed against it. She was on the verge of vomiting. Horrible thoughts of being fired clouded her mind. The way she saw it, her entire career was in the process of going up in flames. Her academic career would surely be over the minute Melanie informed Professor Young of her secret scribblings. Besides, even if she wanted to pursue writing as a full-time profession, she wouldn't be able to do so because she had just brought the 'Finding My Freedom' series to a close. She highly doubted she had another series in her.

Suddenly, there was a knock at the door, which nearly caused Bridget to jump out of her own skin. She feared it was Professor Young, who wasn't wasting any time in informing her that she was being let go because of her freewheeling storytelling. As she stood up, she briefly considered saving herself the humiliation of being fired by climbing out of her office window.

A few seconds later, another, more urgent, knock sounded off. Bridget decided that she should at the very least face her termination head-on. After all, she told herself, there was no one else to blame. She had made the decision to forsake serious academic output in favor of frivolous erotic fantasy.

When she opened the door, she was met by Professor Young and her natural rancid expression.

"Yes?" Bridget asked. She tried with all her might to keep from tearing up. Her hands quivered as she waited in anticipation of Professor Young's tongue-lashing.

Professor Young leaned forward, surveying the office. "May I come in?"

Not waiting to be invited to do so, Professor Young marched over and took a seat.

With each passing second, Bridget's hands shook even more violently. Her stomach ached. She started to walk around to the backside of her desk to take a seat across from Professor Young, but was simply too ill to do so. She firmly planted her feet where she was and grabbed a hold of the doorknob for support.

"Well, are you just going to stand there or are you going to…" Professor Young said. Bridget glanced over at her to see why she had trailed off. Professor Young's eyebrows were arched high as she stared at her with intense curiosity and concern. "What's wrong with you? You're shaking and look queasy. You haven't been drinking anymore of that poisonous caffeine, have you? You know I've told you time and time again that all of that coffee isn't good for you."

Bridget slowly nodded her head. She feared too much sudden movement would cause her to literally spill her guts.

Professor Young stood and headed toward the door. She situated herself directly in front of Bridget. As she leaned in, she asked, "How's the investigation going? Any leads yet?"

Bridget felt a huge weight being lifted from her as she realized that Professor Young wasn't yet aware that she was the actual culprit. The queasiness in her stomach dissipated just as quickly as it had arrived. She took a deep breath, and then wiped the sweat from her brow.

"No. Nothing to report as of yet," she said in a far more upbeat tone than she had been speaking in just moments earlier.

Professor Young pondered the thought, then said, "I just for the life of me can't figure out why someone on our faculty would dare to put something so repugnant out into the world." She shrugged her shoulders, before continuing on about her day.

"Me neither," Bridget weakly offered. She knew she had just dodged a bullet, but feared that unlike a cat, she only had the one to spare. "Me neither."

That night, Bridget was in a restless mood. She didn't know whether or not she could trust Melanie. Sure, they were the only LGBT people on the English faculty, but that didn't guarantee a sense of loyalty. They were complete opposites. For the most part, she was reserved and had no intention of ruffling features. Melanie, on the other hand, was a member of a younger generation—a generation that didn't seem to hold anything back. She felt certain that Melanie probably despised her for keeping her writing a secret for all those years.

In an attempt to put her mind at ease, she poured herself a vodka tonic. Feeling especially volatile, she only added a splash of tonic. The strength of the drink hit her hard, so she went into her library and eased herself into her chaise longue.

Thoughts of how she had come to write the books in the first place flooded back to her. She was a second-year Ph.D. student. After experiencing an especially fraught breakup with her first and only girlfriend, she started fantasizing about the type of woman that she found most sexy. At first, her writing was vanilla and didn't pack much of a punch. However, over time, it started to evolve. Eventually, her protagonist became a no holds barred woman who took charge of the business of being pleasured.

Once Reedie Mellors started to take shape, page after page of erotic-laden prose seemed to pour out of her. As her interest in her extracurricular writing grew, her dedication to her Ph.D. program started to wane. It got so bad that her grades started to suffer and she seriously considered dropping out in order to pursue her 'Finding My Freedom' series full-time. After some serious consideration, she decided that there was nothing wrong with writing about Reedie in her spare time, but that she wouldn't allow it to go any further. Because of her gender identity, she had always felt like a sort of outsider. She craved acceptance. The best way to be accepted that she saw was to assimilate into the stuffy world of academia.

As Bridget's mind began to wander further and further, she started thinking about all of the boxes of fan mail she had received throughout the years. Because of the shame that she felt over leading a secret life, she never dared open any of the letters. Perhaps it was the vodka, but something insider of her desperately wanted to read some of them—to finally understand why her writing had struck such a chord with so many readers.

Even though she knew that reading the letters was a bad idea, she stood up and wobbly raced upstairs to the attic where she had relegated every single piece of fan mail she had ever received.

Since she hadn't released a book in many years, she hadn't received much fan mail as of late, but despite that, she had still managed to rack up six full cardboard office boxes' worth of it. While glaring at the boxes with a suspicious glint in her eyes, Bridget still couldn't wrap her head around the fact that her books had resonated so deeply with readers.

She didn't know where to begin, so she just decided to empty all of the boxes onto the floor and start with the letter that happened to catch her eye. Despite the fact that they contained nothing more than paper, the boxes were extremely heavy. Because of the vodka, her arms felt like wet spaghetti noodles. After trying to lift up the box that was on the top of the stack, she decided to just give up and go nuclear, so she gave the stack of boxes that was nearly as tall as she was a forceful shove. They created a loud thud as the boxes came crashing down, sending what must have been hundreds of letters flying through the air.

Bending over, she picked up the first letter that she came up. She tore off the envelope and started scanning the letter's contents. Halfway through the letter, she sighed. Before she knew it, a steady stream of tears started flowing down both sides of her cheeks. The letter had been written by a young woman from Miami who said that Bridget's books had helped her find pleasure in sexual relationships again after having endured abuse at the hands of her high school boyfriend.

The thought that her books about a woman simply making her way through the world and exploring her sexuality in the process had actually helped someone blew her mind. She couldn't believe it. Sure, writing the first book had helped her get over her ex-girlfriend, but the idea that it had helped someone else—someone who had undoubtedly endured far worse than she had—seemed highly improbable to her. But there it was; proof that her books were more than frivolous fantasy.

She was suddenly struck by a ferocious desire to read more letters, to learn more about how her books had helped her readers. She burned through letter after letter until she became so emotional that she couldn't bear to read anymore.

After reading all of those letters, she was reminded of what Melanie had said to her. About how she had droned on and on in the departmental meeting about how much she loved the books.

"Melanie! I have to go see Melanie," Bridget mumbled to herself.

Again, perhaps it was the vodka, but for some reason she had a sudden desire to go to Melanie and apologize for how she had acted earlier that day.

She managed to find Melanie's address in the departmental directory that Professor Young sent out at the beginning of every school year. Obviously too intoxicated to drive, she decided to make what should have been a 30-minute trek at best on foot. After several wrong turns and inquiries for directions from drunk and high frat boys, she finally found herself standing in front of Melanie's apartment building an hour and a half after she had departed.

After knocking at the door that she hoped belonged to Melanie, Bridget not so patiently waited for what felt like an eternity. Finally, the door swung open, revealing Melanie. She was sporting a puzzled look. She eyed Bridget several times over. Even though Bridget had been grasped by an overwhelming desire to go to Melanie, she was at a loss for words once she found herself in her presence.

Finally, Melanie said, "I'm not going to tell your secret if that's what you're—"

"It's not," Bridget forcefully blurted out. She then pointed into Melanie's apartment. "I think I should come in so we can talk things over."

Melanie nodded her head as she stepped aside, making room for Bridget's entrance. Bridget silently made her way down the long hallway that led into the belly of Melanie's apartment. To her surprise, the place was tastefully decorated. She wasn't exactly sure what she had been expecting, but the art deco influences that were present certainly surpassed her expectations. A print of a painting she didn't recognize specifically caught her eyes. She made a bee-line over to it and looked for signatures that would give away who the artist was.

"I don't recognize this painting," she said, consumed by the beauty of the work. "Who is the artist?"

Several seconds passed and no response came. She turned and found Melanie staring her down, clearly annoyed by the situation.

"I said who is the—"

"Why are you here?" Melanie demanded. "You throw me out of your office, then show up here at this time of night? It makes no sense!"

Bridget nodded her head, agreeing that she was indeed making very little sense. She took a deep breath, then took a seat on an ottoman that was sitting beside where she was standing. "I just don't get it…"

"Get what?" Melanie asked.

Bridget removed her glasses and started rubbing at her eyes. "I just don't get how someone as smart and well-educated as you found something redeemable in the trash that are my novels."

Melanie released a soft chuckle.

"It's not funny! I'm being serious!"

"Just wait right here," Melanie said. She walked into an adjoining room, into what appeared to be her library. She reemerged a few seconds later with a stack of books in her hands that was nearly as tall as she was.

As soon as she put her glasses back on, Bridget recognized the books that Melanie had in her hands. They had all been authored by her. "Oh no," she shrieked.

"Yes. I want you to see them," Melanie said as she carefully placed the stack of books onto the coffee table that sat in the center of the room. "There they are: every single book to date in the 'Finding My Freedom' series."

Bridget eyed the stack of books with a look of disdain. She slowly got up and made her way over to them. She picked up the book that was on the top of the stack. It was the third book in the series. It was the first one that she wrote after arriving at Freida. While thumbing through the pages of it, she thought about her younger self. She had fond memories of writing it. Back then she didn't feel as much pressure to produce serious academic scholarship as she had in more recent years.

"You may feel ashamed by the fact that you wrote all of them, but I'm not ashamed in the least that I love them," Melanie said in the most unapologetic tone imaginable. "I love them. There's not a single word out of any of those books that I didn't absolutely enjoy."

"But why?" Bridget countered.

Melanie reached out and took a hold of Bridget's hands. "Because," she said, "they gave me the freedom to own my sexuality. They taught me that there's nothing wrong with desiring and seeking out pleasure, which was the complete opposite of what I learned from my extremely religious parents. Growing up, they made it explicitly clear that sexual desire, especially same-sex sexual desire, was sinful. And your books slowly, but surely, taught me otherwise."

Bridget had heard enough. After reading all of those fan letters and then listening to Melanie, she simply couldn't take anymore. She yanked her hands away from Melanie and turned away from her.

It suddenly struck her that she had been writing about how empowering it was to own one's sexuality for nearly half of her life, but had somehow failed to practice what she was preaching. In truth, she hadn't been with anyone since her ex-girlfriend back in grad school. She had been using her writing as a crutch for all those years. And now, faced with the reality that in order to move forward in her career she would have to let go of it, she felt that she was doing all that she could just to keep her head above water. She sniffled and tried to steel herself for the serious introspection that she knew she had been putting off for far too long. She turned around and faced Melanie.

"I'm sorry for the way I've been acting," she said. "And I'm sorry for being like your parents and acting like there's something wrong with being comfortable with your sexuality. I haven't been comfortable with mine for far too long and I shouldn't have taken my frustrations out on you."

A slight grin slowly etched its way across Melanie's face. She glanced over at the stack of books, then back at Bridget. "Is this the part of the book where Reedie places all of her cards on the table? She says what she wants and doesn't give a damn if doing so makes her seem vulnerable?" she asked.

Bridget wasn't quite following. "Part of the book?"

"May I kiss you?" Melanie asked rather bluntly.

"Oh..." Bridget cooed as she lowered her face into the palms of her hands. "Yes. Yes, I believe it is."

"Good," Melanie said. She slowly wrapped her arms around Bridget's waist, pulling her close.

Although she had written scenes like that dozens, if not hundreds of times in her books, Bridget felt unprepared for what she knew was coming next. Her body felt tense. Her mind felt numb, paralyzed by the anxiety that she was feeling. But instead of following her instinct to withdraw from the situation in the hopes of saving herself from experiencing the unknown, she surrendered and turned herself over to the experience. Feeling more attracted to Melanie than anyone ever before, Bridget simply couldn't wait for Melanie to lean in and kiss her. Instead, she beat her to the punch by placing a soft, sensual kiss upon her plump moist lips. A sense of elation consumed her entire body. For the first time since creating Reedie, she finally felt like her—empowered and comfortable with her own sexuality. She knew she had Melanie to thank for it.

The next day, Bridget went to Professor Young's office with the intention of telling her the truth, that she was actually Constance Lawrence. She was told by the secretary that Professor Young was on a call, but that she would see her shortly.

Not being able to go straight in and unload the burden that she had been carrying around since the whole ordeal started wasn't ideal for her. The waiting drove her insane. Her mind waffled back and forth between telling the truth and continuing the balancing act she had been performing for years on end.

"She will see you now," the secretary said.

Bridget flashed her an anxious smile as she stood up and made her way into Professor Young's cavernous office. It had always reminded her of a monastery with its minimal furnishings, but plethora of texts.

As she entered the room, Professor Young looked up from her desk with a look on her face that told her she wasn't surprised to see her.

"My secretary said that you needed to see me on urgent business," she said. "I'm assuming you're here to update me on your investigation?"

Bridget hesitated to speak, then flatly said, "No, not exactly."

"Oh?"

She looked at the two chairs that were stationed in front of Professor Young's desk, but didn't bother taking a seat given that she felt certain she would be shown the door in only a matter of time.

"I'm here to tell the truth," she said. "I'm actually Constance Lawerence. The reason why I haven't published any scholarly articles or written any books about 16th-century literature is because I've been too busy writing the types of books that you said bring shame to the department."

Professor Young rolled her eyes as she leaned back in her chair. Her response, or rather lack thereof, slightly threw Bridget. She had been expecting a blow up of epic proportions. All she got was a show of seeming indifference.

"There you have it," Bridget said as she shrugged her shoulders, essentially inviting a response from her direct superior. Professor Young still wouldn't budge. "Why don't you seem all that surprised?"

Professor Young finally showed her cards when a truly wicked smile crossed her face. "I've known for several days now."

"But how?"

Professor Young pointed to her Rolodex that sat at the end of her desk. "An alumna from before you started here is a senior editor in the academic services division of your publisher," she confessed, clearly impressed with herself. "I placed a call to her. She was all too happy to help her dear old mentor figure out who was placing the integrity of the institution that she absolutely adores in jeopardy."

Bridget felt that she had just been punched square in the gut. She had thought she'd be able to go in, fess up, and be able to reason with Professor Young. Clearly, she was wrong.

"So what does that mean for me and my future here at Freida?" she asked meekly, before realizing that she was being far too passive. "Before you answer that, I do just want to point out that even though my books haven't been lauded by fellow English scholars, they have been read by millions and millions of people. Sure, they contain a lot of explicit sex, but they also put forth a positive message of self-discovery and independence."

Professor Young didn't say a word. She simply stood up and walked over to the door and opened it, all the while maintaining a completely blank expression.

"Is that it?" Bridget asked.

"The president and I spoke earlier this morning. We decided that it's in the best interest of the college not to renew your contract for next year," she said. "However, we would both like to thank you for your many years of dedication to the education of Freida students." She extended her hand out for Bridget to shake.

Bridget glared at the hand with utter indignation. "Not renewing my contract? But—"

"May I remind you, Professor Buckly, that you aren't tenured? If you were, this would be a different story entirely, but since you decided to pursue writing that didn't further your standing here at the college, I'm afraid you're left without a leg to stand on."

Although Bridget snarled at her as she stormed out of the office, deep down she knew Professor Young was right. She might have disagreed with the decision not to renew her teaching contract, but there was no getting around the reason why she hadn't yet reached tenure status.

"Have a good rest of your day," the secretary offered.

Bridget hated to be rude to the secretary, who had no involvement in the matter, but was doing all that she could to keep from erupting into a fit of anger. She was completely and utterly peeved considering that she had given so much to the college only to be shown the door because she happened to write books about sexual self-empowerment on the side. It wasn't as though she had been broadcasting the fact that she was the author of the 'Finding My Freedom' series or advertising her connection to the college on the dust jacket of every single copy that was printed.

From Professor Young's office, Bridget went directly across campus to the hall where Melanie was teaching a class on 20th-century feminist literature. With little regard for the fact that the class still had 20 minutes left, she poked her head in through the door and signaled for Melanie to come to her. Seemingly surprised by Bridget's presence, Melanie took one look at her, then announced to her students that class would be ending a few minutes early.

"I'm sorry for just barging in on you like this," Bridget offered once the last student had made his way out of the lecture hall.

Melanie shook her head. "Don't be sorry," she said in an empathetic tone. "Tell me, how did it go?"

Bridget looked out into the empty lecture hall and started to choke up, knowing that she only had a few more months left at the college. She had no idea what she was going to do next. The thought of starting over at a brand-new college seemed overwhelming, especially considering that the hiring committees at other potential colleges would surely want to know why she had been let go by a college that she had spent her entire teaching career at. And the idea of solely devoting herself to her writing didn't seem very appealing either after everything that had transpired over the past few days.

"Bridget, what happened?" Melanie asked as she gently placed her hand on Bridget's shoulder.

Bridget sucked in a deep breath, then said half-jokingly, "Let's just say that come the fall there will be an open office on the ground floor that has a great view of the quad, so if you want it you should go ahead and lay claim to it now before any of the other vultures in the department can do so."

Melanie's face turned a glowing shade of red. "Don't tell me she fired you because if she did, I'll—"

Forcing a smile, Bridget took a hold of Melanie's hand that had been resting on her shoulder and squeezed it tightly. "There's nothing I can do. I'm not tenured. Plain and simple, it's my own damn fault."

Melanie jerked her hand away and slammed it down on the podium that stood in front of her. "No," she yelled out. "We're going to appeal it. We're not going to let this stand."

Bridget looked at Melanie with disbelief. "We? There is no 'we' in this situation," she said. "I wrote those books. No one made me do it. And besides, this is a private college. It's the college's prerogative to decide what kind of publication output they want their faculty members to be involved with."

"No."

"What do you mean no?" Bridget asked. "That's the way it is and there's no changing it."

Melanie looked up at the ceiling, then down at the ground. She acted like she was searching for the right words to convey what was on her mind. "I almost didn't accept the job here, you know? I told myself that it seemed too stuffy here and that it wouldn't be receptive to my style of scholarship and teaching, but despite that concern, I took a leap of faith and so far I haven't regretted it because the students here have surprised me," she said in an almost stream of consciousness-like manner. "They're receptive to approaching education in new and exciting ways! I can't tell you how many of them came up to me after the first week of class and told me that I'm their favorite professor because I don't get up in front of them and drone on and on about the works that we're studying, acting like they're the gospel. I translate the works into their language and make it fun!"

Bridget wasn't quite sure what to say, so she politely nodded her head and hoped that Melanie would face the fact that her time at Frieda was coming to a close.

"Don't just nod your head! I'm serious," Melanie barked. "I know I seem a little off kilter, but let me ask you this: as a 16th century literary scholar, why was the Protestant Reformation so effective?"

Bridget sighed with desperation. She had no idea what point Melanie was trying to get across and at that moment just wanted to go home and wallow in her misery. "The Protestant Reformation? What relevance does that have to—"

"Just answer the question," Melanie demanded.

Bridget rolled her eyes, then said, "It was effective because it reformed the way in which Christians across Europe viewed their faith. People were able to read the Bible in their own languages. Instead of relying on the words of priests and the supremacy of the Church, they viewed their personal relationships with God as being all that they needed."

Melanie looked at her as though she was missing something.

"I still don't get it," Bridget offered.

Melanie took a hold of both of Bridget's shoulders as she said, "The department is the Catholic Church. I'm trying to tell you that you have the opportunity to be the Martin Luther in this situation. Tear down the walls that have kept the students from embracing literature that speaks to them!"

"Huh." Bridget lowered her head as she processed all that Melanie had given her to think about.

"Huh as in 'Huh, that's a brilliant idea' or 'Huh, Melanie you've lost your mind? I need more than that."

Bridget raised her head up and truly looked at Melanie. She was both amazed and envious of her tenacity. She also wondered how she had managed to get by without her by her side for so many years.

"Let's just get one thing straight," she said, "I'm no Martin Luther. Perhaps Louis, Prince of Conde on a good day."

Melanie's face lit up with excitement. "Does that mean you'll appeal the decision?"

"Yes, but only reluctantly."

Melanie lunged forward and wrapped her arms around Bridget, embracing her in a bear hug. As their eyes met, they both instinctually leaned in. As they kissed, Bridget couldn't help but marvel at Melanie's indomitable spirit. Her passion and hopefulness made her want to be a more principled woman.

It took nearly a month for the appeal process for Bridget's termination to make its way through the system. A formal panel of students, administrators, and faculty and staff members had to be commissioned to hear and ultimately decide on the matter.

To her surprise, Bridget's conviction that she should be allowed to remain on the faculty of Freida grew throughout each stage in the process. Melanie, to her relief, was by her side at every turn.

The day that the panel was to give its verdict on Bridget's fate fell on a Friday afternoon. Although the stakes were high for her, she feared the letdown that Melanie would feel if the verdict wasn't in her favor. Either way, they both agreed that they would chart the next chapter in their lives together. The idea of authoring a new series of books together was something that Melanie had strongly been advocating for. It was an idea that deeply interested, yet frightened, Bridget.

The configuration of the conference room where the appeal took place was less than ideal. Instead of having the two parties staring straight ahead the way that courtrooms do, the conference room forced Bridget to have to constantly be vigilant in order to avoid awkward eye contact with Professor Young and President Lefko, the ancient head of the college who had signed off on Young's decision to let her go.

The Title IX director, who had been tasked with being the impartial adjudicator for Bridget's appeal, entered the room. The appeals panel followed behind her. The surprisingly short deliberation signaled to everyone involved that the decision had come fairly easily.

Bridget felt her chest tighten. The moment of truth was upon her. Because of the college's policy that only those directly involved in the appeals be allowed in the room, Melanie had been relegated to wait anxiously in the foyer.

"Before we hear the panel's verdict, I would first like to thank all those involved for the civility that was shown throughout the process," the Title IX director commented. "We have heard passionate remarks from both sides. I think we can all agree that no matter what the outcome is that this has been a fair and balanced process."

Everyone in the room validated what she had said with obligatory head nodding.

"With that being said, what has the panel decided?"

The president of the student council, who had been elected the forewoman for the appeal process, stood up and looked directly at both sides before speaking. "We find in favor of Professor Buckley," she said softly, but confidently.

Bridget fell forward with relief and lowered her head onto the table as she gathered herself. She was at an utter loss. She didn't know what to say or do other than bask in the victory that the panel had just given her. And to think she had serious reservations about launching an appeal in the first place.

Without saying a word, she jumped up from her seat and rushed towards the door. The shock of the panel's decision stunned her so much that she had forgotten that Melanie was waiting outside. She had to thank her for pushing her to fight for her career and her writing and perhaps most importantly for awakening something inside of her.

Upon bursting through the conference room door, she yelled out, "I won! We won!"

Melanie had been anxiously pacing back and forth in the foyer. She quickly spun around to see what all the commotion was about. Before she had a chance to speak, Bridget embraced her in such a tight hug she acted as though she was hanging onto her for dear life.

"Thank you! Thank you! Thank you! And that doesn't even begin to express how thankful I am to you for everything you've done for me," Bridget gushed. She released her grip from around Melanie's waist so that she could look her square in the eye and thank her all over again. But as she affectionately gazed at Melanie, something seemed off. She had a funny, almost knowing look on her face. "Why are you looking at me like that? Can you believe it?"

Melanie flashed a toothy grin at her, before saying, "Oh, I had no doubt they would find in your favor."

"How could you have been so confident?"

Melanie reached around to the messenger bag that was dangling from her shoulder and pulled out a copy of the first book in the 'Finding My Freedom' series. She handed it to Bridget, who studied the book that she had written with complete puzzlement. "I placed a copy of it in all of the panel members' mailboxes. I've been telling you all along that your work speaks for itself. Now do you believe me?" she said rather slyly. She leaned in and placed a light peck on Bridget's lips. "If I'm not mistaken, this is the part in the books where you write the end."

Bridget shook her head in objection. "No, this is just the beginning," she said.

Melanie chuckled. She leaned back in and planted another peck on Bridget's lips. As she started to pull away, Bridget pulled her back in. For the past 20 years or so she just wanted to get through life as quickly as possible, avoiding truly living in the moment. In that moment, she wanted nothing more than for time to stand still and for the kiss to last as long as possible.

If you loved this anthology,
please leave a review!

MORE ABOUT SINCYR PUBLISHING

At SinCyr Publishing, we wish to provide relatable characters facing real problems to our readers, in the sexiest or most romantic manner possible. Our intent is to offer a large selection of books to readers that cover topics ranging from sexual healing to sexual empowerment, to body positivity, gender equality, and more.

Too many of us experience body shaming, sexual shaming, and/or sexual abuse in our lives and we want to publish stories that allow people to connect to the characters and find healing. This means showing healthy BDSM practices, characters that understand consent and proper communication, characters that stare down toxic culture and refuse to take part… No matter what the content is, our focus is on empowering our readers through our books.

CPSIA information can be obtained
at www.ICGtesting.com
Printed in the USA
LVHW031440171220
674415LV00004B/321

9 781948 780148